PRAISE FOR

"Teenage boys will relate to Lucas as he struggles to live up to
larger-than-life expectations, and they will also salute his bravery in the face of danger."
—*Kirkus Reviews*

"A solid genre-blender that has appeal to superhero comics fans, suspense lovers, and even
those who just want a YA problem novel with a character looking for his identity."
—*Booklist*

LEGACY

THOMAS E. SNIEGOSKI

BLUEFIRE

Text copyright © 2009 by Thomas E. Sniegoski
Cover art copyright © 2011 by Victor Gardino

Visit us on the Web! www.randomhouse.com/teens

Educators and librarians, for a variety of teaching tools, visit us at www.randomhouse.com/teachers

The Library of Congress has cataloged the hardcover edition of this work as follows:
Sniegoski, Tom.
Legacy / Thomas E. Sniegoski. — 1st ed.
p. cm.
Summary: Eighteen-year-old Lucas is reluctant to take on his father's superhero mantle, but changes his mind as he comes face-to-face with evil after his mother is killed.
ISBN 978-0-385-73714-2 (trade) — ISBN 978-0-385-90648-7 (lib. bdg.)
— ISBN 978-0-375-89387-2 (ebook)
PS3619.N537 L44 2009
[Fic] — dc22
2008044867

ISBN 978-0-375-84606-9 (pbk.)

RL: 4.5

Printed in the United States of America

10 9 8 7 6 5 4 3 2 1

First Bluefire Edition 2011

For Stephanie and Dan,
a true dynamic duo

Gigantic gobs of gratitude to LeeAnne, my lovely and tortured wife, and to
Mulder the wonder dog, for continuing to put up with my shenanigans.

Thanks are also due to my brother from another mother, Christopher Golden,
Liesa Abrams, James Mignogna, Kenn Gold, Dave *"who threw the pies"* Kraus,
Mom and Dad Sniegoski, Mom and Dad Fogg, Pete Donaldson,
Sheila Walker, Mike, Christine and Katie Mignola, Abby and Kim,
and Timothy Cole and the League of Justice down at Cole's Comics in Lynn.

Up, up, and away!

prologue

He could always see it in their eyes.

The look that said, *Why would anybody put on a costume and fight crime?*

He wanted to tell the poor slobs, *If you have to ask that question, you'll never know.*

You'll never understand.

{1

The masked man, dressed in the tight-fitting costume of red and black, perched at the edge of an office building and surveyed the city sprawled below him.

Seraph City.

They—the citizens he protected—called him the Raptor, a sleek bird of prey feeding upon the vermin infesting the city.

His city.

They might not have understood him, but they were grateful for what he did, how he allowed them to sleep safely in their beds knowing he was out there.

Protecting them from evil.

The Raptor looked at his partner beside him.

His sidekick.

The newspapers called him Talon.

The Raptor and Talon; it had a nice ring to it. They'd inspired other crime fighters in cities across the world. For there was only so much that law enforcement could do. No matter how hard the police fought, some bad guys would always slip through the cracks.

It was up to the Raptor and Talon, and others like them, to pick up the slack.

Talon noticed that the Raptor was staring at him and met his gaze. "What?" he asked.

"Nothing." The Raptor turned his eyes toward the rooftop of the building below them.

The object of this evening's mission.

While the Raptor had indeed inspired the birth of heroes, these superheroes had in turn inspired the birth of a new class of criminal, a kind of evil the world had never seen before.

Flamboyant. Colorful. Powerful. *Deadly.*

The Raptor refused to accept responsibility for these new and dangerous criminals, convinced they would have arrived even if he hadn't. The world was changing, and these villains were simply products of that change.

Just as he and the other costumed crime fighters were.

One side couldn't . . . *wouldn't* exist without the other.

"So you think they're down there?" Talon asked.

The building below them had been designed to be Seraph City's new convention center, a showplace to announce to the world that a restored Seraph was on the rise. That the dangerous, crime-ridden place of old was a thing of the past.

But that was before construction workers discovered that

the earth beneath the building had served as an illegal dumping ground for years, poisoning the area with toxic waste.

The project had been stopped cold, leaving an abandoned, decaying shell, a perfect home for all manner of vermin.

"They're down there, all right," the Raptor confirmed.

He had been searching for the Terribles for more than a week, and finally, thanks to his many informants, he had located his prey.

"Slippery Pete saw the Frightener and the Blade Master going in less than an hour ago," the Raptor said.

"Good old Slippery Pete," Talon said with a chuckle. "It's a good thing he's more afraid of us than of the Terribles."

The Terribles had held the city in a grip of fear for weeks. Their recent armored car attack had left two civilians close to death and another badly burned.

It was high time their reign of terror was brought to an end, and over the last three nights the Raptor had forgone sleep to spend every moment tracking the Terribles.

Now he had found them.

A thrill vibrated through his body as he readied himself to strike. He always felt this way before he went into battle; he always felt this good.

There was movement in the shadows below them, and he and Talon both tensed, watching with predators' eyes.

The Raptor reached up to his mask, gently tapping the side of his head to activate the Owl's Eye lenses in his face mask, which turned the night as bright as day.

Below him, lighting up a quick smoke, was the Muscle.

This villain was ten times as strong as a normal man, and twenty times as dumb. He would be the least of their problems.

The criminal finished his smoke and returned to the protection of the nest.

"It's time," the Raptor announced, spreading his arms to activate the flight sensors woven into the protective mesh of his costume. Talon did the same, and they leapt from the rooftop, riding the air currents to the unfinished convention center below.

Silently they touched down in the cool darkness of the center's entryway. A set of double doors secured with corroded, rust-covered chains and padlocks was now all that stood between them and their quarry.

Talon looked at him, a glimmer of excitement in his eyes.

"It's all yours," the Raptor said. It was like throwing a bone to a hungry dog.

He smiled as he watched the boy lunge. The strength-enhancing exoskeleton built into the costume he wore allowed the boy to tear the doors from their hinges with ease.

He was good; maybe good enough to carry on the legacy when it came time for the Raptor to step down.

Of course, the crime fighter hoped he wouldn't need to think about that for many years. There was far too much evil in the Angel City for him to think about stepping down as its protector.

With a powerful leap, the Raptor bounded through the doorway to join his partner. Oddly, there was no sign of the Terribles.

"What, did they see you and surrender?" he asked, coming to stand beside Talon.

"Something's wrong" was all Talon had to say. Suddenly the darkness was dispelled by a bright, almost blinding light as multiple spotlights set up all around the cavernous first floor were illuminated.

Stunned, the Raptor realized almost at once what he and Talon had done. How could they have been so stupid? So overconfident?

There were five chairs set up across from them, with five people bound and gagged in them. He knew each and every one. They were his agents, his informers, people he used and trusted to collect information to eliminate the criminal element from the city.

Justin Spiewack, the incorruptible beat cop with a wife and two infant daughters; Patricia Doughtery, tough-as-nails reporter for the *Seraph Sun*; Brucie Mitchell, owner of the Ballentine club, Seraph City's hottest nightspot; Dr. Lita Coughlin, personal physician to some of Seraph City's most powerful criminal figures; and Slippery Pete, one of the greatest con men of the twentieth century.

All of them tied to their chairs. All of them clearly terrified as the small digital clocks connected to explosive devices resting in each of their laps counted down the last seconds of their lives.

Eight . . . Seven . . . Six . . .

"What do we do?" Talon asked, his earlier excitement replaced by fear.

Five . . . Four . . .

A thousand and one scenarios ran through the Raptor's

mind. But he knew that none would be successful. "It's too late," he said.

Three . . . Two . . .

This isn't how it's supposed to be, he thought, frozen in place, feeling the fear emanating from those who had aided him in battle.

The Raptor and Talon were supposed to charge into the dilapidated building, defeat the bad guys, and bring them to justice.

That was how it was supposed to be. How the game was played.

How it always had been.

One.

The world around the Raptor was consumed in fire and smoke, and a sound that could very well have signaled the end of the world.

The end of *his* world.

Evil had changed the rules.

1

Even with the industrial-sized fan blowing, it was hot as hell inside the garage of Big Lou's Gas Up & Go.

Lucas Moore was under the hood of Jeb Dolahyde's old Ford truck, using a ratchet wrench to tighten the spark plugs he'd just installed. He could feel trickles of sweat tickling the scalp of his shaggy head, eventually dripping down to and across the bridge of his nose. It was days like this when he wished he had the courage to get a crew cut, to shave it all off, but the ladies seemed to like his untamed, curly black hair.

And what the ladies liked, he kept.

He stood up and pulled a red bandanna from his back pocket, wiping the sweat from his face. All he had to do was change the fluids and he'd be done with the first car of the day, leaving only five more to go.

His head pounded and his stomach was becoming increasingly sour. He knew he should probably have something to eat, but the thought only made him queasy. Lucas wanted to blame his misery on the blazing Arizona heat, but he knew it was more likely the beer and whiskey shots from the night before.

He headed to the workstation in the corner of the garage, stopping in front of the fan and closing his eyes. The warm air didn't provide much in the way of relief, but it was better than nothing.

Head throbbing, he pulled himself away from the fan and dropped the wrench on the workbench. His stomach burbled, and again he considered getting something to eat at the diner across the way, but then he realized that would mean seeing his mother, and he thought better of it.

He flashed back to earlier that morning when his mother had been preparing to leave for work at the Good Eats Diner (also owned by Big Lou). She had started to lay into Lucas about how he had come in drunk, and how he wasn't even old enough to be drinking, and pretty soon that had led into how he wasn't doing anything with his life, and how he would never amount to anything without a high school education.

The fact that Lucas had dropped out of high school earlier that year was a real sore spot for his mom, but Lucas saw it as looking at things realistically. He believed high school wasn't going to teach him anything that was going to help him much in life, especially when he more or less knew he was going to end up fixing cars in Big Lou's garage anyway.

Dropping out of school had just helped him on his way to an inevitable career path. But try telling his mother that.

He was walking over to a display of radiator fluid when he heard his name called.

Lucas turned to see Richie Dennison and two of his punk friends, Teddy Shay and Vincent Clark, saunter into the garage.

"What can I do for you, Richie?" Lucas asked, taking a plastic container of radiator fluid over to the pickup.

"I told you last night it wasn't over," Richie said. He stood with his hands out to either side, like a gunfighter ready to draw.

Lucas's head immediately began to throb harder. "What wasn't over?" he asked, setting the container of coolant down in front of the truck and approaching the three.

"You know what I'm talking about," Richie snarled. "Playing stupid isn't going to help you."

Seeing Richie had begun to stir up some memories from the night before, but they were buried pretty deep. Lucas vaguely recalled making a comment about Richie's girl-friend. "This doesn't have anything to do with something I said about Brenda, does it?" he asked.

"I told you never to say her name to me again!" Richie shouted, coming at Lucas with his fists clenched.

Lucas backed up, throwing his hands in the air. "Hey, look, I'm sorry, all right? I don't even remember what I said. But I'm sorry. Okay?"

Richie smirked and his friends chuckled.

"Figured you'd try to get out of it once your buddies weren't around to back you up," he said.

"Look," Lucas began, "I don't remember much about last night. . . . I guess I was a little drunk."

"Not too drunk to run your mouth and talk trash about my girlfriend," Richie replied.

Lucas thought for sure he was going to throw up. The heat and his hangover were making him feel sicker by the second. "What do you want from me?" he finally asked, trying to keep the annoyance out of his tone. "I said I was sorry. I shouldn't have talked trash about Brenda."

Richie moved more quickly than Lucas expected, slamming a fist into his jaw and sending him stumbling to one side.

But he didn't go down.

"I told you not to say her name," Richie said menacingly.

Lucas held the side of his face. "I think it's time for you all to get the hell out of here," he said, jaw throbbing.

He knew he'd been wrong the night before, even though he couldn't remember exactly what he'd said. He did have a tendency to run his mouth after a few beers, and probably deserved that punch.

But no more.

"We'll get out, all right," Richie said as he and his buddies came at Lucas. "Just as soon as we're done stomping your ass."

Lucas liked a good scuffle as much as the next guy, but three against one? That just wasn't right.

He ducked his head low and charged. Teddy tried to hold

Lucas's arms behind his back, but Lucas drove the heel of his heavy work boot down onto Teddy's sneakered foot. The kid screamed, limping backward, giving Lucas a chance to concentrate on the other two.

Vincent knocked him back with a punch that grazed his cheek, but it gave Lucas the opportunity he needed. He dove at the guy, grabbing him around the waist and bringing him down to the ground. He pinned Vincent to the floor and put everything he had into a punch to the kidneys.

Richie threw his arms around Lucas's thick, muscular neck, pulling him from his friend, who now writhed on the floor, moaning. Lucas jabbed his elbow back into Richie's stomach, loosening Richie's grip enough that Lucas was able to turn and throw a right cross into the guy's face, sending him sprawling to the floor.

Breathing heavily, Lucas stood unsteadily as he watched Teddy help Vincent up from the floor. Both eyed him cautiously.

"Get out," Lucas said, spitting a wad of bloody saliva onto the concrete floor.

They didn't move, waiting as their ringleader got to his feet.

"Don't make me tell you again," Lucas warned. He really wasn't ready for round two, but he didn't think the three of them had it in them either.

"This isn't over," Richie said, his back to Lucas.

What happened next was a blur.

Lucas thought the boy was leaving, but Richie spun around. Something glinted in the glow of the fluorescent lights as he surged toward Lucas. Lucas tried to block the thrust, but he wasn't fast enough, and suddenly there was an explosion of pain, followed by a cold numbness in his stomach.

Lucas looked down at himself as Richie stepped back. He could see the new hole in his T-shirt, a scarlet stain starting to expand around it.

"What did you do?" Lucas asked, horror beginning to sink in.

He looked up to see the three wearing expressions of shock as they started to back toward the garage exit. Richie was still holding the blood-speckled knife in his hand.

Jeb Dolahyde appeared in the entrance just then, his ample belly making it around the corner before the rest of him. He was taking the plastic wrapping off a pack of discount cigarettes but stopped short when he noticed Richie and then Lucas across the room.

"What the hell . . ."

The punks bolted from the garage.

Lucas could smell the blood from his wound. He stared at the scarlet blossom on the belly of his T-shirt until his eyes began to blur. For some reason it no longer hurt as much as it had, and he knew that had to be a bad thing.

"Lucas?" Jeb called to him, his cowboy boots clicking across the concrete floor.

Lucas continued to stare at the stain on his shirt, afraid to look beneath the fabric. Outside he heard the screeching of tires as Richie and his friends fled.

"Lucas, you all right?" he heard Jeb ask. "Do you need me to call 911?"

Lucas didn't answer. He was distracted by the fact that he

could no longer feel any pain. Gathering his courage, he grabbed hold of his bloody shirt and lifted it. His exposed stomach was smeared and sticky with blood, but no matter how hard he searched, he couldn't find the wound.

With a tentative hand he reached down and began to feel around, expecting a lightning bolt of pain that never came.

There was nothing there.

"No," he said finally, looking up into the concerned face of Jeb Dolahyde. "It . . . it looks worse than it is."

It was like he hadn't been stabbed at all.

It was a good thing Lucas kept a spare shirt in the back of his truck. He threw the bloodstained T-shirt into one of the barrels inside the garage.

He quickly returned to the job of finishing Jeb's truck.

Jeb hovered for a while, asking a lot of questions about what had happened, but he finally gave up and went outside when it became clear that Lucas wasn't giving any answers. It wasn't that Lucas was intentionally being rude; it was just that he really couldn't explain it. No matter how hard he thought about it, he always came up with the same answer.

Richie Dennison had stabbed him.

But if that was the case, why wasn't he hurt?

Lucas threw himself into the job, changing the radiator coolant, then topping off the fluids for the wipers and the brakes. And all the while, the questions kept right on coming.

It wasn't that he hadn't been hurt. He'd been hurt, all right. He'd felt the blade go in—it was one of the most painful things he'd ever experienced. And he'd bled like a stuck pig, too.

But in the time it took Jeb to come into the garage, something had happened.

Lucas cleaned up and tossed the trash into the barrel. He saw his bloody T-shirt among the discarded air filters and auto-parts packaging.

Pulling his eyes away, he went outside to find Jeb.

At first he didn't see Jeb anywhere, but then he caught sight of the large man ambling across the parking lot of the Good Eats diner with an iced coffee.

"Truck's all set," Lucas called out, wiping his hands on the bandanna from his back pocket.

"Good job," the man said, eyeing him curiously. "You sure you're all right? That was a helluva lot of blood."

Lucas forced a smile. "I'm fine. Think I just got a good scrape when me and Richie were fighting. You know how those things bleed."

Jeb nodded, but Lucas could see he really didn't understand. Truth be told, neither did he.

Lucas was writing up Jeb's receipt and collecting his cash when it came over him. He was suddenly absolutely ravenous. As he said goodbye to Jeb, he actually stumbled a bit, catching himself on the corner of Big Lou's metal desk. His legs were shaky, and he wasn't sure he had ever been this hungry before.

Placing the BE RIGHT BACK! sign on the door to the office, Lucas made his way across the street toward the diner, wondering if there was enough food in the place to satisfy his hunger.

As he stepped into the air-conditioned space, his eyes scanned the crowded diner for a place to park himself. His mother stood at the back of the restaurant, a full pot of coffee in one hand.

Cordelia Moore was staring at him with eyes that just about *screamed* he was in trouble. She pointed to a spot that was being vacated by an old man and his wife, and shot him a look that said Lucas had no choice.

The smells inside the diner were overwhelming, and Lucas's belly gurgled and growled uncontrollably. He had to eat soon.

His mother approached the table, rag in hand, and started to wipe it down.

"Hey," he said by way of greeting.

"What's this I hear about a fight over at the garage?" she asked.

"You talked to Jeb, eh?" His stomach was aching, and he almost told her to knock off the small talk and bring him one of everything on the menu.

Almost.

"Yes, I did, and he seemed to think you might've been hurt pretty bad."

She'd finished the table and stood staring at him with those angry eyes, hands on her hips.

"I'm fine," he said, frustrated that he had to explain himself again. "He knew I was fine. . . . I told him I was fine."

"Well, he didn't seem to think you were fine." She reached out and grabbed his face. "Let me see."

He wrenched his face from her hand. "I told you . . ."

"I know, you're fine."

His stomach grumbled so loudly that his mother heard it over the din of the crowded diner.

"Sounds like somebody's hungry," she said.

He nodded, pressing a hand to his aching abdomen. "Like you wouldn't believe."

"How's about the Hungryman's Platter and a cup of coffee?"

"As fast as you can get it," Lucas said, looking up to meet her gaze. "Please."

She gave him the look again, then turned and headed toward the kitchen to place his order.

"And he wonders why I'm so upset about him dropping out of school," Lucas heard her grumble as she walked up the aisle. "Big trouble is going to find him one of these days."

Lucas shook his head as he watched her go. Diners seated nearby had heard her scolding him and were casually looking his way.

"Big trouble, huh?" he called after her. "What kind of trouble would come looking for me here?"

The private jet taxied down the single runway of the La Cholla Airpark, coming to a gradual stop in the blazing Arizona sun.

The door opened and a retractable stairway unfolded to the tarmac. Within moments a tall, white-haired figure leaning on a silver-topped cane stood in the doorway, looking out across the private airfield.

"May I help you, sir?"

The gentleman looked over at his pilot, who had joined him at the door.

"No need, Jeffrey," the man said, limping from the doorway and slowly making his way down the steps.

"Should I arrange a ride for you?" the pilot asked, following.

"I'm way ahead of you," the white-haired man said from the bottom of the stairs.

A navy blue Crown Victoria appeared just then, driving across the airfield toward them.

"Very good, sir," Jeffrey said.

The man waited until the driver emerged, walked around the car, and opened the back door.

"Any idea when you'll be wanting to return to Seraph?" Jeffrey asked as the old man was about to climb into the car.

The old man stopped, considering the question.

"If all goes according to plan, it shouldn't take long," he said, then entered the coolness of the limousine.

{17

But one can never tell with things like this, the old man thought as the driver climbed back inside.

"Take me to Perdition," the old man instructed.

And without a moment's hesitation, the car was on its way.

2

Lucas considered heading over to the Hog Trough for a few drinks after work but thought better of it.

The business with Richie was still gnawing at him, and then there was his mom. Did he really want to have another run-in with her tonight?

Nope, he just didn't have the patience.

He sat behind the wheel of his truck, windows rolled down to catch the breeze as he headed home for an early night.

This is a good thing, he thought, driving fast down the bumpy dirt road that would take him to the Perdition Trailer Park (also owned by Big Lou).

Lucas's mind scrolled through all the things he could do with the extra time tonight—stuff he'd been meaning to do but never quite got around to. He could start the Lord of the Rings books. He'd read *The Hobbit*, but not the Rings trilogy—although he had seen the movies and thought they were awesome. Or he could catch up on his laundry. Not as fun as reading, but it had to be done. And then there was the whole just-spending-time-with-his-mother thing.

She was a good mother, and she had done a lot for him, but they'd sort of drifted apart in the time since he'd left high school.

He drove slowly through the metal arch that served as the entrance to the trailer park, watching for stray kids and animals. It wouldn't be the first time one or the other had darted out in front of him.

He pulled up beside the powder blue double-wide he and his mother called home, and saw old Mrs. Taylor sitting in front of her place across the street. By the way she was staring, he knew she was waiting for him.

"Hey, Mrs. Taylor," Lucas said as he climbed from his truck.

She was wearing a lovely flowered housecoat and a blond wig that sat crooked on her head, like some sort of furry hat, with tufts of gray poking out underneath.

She got up from the white plastic lounge chair and motioned for him to join her.

"What's up?" he asked, crossing the dusty street.

"Somethin's wrong with my AC," she said, bony hands on even bonier hips. "Take a look at it, will ya?"

Lucas didn't know squat about air-conditioning, but there was no sense in arguing with the lady. As far as she was concerned, he could fix just about anything.

"Sure, no problem," he said, climbing the three steps to the front door.

He stopped short, peering through the screen at Fluffles, Mrs. Taylor's nasty cat. The thing had more attitude than a pit bull with a toothache.

"Fluffles is at the door," he told Mrs. Taylor.

"He won't hurt ya," the old woman said. "You just gotta show 'im who's boss."

She was standing beside him, looking in through the door.

"Why don't you show 'im?" Lucas suggested.

Mrs. Taylor went in first, kicking at the cat with her slippered foot. "Go on, shoo!" she said.

Fluffles hissed like a cobra, trying to get around her to come at Lucas, but the old woman managed to block the attack.

"Behave yourself, cat!" she exclaimed. Her foot connected with the side of the white-furred beast, sending it running with a shrill squeal.

"I'll be payin' for that tonight," Mrs. Taylor said, walking from the entry through the tiny kitchen and into the living room. "Damn thing will probably suffocate me in my sleep."

The idea was horrible but not all that far-fetched.

It was stiflingly hot inside the cramped living room. The news blared from an old twenty-five-inch television set in the corner.

"There it is," Mrs. Taylor said, pointing out the old air conditioner in the wall. "Nothing cool comin' out of that."

"Not sure what I can do," Lucas said, walking over to give it a look. The machine was old, and he was surprised that it had worked as long as it had. When he turned it on, it made a low humming sound, sending warm air out the vents.

On the news, a Chicago woman and her child were describing how they had been saved from an apartment fire by a superhero called the Winged Champion. Lucas looked up, finding himself pulled into the story. He watched the grainy cell phone footage of the superhero with enormous white wings swooping down out of the sky to pluck the woman and her daughter from the rooftop of the collapsing building.

"Wow," Lucas said.

"Yeah," Mrs. Taylor agreed. "Wonder if one of them super-types could figure out what's wrong with my AC."

Lucas took the hint and returned his full attention to the old woman's air conditioner. He pulled the plastic face from the front of the unit and curled his nose with distaste.

"Fluffles doesn't happen to like sitting on the AC, does he?" Lucas asked.

The inside of the unit was clogged with tufts of white fur, the old filter completely covered.

"Matter of fact, he does," Mrs. Taylor confirmed.

Lucas pulled the filter from inside the AC and brushed most of the fur into a barrel that Mrs. Taylor brought from the kitchen.

"This might help," he said, putting the filter back. "I think it might've just been clogged."

He reattached the unit's front piece. "Fingers crossed," he said, flipping the switch and feeling a blast of much cooler air flow from the vent openings. "I think that did it," he said proudly.

"You're a lifesaver," Mrs. Taylor said happily. She reached inside the pocket of her flowered housecoat and removed a change purse. "How much do I owe you?" she asked, unzipping the purse and removing a wad of crumpled bills.

"You don't owe me anything," he answered.

Every time he did something for the woman, she tried to pay him. But Lucas wasn't interested in taking the old lady's money. He knew she barely had enough to support herself as it was.

"What, do you think you're one of them super-types?" she asked, gesturing toward the television. "Swoopin' in to save the day?"

Lucas laughed. "Not me," he told her. "Think of me more as a Boy Scout."

"You're too good to me, Lucas," she said with a smile, returning her small purse to her pocket.

"My pleasure." Lucas cautiously headed for the door, watching for Fluffles.

"Word to the wise," Mrs. Taylor whispered. "Think your mom's been hittin' the hooch." She made a gesture as if drinking from a bottle.

Lucas nodded and his stomach sank. He hated when his mother drank; it always ended with her crying.

As he crossed the street toward their trailer, he'd almost decided to take his truck and head to the Hog Trough. But then he saw her, glass in hand, standing in the doorway waiting for him.

And he didn't have the heart to leave her alone.

* * *

Lucas leaned into the refrigerator, looking for something to eat. He found some old pizza and leftover spaghetti and meatballs.

"Did you eat yet?" he asked his mother, carrying the leftovers to the microwave.

Cordelia was sitting at the small kitchen table, a nearly empty glass of whiskey in her hand.

"I had a big lunch," she answered, her eyes riveted to the melting ice in her glass.

"Lucas, do you hate me?" she asked suddenly.

He rolled his eyes as he put the spaghetti in the microwave and hit the two-minute button. He hated when she got like this. It didn't happen very often, but when it did, it was the worst.

"No, I don't hate you. Why would I?" he said. He could hear the ice in her glass tinkle like Christmas bells. He tried to concentrate on the spaghetti.

"If it wasn't for me, you wouldn't be in this place," she said, her words slightly slurred.

Lucas wondered how many drinks she'd had.

"It's fine, Ma," he said. "Don't worry about it. All I know is Perdition. I don't know what I'm missing."

She nodded, getting up from her chair and going to the counter, where the bottle of whiskey was waiting.

"And that's exactly it," she said as she unscrewed the cap and splashed more of the golden liquor over the ice. "You are missing stuff . . . lots of stuff. . . . You're wasting your life away working in a crappy garage because I wasn't strong enough to—"

{23

The microwave alarm went off.

"Ma, enough," Lucas said, replacing the spaghetti in the microwave with a paper plate that held three slices of cheese pizza. "I don't know why you keep blaming yourself for coming here."

This was the pattern. She got a little bit drunk and started talking about how she had to run from her past in Seraph City. No matter what he said to console her, it never helped.

And really, Lucas had never blamed her for leaving. Sure, he was curious about the specifics, about a father he knew nothing of, but he always figured she had done what she had to do, nothing more or less than that.

She was adding ice to her drink as he sat down to eat. He didn't want to talk about this stuff anymore, but when she was like this, there was no stopping her.

"You know how sorry I am, right?" she asked, practically falling into her chair.

"Be careful," Lucas said, spearing a meatball and starting to eat.

She reached out to touch his hand. Hers was damp and cold from the condensation on her glass, and Lucas almost pulled away, but then realized how that would look to her.

"There's no reason for you to be sorry," he said, grabbing a slice of pizza with his other hand.

"I always wanted the best for you." She had tears in her eyes now. "But I had to get away from the city . . . as far away as possible or . . ." She fell silent, staring into her glass once again. And then she had some more to drink.

"Ma, I don't know how many more times I have to tell you this," Lucas began. "But I like it here. This is my home. It's the only home I've ever known."

"But—" she started to argue.

"No buts," he interrupted. "Perdition is fine. Everything I could ever want is here." He got up and took his dirty dishes to the sink. "End of story."

He returned to his mother, put his arm around her, and gave her a kiss on the top of her head.

"You might want to think about making yourself some coffee or something," he said, heading toward his room. "I'm gonna call it a night."

And he left her there alone.

Alone with the memories of her past, and what she believed to be her failures.

{25

Shaking off the cobwebs of deep sleep, Lucas pulled himself from beneath the sheet and saw that it was after eight.

The garage was supposed to open at eight.

He threw on some clothes, grabbed his wallet and his keys, and pulled open the door to his room.

He half expected to see his mother still sitting at the kitchen table, but from the looks of it, she'd managed to get up and make it out to the diner on time. Lucas half recalled somebody knocking on his door and telling him it was time to get up, but he had decided it was only a dream and had rolled over.

Locking up the trailer, he went to his truck.

Mrs. Taylor was outside again, this time watering her

plants in a spectacularly colored housecoat and a new, brunette wig. "Late again," she called out, and began to cackle.

Lucas shrugged and climbed behind the wheel of his truck. Within seconds, he peeled away from the trailer and was on his way to work.

3

Lucas breathed a sigh of relief as he pulled into the gas station and saw that Big Lou's gas-guzzling SUV was not in its usual spot alongside the office.

But then he noticed the black Ford Mustang parked in front of the garage doors.

A customer, waiting.

Lucas parked his truck in the back and quickly ran to the front, searching through his key ring.

He unlocked the door to the main office first, then flicked the switch to raise the doors to the service bay.

A man had stepped from the waiting car, watching Lucas with an intense stare.

"Morning," Lucas said, walking around the garage and flipping on the lights. "What can I do for you?"

The older man was dressed in black and walked with a cane. The haircut, clothes, and car all screamed that the guy was from the city, maybe from Texas.

"It says you open at eight," he said.

"Yes, it does," Lucas agreed with a polite smile.

The man looked at his fancy watch. "And here it is close to eight-thirty."

Lucas looked at an imaginary watch on his own wrist. "Huh," he said, tapping his wrist. "Must be slow."

The man chuckled. "I don't mean to be rude, it's just that I've been waiting for some time."

"Yeah, and I'm really sorry about that," Lucas said. "Why don't you tell me what I can do for you?"

The man looked from Lucas to his car and back. "My car seems to be running a bit rough."

Lucas nodded. "Would you mind driving it in?"

The older man limped back to the car, got behind the wheel, and drove the Mustang inside.

"Leave it running and pop the hood, please," Lucas told him.

The old man silently did as he was told, then limped over to the workstation and leaned on the table to watch Lucas work.

Lucas stuck his fingers beneath the hood, found the latch, and pushed it up, peering down into the engine. He immediately went to work checking off mental boxes as each item on the list met with his satisfaction.

"Live around here?" the man asked from behind him.

"Yeah," Lucas responded as he checked the various hoses.

"Lived here your whole life?" the older man continued.

"My whole life," Lucas repeated. He listened to the engine. It sounded fine to him.

"Still in school?" the man asked.

Lucas answered before he could really think about the question. "Should be, but I dropped out to work full-time."

"Hmmm, not too smart, was it?"

Lucas pulled himself from beneath the hood. "I think it was," he answered with annoyance. *Who the hell does this guy think he is?* "Wasn't learning anything that would help me in the future, so I decided to start my career early and make some money."

The man looked around at the old garage. "Such a career," he said with a chuckle.

Lucas felt his annoyance turn to anger. "Sorry," he said, leaning through the driver's-side door to turn off the engine. The new-car smell hit him immediately. "Can't find anything wrong with your car. Maybe you should take it to a more educated mechanic."

"Didn't think you would find anything," the older gentleman said, pushing off from the worktable and limping closer to Lucas. "I just bought it yesterday."

"So what the hell did you have me looking under the hood for?" Lucas asked, temper flaring.

"I wanted to see you," the man said, limping closer still. "I've traveled pretty far just to talk to you."

"What did you want to talk to *me* for?" Lucas snarled.

The man just stared.

"I'm your father," he said finally. The words seemed to suck all the sound from the garage.

Lucas stumbled back, feeling as if he had been slapped across the face. "Wha—what did you just say?"

"You heard me," the man said. "I'm your father, and I've come to speak with you about—"

Lucas was suddenly moving. First he slammed the driver's-side door, and then he walked to the front of the car.

"You'd better go," he said. He couldn't think. He pictured his brain exploding into sparks like those computers did in the old movies.

And then he pictured his mother, drinking herself into oblivion as she thought about the bad old days. Days that this guy probably had something to do with, if he was indeed who he said he was.

"We have to talk," the older man urged, his limp more severe as he tried to step closer.

"Get out," Lucas yelled, slamming the hood of the Mustang.

"Everything all right in here, Lucas?" Big Lou's massive bulk suddenly filled the doorway between the main office and the garage.

The old man glanced quickly at Big Lou, then turned his eyes back to Lucas.

"Yeah, everything's fine," Lucas said, his gaze not leaving the old man. "I was just giving this guy directions to the highway. You got those all right, old fella?" he asked, venom dripping from every word.

The old man nodded slightly and walked to the driver's side of the car. "I've got it," he said, opening the door and carefully lowering himself behind the wheel. "Nice talking with you."

Lucas suddenly wanted to say so much more to the man . . . wanted to slice him apart with the savagery of the words that now filled his head. Instead, his eyes followed the Ford Mustang as it backed from the garage, into the lot, and onto the road out front.

I'm your father. The words reverberated inside his skull, pounding like the worst migraine he'd ever had.

I'm your father.

And suddenly Lucas was sick, leaning over while what little there was in his stomach spewed from his gaping mouth into the garbage barrel.

Lucas didn't know how long he'd been standing in front of the Good Eats Diner.

The morning was a complete blur. As soon as the old man . . . *his father* . . . had left the garage, Big Lou had been on him to straighten up the shop and work the pumps.

It had been pretty insane the last few days—first the business with Richie Dennison and now this. If things kept going the way they were, he was pretty much certain he wouldn't be able to keep a straight thought in his head.

Things are just getting too freakin' weird.

And now, standing out in front of his mother's place of employment, he had the chance to make them even weirder.

Lucas had no idea what to do. Should he tell his mother what had happened across the street—who had paid him a visit?

His thoughts flashed back to the night before. She had drunk herself into a stupor over something that had happened years past. He'd never really asked for specifics, because he'd never really cared. Something had made her leave Seraph City, and he guessed it had something to do with her being pregnant, and with the guy who had just introduced himself.

But doesn't she have the right to know that this guy was around? What if he's dangerous or something?

He paced back and forth, disgusted with himself for wanting to know more about the guy. He'd never really cared before, or at least, that was what he'd convinced himself of. But now, there had been a chance to get answers and . . .

"You comin' in or are you just gonna walk back and forth in front of the window until your lunch hour's done?" his mother suddenly asked.

Startled, Lucas looked up to see her holding the door open.

"Get in here," she said, waving him inside. "Before I let all the air-conditioning out."

He did as he was told.

"What's your problem?" she asked as he passed her.

"Got a headache," he said, still not sure how to approach this.

"You and me both," Cordelia responded. "Why'd you let me drink so much last night?"

She led him to a booth and sat him down.

"Like I can stop you," he said, grabbing a menu and pretending to read it. He wasn't seeing anything at the moment.

She left and returned with a large glass of water. "Here, drink this," she said. "It should help."

He took a sip as she stood there watching him.

"I should probably say I'm sorry about last night," his mother said.

Lucas shook his head. "Don't worry about it."

"It's just that I get thinking about you, and how we're kind of at a dead end here, and how we'd probably be doin' so much better if I'd stayed in Seraph and—"

He raised his hand and stopped her.

The words were almost there, trickling down from his fevered brain to the back of his throat. They were coming now, flowing over his tongue and about to escape . . .

"You never have to apologize for what you did," he found himself saying. "You did what you did because you thought it was best for you and for me. That's it. End of story."

He could see she was about to argue with him, so he looked back at the menu.

"Think I'll have the double bacon burger today," he said, closing the menu. "Medium well, with extra onions."

He looked at her again and smiled, bringing their conversation to a close.

She returned the smile and nodded.

"All right then," she said. "A double bacon burger, medium well, with extra onions."

She hustled off to the kitchen to place the order, and he took a large, numbing gulp of his ice water.

At the last moment he'd decided not to tell her. Why put the poor woman through the trauma?

Nope, he would keep this his little secret.

No matter how hard he tried, Lucas couldn't forget even for a minute what had happened at the garage that morning. It kept replaying in his mind, like a flashback in a movie.

He was grateful that Big Lou hadn't given him anything

complicated to work on. Pumping gas and washing wind-shields was about his speed today, and there hadn't even been a lot of that to do, which gave him plenty of time to think.

By quitting time he thought his skull would explode, and he figured the only way to save himself would be to kill the pain with beer.

At the Hog Trough, four beers and ten games of darts later, Lucas was feeling no pain.

It was a good idea to come here tonight, he thought as he finished a beer and gestured at Trixie for another.

The drinking age in the state of Arizona was twenty-one, but Trixie was a saint, letting him drink there even though he wasn't of age.

He loved her like a fat kid loves cake.

His troubling thoughts were numbed by the alcohol and the company of his bar mates, but they were still there, mak-ing his brain itch whenever he had a down moment.

Trixie brought him his new beer, and he thanked her, yelling over the country music playing on the jukebox.

He took it carefully, sipping from the edge of the tall, frosted glass so that he wouldn't spill a drop. He looked around the Trough. Most of his friends had already called it a night. But Lucas didn't care. He needed this.

Richie Dennison and his girlfriend, Brenda, had been in earlier, but after seeing him sitting at the bar, they didn't stay too long.

Imagine that.

He held his beer in one hand, scratching his stomach through his T-shirt with the other. He'd pretty much convinced himself that he'd just been grazed by Richie's blade, that the edge of the knife had given him a kind of paper cut on his stomach that had bled like crazy—as some paper cuts do—before healing up.

He could buy something like that. It was the only thing that made sense.

But he still could remember the feeling of the blade piercing his skin.

Shaking away the disturbing recollection, he saw that his glass was almost empty. He downed what remained and returned to the bar.

"Trixie!" he called out, his voice louder than he had intended in the sudden silence between jukebox tunes.

The barmaid turned and ambled toward him with a smile on her face. "Don't you think you've had just about enough?" she asked, taking the empty glass and wiping down the counter with a damp rag. "Remember, you've got work tomorrow."

"I know I've got work tomorrow," he answered, feeling perturbed. "But I would like another."

Trixie made a face, and he could tell she was deciding whether or not she should serve him one more.

"I don't know," she said with a drawl.

"One more, Trix," Lucas begged, trying not to slur. There was a little voice inside his head trying to tell him he'd had enough, but he'd never really cared for that voice. He gave Trixie his cutest smile, the one that seemed to work on all the ladies . . . well, it worked on his mother, anyway.

She caved and gave him another.

He found an empty stool at the bar and sat. This beer

tasted good, the best one that night, and that was probably because he had to really work for it.

The final sips seemed to hit him hard. A kind of fog settled over his brain, and there was nothing he wanted more at the moment than to lay his spinning head down on a pillow and go to sleep.

"That's it for me," he announced, sliding from the stool. He reached into his pocket, searching for his keys.

"You all right to drive?" Trixie asked warily as she dried a beer mug with a dish towel.

"Don't worry about me," he said, heading for the door. "Only heading down the road a bit. . . . I'll be fine."

The old man was standing in the doorway watching him. For a moment Lucas thought it had to be some sort of hallucination, but soon he realized the man was most definitely standing there.

"I thought we might be able to talk," the man said. "But I guess this isn't a good time."

And then he was gone, the door slowly closing behind him with a hiss.

Swearing under his breath, Lucas quickened his pace to the door and pushed it open, searching the steamy Arizona night for the man.

He found him crossing the parking lot to that damned Mustang.

"You!" Lucas bellowed, stumbling a bit as he lunged across the lot.

The man stopped and slowly turned to face him.

"You hold it right there," Lucas called out. "Who the hell do you think you are, following me?"

"We need to talk . . . Lucas. It is Lucas, isn't it?"

"I didn't tell you my name," Lucas bellowed.

"No, but I heard your boss say it this morning before I left the garage."

"Whatever," Lucas said, one of his arms flailing. "I want to know why you're following me."

"Like I said, we need to talk."

"I don't want to talk to you," Lucas said. He could feel himself getting angry, his need for answers clouded by the alcohol. Just looking at the white-haired man standing there in his fancy, dark clothes, leaning on his fancy cane, made him furious.

"Now isn't a good time anyway," the older man said. "Maybe when you're not drunk."

He turned to his car.

"Drunk?" Lucas said. "Who the hell is drunk?"

The man turned briefly. "You are," he said with a condescending laugh. "And I hope you're not planning to *drive* in that condition."

It was like somebody had flipped a switch inside his head and all Lucas could see was red. How dare this man . . . this old man . . . tell him he was too drunk to drive?

Before he knew what he was doing, Lucas charged at him. "I'll show you my condition," he slurred drunkenly, raising his fist.

Lucas knew he was going to regret what he was about to do, but he couldn't stop. He was going to hit this guy . . . probably more than once.

And after the day he'd had—after the few days he'd had, really—he was going to *enjoy* it.

Lucas let his fist fly toward the man's face, but his face suddenly wasn't there anymore. Lucas stumbled forward with the ferocity of the punch and spun around, searching for the object of his rage.

But as he turned, there was a blur of movement in front of him, something so fast that his drunken eyes couldn't follow it.

Before he could even react, Lucas was punched, one blow knocking his face violently to the left and another doing the same to the right. Then a kick to the stomach propelled him backward through the air. He landed hard on his butt, dazed and confused and trying desperately to remain conscious.

"You're not even close to being ready for that," the old man said as he limped toward Lucas and squatted down with the help of his cane to fish the truck keys from Lucas's pocket. Finding the keys, he tossed them across the Trough parking lot. "Hopefully you'll find them when you're sober," the old man said as he climbed into his car and backed out of the lot in a cloud of dust and gravel.

"You better run," Lucas slurred, slowly slumping over, unconscious before his head even touched the ground.

NASCAR was racing inside his head.

Not just the cars from a particular race, mind you; nope, all the cars that ever participated in a NASCAR race—past, present, and future—were driving through the furrows of his swollen and pulsing brain, causing one of the most excruciating headaches he'd ever had the misfortune to experience.

Lucas came awake with a dry snort, lifting his head to figure out where he was and why he felt like he was going to die.

He hit his head on the steering wheel of his truck. It wasn't a bad bump, but his brain was throbbing so badly that he was sure it was about to detonate, taking off the top of his skull.

At least then the pain would stop.

Lucas awkwardly pushed himself into a sitting position.

His tongue felt as though it had been wrapped in trash bags, and his breath smelled like something that belonged inside one.

He looked out the window. He was still in the parking lot of the Trough. The memory of the confrontation with the old man—his father—suddenly rushed to fill his thoughts. He touched his jaw where he'd been struck multiple times the night before and moved it from side to side; it didn't feel as bad as he remembered it should. The old man had certainly packed a decent punch.

Sitting up, he gazed through the rearview mirror at the Hog Trough behind him and could just about make out the old, dusty Budweiser clock in the window, and the time.

He was going to be late for work again.

"Crap. Crap. Crap," Lucas said in a panic. He fumbled through his pockets but didn't find his keys. He then recalled that the old man had tossed them somewhere in the lot so that he wouldn't drive drunk.

On the verge of believing the situation was hopeless, Lucas suddenly remembered. His mother had given him something pretty goofy last year for his birthday, something she'd picked up from one of those television shopping networks. It was a plastic case for an emergency car key that you could stick underneath your car with a powerful magnet. He'd thought it was a pretty crummy present, but he'd humored her. She'd even gone out and had another key for his truck made.

He climbed from the truck and bent down, reaching beneath the frame and fishing around for the case, hoping it hadn't fallen off over the course of the year.

"Bingo!" he said aloud, finding his present, sliding open the mud-caked case, and removing the key. *Maybe it wasn't such a stupid present after all,* he thought as he climbed back inside his ride. Racing the clock, Lucas turned the truck's engine over and pulled out of the parking lot, tires spinning and gravel tossing.

He would have loved to go home to shower and decontaminate his mouth, but he didn't have the time. This was getting to be a habit, and he hoped he didn't stink too badly.

He swung into the garage lot and his heart sank. He wasn't going to be so lucky today—Big Lou's SUV was parked alongside the main building.

"Crap," he barked again, slamming the palm of his hand down on the steering wheel. He was going to get the "a person's got to learn responsibility" speech for sure.

Lucas parked the truck and poured himself from the seat, plodding across the lot to the main building. The garage doors were already up. Big Lou's Gas Up & Go was open for business; too bad the mechanic wasn't in yet.

This is gonna be bad.

Lucas considered sneaking in through the bay, but he thought better of it. Might as well confront Big Lou and get it out of the way. He entered through the office door.

As he pushed the door open into the air-conditioned room, a bell clanged happily, sending a spasm of pain through his skull.

Big Lou was settled in behind the front desk, receipts and bills spread out before him as he got ready to do the monthly books. His trademark cowboy hat was atop his gumdrop-shaped head; from beneath it, he stared at Lucas with beady eyes. An unlit cigar—he was trying to quit—protruded from the left side of his wide mouth.

"What'd you do, sleep in your truck?" he asked, his nose wrinkling in disgust.

"Matter of fact—" Lucas began.

"Your mom's looking for you," Lou interrupted, placing a yellow receipt on a stack of others.

"Let me go over and speak with her, and then I'll get right to work," Lucas said, turning eagerly toward the door.

"You can talk to her later," Lou said.

Lucas turned his head, certain that more info was coming.

"I want you to take the tow truck out to Garrick Road. Got a call a little while ago that somebody's broke down out there and needs a tow back here."

"Sure," Lucas said as Big Lou maneuvered his gigantic belly out of the way of the desk drawer to fish around for the tow truck keys inside. He tossed them to the boy.

"Make it quick," Lou said as Lucas caught the key ring. "Gotta get some money into this place before I lose my shirt."

Without another word, Lucas was gone, leaving the office and crossing the lot to where the tow truck was parked. If anything should have made him feel better, it was the fact that he didn't have to listen to Big Lou's words of wisdom.

Maybe it wasn't going to be such a disastrous day after all.

But then he thought about his mother and how he'd stayed out all night without giving her a call, and he knew that was wishful thinking. That meeting would go exactly as expected. Badly.

It took him less than ten minutes to get to Garrick

Road. His eyes searched the lonely stretch, and as he caught sight of an all-too-familiar car awaiting his arrival, his day moved from the disastrous category into one of the worst in his life.

He knew that black Ford Mustang; no amount of road dust could disguise it.

"You have got to be kidding me," Lucas grumbled beneath his breath as he pulled up behind the vehicle.

Inching the tow truck as close as he could, Lucas lay on the horn. The blaring sound nearly caused him to pass out from pain, but it would have been worth it to scare the old man into a heart attack.

Through the grimy, bug-spattered windshield, he watched the guy slowly emerge from the driver's seat, using the cane to help him stand.

Didn't need the cane to beat my butt last night, Lucas thought, watching as the old man slammed the car door closed and stood there. *Like to see him try that again when I'm not drunk.*

Lucas could feel himself growing angry already. He opened the door and climbed from the truck.

"What's wrong with you?" Lucas demanded.

"Sorry about the keys," the old man said, handing them back to Lucas. "You weren't in any condition to drive."

"I'm done with this," Lucas said, grabbing the keys and getting up into the old guy's face. "I want you to stop following me . . . or whatever it is you're doing. I bet you don't even need a tow, do you?"

The older man sighed, crossing his arms.

"No."

"Dammit," the boy cursed, kicking at the dirt angrily. "I don't know what you want from me, but I don't have it, all right? Go away, back to wherever it was you came from. I don't need you in my life now or ever and—"

"We need to talk, Lucas," the man interrupted him.

"See, that's what I mean. No, we don't need to—"

"We need to talk because I'm afraid your life, and the life of your mother, could be in danger."

Lucas couldn't believe his ears.

"What did you just say?" he asked, his voice becoming louder. "Did you just *threaten my mother?*"

The man lifted one hand while leaning on his cane. "I did no such thing," he explained. "What I said was there is a chance that you and your mother could be in danger . . . because of me, which is why we need to talk."

At first Lucas thought this was some sort of twisted joke. Judging by the serious expression on the man's face, though, he seemed to mean what he was saying.

"You expect me to listen to this?" Lucas asked. "I don't even know who you are. Why would I—"

"Clayton Hartwell," the man said, extending a hand for Lucas to shake.

Bells—very loud bells that hurt like hell—went off in Lucas's head. Clayton Hartwell—where had he heard that name before?

And then it came to him.

"Holy crap! You're like a billionaire or something."

"Or something," the man agreed.

"You're lying," Lucas accused. "Prove that you're who you say you are."

The older man sighed, reaching into his suit-coat pocket to produce a wallet. He riffled through it, found his license, and handed it to the boy.

"If we could just make this quick. There really is an awful lot I need to share with you before—"

"It *is* you," Lucas said, staring at the photograph.

"Imagine that," Hartwell said, reaching out to take the license back from the boy.

Lucas watched as the man put the identification back into the wallet and returned both to his coat pocket.

"Satisfied?" the older man asked.

"Why?" Lucas suddenly said.

"Why?" Hartwell repeated. "Why what?"

"Why now?" the boy questioned. "Eighteen years I've been on this planet. Why *now* do you decide to come and find me?"

Hartwell chuckled. "You get right to the point," he said. "Definitely a Hartwell trait."

"Yeah? Do you have a bad temper too?" Lucas asked. "'Cause if you don't start telling me what this is all about, you're gonna see an example of mine."

"I'm dying," Hartwell said unemotionally. "Let's cut right to the chase."

Lucas felt a bit unsteady on his feet, but he blamed it on the escalating heat and the fact that he was still feeling the effects of last night's drinking.

"You're . . . That sucks," he said, regretting his words, but he had no idea how to react. It wasn't as if he knew this guy. It was like being told a total stranger was about to get hit by a bus.

So what?

"It does at that." Hartwell nodded. "And it's also the reason I needed to find you."

"You wanted to track me down to tell me that it sucks to be dying?" Lucas asked.

"No, I wanted to track you down to give you something."

Lucas's heart started beating a little bit faster. This guy had more money than God, and if he was looking to give some of that away . . .

"Is this about your will or something?" he asked.

"Much more than that," Hartwell explained. "Let's just say I've lived an extreme life, one filled with excitement and often great danger. But now it's coming to a close."

The man paused, as if considering his next words.

"The world needs to have somebody like me in it," Hartwell explained. "I have to pass my legacy on to someone else before it's too late."

"Your legacy?" Lucas asked. "What, like the family business? I don't know anything about running a business. I can't even give out the right change at the gas station."

And then he noticed the man had removed his suit jacket and draped it over the roof of his car.

"Hot or something?" Lucas asked, a little startled as his father began to unbutton his shirt.

"I have something to show you," the man said. "And then hopefully you'll understand."

Lucas started to freak. All he needed now was to have one of his buddies drive by and catch him standing on the side of the road with a half-dressed old dude.

"Look, leave your shirt on, okay?" he said. "If you're hot, we can go sit in the car."

The man, however, pulled his shirt open to reveal something strange. At first Lucas thought it was a red and black T-shirt, but then he noticed the symbol.

An open bird's claw.

A talon.

"What's that?" Lucas asked.

"It's my insignia," Hartwell said.

"Your *insignia?*"

The older man nodded.

"I'm the Raptor, Lucas."

Lucas continued to stare. He nodded slightly to show he understood, but inside his head, he was screaming.

Holy crap, my father is a superhero!

"This is a joke, right?" Lucas asked, fighting the urge to turn and run. "Like, maybe some reality show or something?" He looked around, searching for hidden cameras, and found nothing but lonely road.

Hartwell shook his head. "No joke," he reiterated. "I am the Raptor. But my days as a hero are coming to an end."

"This is impossible!" Lucas screamed. "I can't believe you're standing here in front of me telling me this crap! If you're the Raptor, prove it."

"I'm an old man and I kicked your butt last night in a parking lot," Hartwell said. "Isn't that enough?"

"No," Lucas spat. "I was drunk and . . . and you could've gotten lucky."

Hartwell sighed.

A strange hum filled the air.

"Is this enough?" Hartwell asked as bolts of crackling power leapt from his wrists, striking an old tree about ten feet away. The tree exploded into flames, as if it had been hit by lightning.

"How's that?" he asked calmly. "Do you believe me now?"

The tree at the side of the road was still burning, and Lucas watched it wither away as the flames consumed it.

"You're a superhero . . . and you . . . and you want me to take over because you're dying."

"That's the gist of it," Hartwell said. "You're my son, and that makes you special. You're one of the few people in this world who can pick up where I leave off."

Lucas felt numb, like he was trapped in some sort of bizarre fever dream. "What does this have to do with my mother?" he finally asked, all emotion sucked from his voice.

"Let's just say that doing what I do has made me some enemies over the years. Enemies who might try to target those who mean something to me."

Lucas stirred from his funk to stare at the man. "She hasn't had anything to do with you in close to twenty years."

Hartwell shrugged. "They'll lash out at anything that could even remotely hurt me."

"So you've put her . . . *us* in danger by coming here?" The realization was slowly dawning on Lucas.

"Yes, but it was necessary that I find you. The Raptor can't die, and he won't if—"

Lucas had no idea why he did it, but he couldn't stop himself. He stepped closer to Hartwell and threw a surprise punch that knocked the old man backward into the Mustang and then to the ground.

Shaking the sharp pain from his fist, Lucas stood over the fallen figure. "I can't believe you," he snarled. "I've never even met you before, and you come here and dump this in my lap . . . as if I'd even want it."

Hartwell grabbed the car's bumper and pulled himself to his feet, blood running from his nose to his lips. "I understand how upset you are, but there's more at stake here than—"

"No," Lucas interrupted flatly, silencing the man. "There's nothing else to say."

He turned and headed for the tow truck.

"Lucas, please," Hartwell called after him. "There's still so much I have to explain."

"I'm done," Lucas said, climbing into the truck. "Get out of my life and take your stupid legacy with you."

He backed down the road and turned the truck toward the garage.

The image of the old man with a dark secret gradually diminished in the rearview mirror, until finally it was gone.

That afternoon, Lucas went home sick.

Big Lou wasn't very happy, but since Lucas had never taken a sick day, and had agreed to finish the waiting repairs before he left, Lou grudgingly agreed to let him go.

Upon returning to the garage that morning, Lucas had gone about his work on a bizarre kind of autopilot, his mind filled with images of that strange meeting on a lonely stretch of road. It was bad enough his deadbeat dad had found his way back into his life, but to claim he was a superhero—who wanted Lucas to carry on his legacy—well, c'mon. Enough was enough.

So Lucas went home to figure out how he was going to talk to his mother about this. There was no way he could avoid it, especially after Hartwell's threat.

He must have sat at the kitchen table for at least two hours, staring into space. No matter how he approached it, what he had to say sounded completely insane. Unless his mother knew her old boyfriend was a superhero?

That just complicated things all the more. If she knew about his extracurricular activities, why hadn't she shared that information with Lucas? Didn't he have the right to know his father was the Raptor?

Lucas grabbed the sides of his head. He had thought his hangover was bad; this information was like an atom bomb ready to explode in his mind.

He closed his eyes and breathed deeply, trying to calm down. But all he could see in his mind's eye was the image of Hartwell, destroying the tree with crackling bolts of electricity.

"Dammit," he sighed, opening his eyes.

Just as his mother came into the trailer.

"Are you all right?" she asked, setting a bag of groceries down on the kitchen counter.

"I'm fine," he answered, not looking at her.

"Big Lou came by for a coffee and told me you'd gone home sick. I was worried."

"No need to worry; just got a headache is all."

"You could've had a bullet in your skull for all I knew,"

she said, taking some milk and butter from the shopping bag and putting them in the fridge. "You didn't come home last night, so I had no idea what kind of condition I was going to find you in."

"I'm sorry about that," he said. "I had a little too much to drink, and I fell asleep in my truck."

"At least you had the common sense not to drive in that condition," she said from inside the refrigerator as she rearranged things. "Did you take anything for the headache?" she asked, closing the fridge.

"No." He shook his head. "I'm just gonna ride this one out."

"Oh, playing the martyr, are we?"

She left the kitchen, heading for her room to change out of her uniform. The whole time she was gone, Lucas tortured himself over how he was going to tell her.

When Cordelia returned, she set about making supper, attempting small talk as she worked. But his answers were short—a word or a grunt—and eventually she just quit trying.

After a while, though, Lucas couldn't stand the silence anymore. "What do you know about my father?" he finally blurted out, watching closely for her reaction.

She was peeling potatoes in the sink with the water running. She stopped for a moment, then continued. "Nothing much, I'm afraid. Just what I've told you in the past," she said with a sad shake of her head. "It was pretty much a one-night stand. I'm not proud of it. I led a wild life back in Seraph. But you know what? If it wasn't for my getting pregnant . . . if it wasn't for you . . ."

"Clayton Hartwell," he said quietly, still watching her.

She dropped the potato and the knife into the sink with a clatter.

"He's that rich guy we see on TV and in the magazines all the time . . . right?" she asked, trying to keep her composure.

"You tell me," Lucas said. "I hear there's a lot more to him than that."

She looked at him; then she left the sink and went to the cabinet, reaching for the bottle of whiskey and a glass.

"Don't do that," Lucas said.

"If we're going to talk . . . really talk, I'm going to need this."

She put some ice in the glass and brought it and the bottle to the kitchen table.

"First off, tell me what you know," she said, pouring the golden liquid over the ice.

"He came to the garage a few days ago and then kept popping up wherever I went," Lucas said.

"So he told you he's your father," she said, taking her first sip.

Lucas nodded. "And the Raptor."

"I can't believe he did that," his mother said with a gasp, setting her glass down before she could drop it.

"He told me, all right," Lucas said, flashing back to his father's display of power. "And he also told me he was dying."

"Dying?" Cordelia asked in a concerned whisper.

"He said he's sick and he needs somebody to carry on his legacy."

Cordelia gasped again and raised the glass to her mouth with a trembling hand. "This is what I've always been afraid of," she said, more to herself than to Lucas.

"What?" he asked. "What are you afraid of?"

"After learning who he was . . . who he really was, I was always afraid the lifestyle would somehow find its way back to you. That some bad guy with an attitude would put two and two together and come after us."

She paused, drink midway to her mouth.

"After *you*."

"And that's why you left Seraph City," Lucas said.

Cordelia nodded. "I ran away. I was pregnant with you, and I couldn't bear the thought of anything hurting you, then or ever . . . so I took off to the most out-of-the-way place I could imagine."

She finished her drink and quickly poured another.

"You said he's sick?" she asked. "How does he look?"

Lucas shrugged. He felt a little put off by his mother's curiosity, but could he blame her? It had been close to twenty years since she'd last seen the man.

"He's kind of thin and pale, but he's still in pretty good shape"—he remembered the kick to the stomach that had sent him sprawling across the Hog Trough parking lot—"for an old guy."

"I was always surprised he didn't come looking for us," his mother said. "But at the same time, I was relieved."

She poked a finger into her glass, playing with the ice.

"Do you hate me?" she asked.

"I don't hate you," Lucas told her. "I just wish I'd known about this. Do you know how hard this is for me to wrap my head around?"

"I know, I know," she said, nodding sadly. "But I did it to protect you."

He was quiet for a moment; then a question came to him.

"Did you meet any of the others?" he asked her.

She stared with a confused expression.

"Any of the other heroes, besides the Raptor? You know, like Talon? Did you meet him?"

She shook her head and had opened her mouth to explain, when her words were cut off by a strange whining sound. It was coming from outside.

"What the hell is that?" Lucas asked, standing up. He tried to see through the blinds covering the window over the sink, but it was dark.

"Sounds like an airplane," Cordelia said, heading toward the door.

Lucas didn't know why, but he was suddenly nervous, frightened by the sound.

"Sit down," he ordered his mother.

She turned and was staring at him in confusion when the first explosion hit, illuminating the kitchen in an eerie orange glow.

"Lucas," she whispered.

"Stay here," he told her, pushing her back toward the table.

He went to the trailer door, his hand on the knob for what seemed an eternity before he finally turned it and went outside.

5

The trailer park was under attack.

Strange vehicles that resembled ATVs without wheels floated above the park on what could only have been columns of air. They darted about like dragonflies, their pilots wearing jumpsuits and black masks with red goggles.

Lucas had never seen anything like it, except maybe in some crazy science-fiction movie.

Some of the trailers at the back of the park were on fire, and Lucas watched in horror as one of the vehicles flew over the Johansons' place and opened fire with a weapon that sounded like the cracking of a bullwhip. A beam of red light shot from the barrel of the weapon and ignited the trailer's propane tanks. The explosion tore apart the Johansons' double-wide and sent Lucas stumbling backward. The heat rushed to fill his lungs and sear his eyes.

He had to get help, and get it fast. Digging deep into his pocket, he searched for his phone but found only some change and his truck keys. He must have left the phone on the table in the kitchen! He spun around but was stopped by the sound of someone calling his name.

Mrs. Taylor was coming out of her trailer, clutching Fluffles in her arms.

"Go back inside!" Lucas called out, running toward her, waving his arms.

The old woman didn't listen, instead heading toward him in a frantic shuffle.

Lucas chanced a quick glance down to the end of the park. The flying machines were heading directly for them now, destroying all the trailers in their path with shots of devastating red light.

It was like being in the middle of a war zone, or at least what he thought a war zone would be like.

A *slaughter* was more like it.

Mr. Niles made it out of his burning home and was aiming a shotgun up at one of the floating craft. He didn't get even one shot off before he was riddled with blasts of laser light that cut him to ribbons.

Mrs. Taylor was screaming, and Fluffles was trying desperately to get away from her. Lucas grabbed them and practically dragged them toward his place.

But Fluffles scratched Mrs. Taylor's face in panic, forcing her to loosen her grip, and the cat sprang from her arms. The old woman let out a cry of dismay and pulled away from

Lucas with a sudden burst of strength, toddling after the flee-ing cat.

Neither made it very far.

"No!" Lucas screamed as one of the vehicles fired on Mrs. Taylor and her beloved cat. Pure instinct kicked in then, telling him to run for his life, but he remembered his mother, still inside their trailer. He turned and felt his blood freeze as he saw her standing in the doorway, a look of horror on her face.

"C'mon!" he screamed over the sounds of destruction, motioning for her to join him.

He could hear the ear-piercing whine of the hovercraft engines as they came closer, and the screams of the dying.

They had very little time. He reached out, roughly grab-bing his mother's arm, and yanked her down the steps.

"What's happening?" she cried, her voice raised in panic. "Why are they doing this?"

Lucas didn't answer. There wasn't time for questions, only action. They had to get to his truck if they were to have any chance of escape. He dragged his mother with him, not bothering to turn around. He didn't want to see how close they were to dying.

The truck was hit with a beam of red, exploding in a ball of flames that threw them backward. Multiple craft buzzed above their heads like flies over a rotting carcass. Lucas could hear his mother's moans beside him and it just about broke his heart. He'd always hated to hear her cry, it made him crazy, but now, it drove him to action.

He didn't know where the strength came from. Before he could even think about what he was doing, he had risen to his feet and picked his mother up from the ground.

"I'm going to get you out of here," he promised her over the humming sounds of the sky vehicles.

"I love you, Lucas," she cried.

He didn't answer, knowing in his heart he would have the time later to tell her how he felt. They would still have all the time in the world together.

Lucas was running now, beams of red light following him, striking the dirt. He darted among them, marveling at his newfound strength. He was certain he'd never felt this strong or fast in his life—although nobody had ever been trying to kill him before either.

But that wasn't entirely true.

Racing for his survival, Lucas suddenly remembered Richie Dennison and the feel of the knife blade in his stomach.

Lucas had somehow survived that. He decided he would survive this as well.

Two of the craft dropped down in front of him, blocking his way, kicking up clouds of choking dust.

Lucas spun around, running back the way he had come, toward the only home he had ever known. Two more of the futuristic vehicles zipped close to his head, and he stumbled and fell. He felt his mother struggle beneath him, pushing away his arm to get to her feet.

"Mom!" he shouted, his voice clogged with dust.

"Save yourself," he heard her yell as she ran straight for the futuristic craft.

"Don't!" he screamed, scrambling to his feet to go after her.

It all seemed to happen in slow motion. The machines fired at her, beams of crimson light blasting first through the corrugated steel of their mobile home and then through the fragile form of his mother. Lucas opened his mouth to scream as he watched the woman he loved, who had sacrificed so much for him, cut down.

He fell to his knees before her, dragging her lifeless body into his arms. He started screaming, begging the ones who had killed her—and all his friends at the trailer park—to kill him as well.

The pilots of the flying machines were more than happy to oblige. They flew in a buzzing circle around him, opening fire, striking him, as well as igniting the two recently filled propane tanks connected to the back of his trailer.

Both he and his mother were consumed in an explosion of hungry fire.

Lucas awoke to the acrid stink of burning metal.

He panicked immediately; he and his mother must still be in danger.

Sitting up, the boy realized he was outside, surrounded by multiple infernos. Everything began to fall into place. He remembered the attacks and what had happened to his mother. The air was thick with oily smoke that obscured his vision, and he crawled on his hands and knees, calling out her name.

He hoped—prayed—that he was wrong, that what he now recalled hadn't actually happened.

That she was still alive.

He found her body in the twisted remnants of their mobile home. She had been badly burned in the explosion. Tenderly, he reached down to take what remained of her body into his arms, but parts of her crumbled to ash.

Lucas screamed. His voice was a ragged roar. An impossible strength flowed through his body, and he tore pieces of twisted metal from the ground, hurling them into the air as if the wreckage weighed nothing, as if the superheated metal burning in his grasp was nothing more than a minor irritant.

How am I still alive? he asked himself. Nearly all his clothing had burned away, and his skin looked different—*felt different*—the only sign he had survived a fiery explosion being the pinkness of his flesh.

When he should have been dead—or at least near death—he felt only a pulsing strength.

As well as an incredible hunger, gnawing in his belly.

He remembered feeling like that after he had been stabbed. The hunger had been almost overwhelming.

Total panic began to sink in.

He started to run blindly, his hands out before him, waving away the choking smoke.

"Help!" he cried, certain the authorities would have arrived by now. "Help me!"

He sensed he was no longer alone and stopped short, listening for signs.

"Hello?" he called out. "I—I need help . . . please. . . ."

Something moved within the smoke, growing more pronounced as it loomed closer.

What if it's them? What if the ones that killed my neighbors and my mother . . . and tried to kill me are still here? They must be searching for survivors.

Eyes darting around for a weapon, Lucas found a broken piece of metal piping lying on the ground and snatched it up.

If he was going to die, he was going down fighting.

A figure emerged from the smoke. It was clad in the colors of darkness and blood.

Lucas immediately recognized the man.

"I was afraid something like this would happen," the superhero said grimly, standing before Lucas like some fearsome demon warrior.

It was the Raptor.

His father.

Lucas let the heavy section of pipe fall from his hands.

"Who—who were they?" he asked. He suddenly felt incredibly dizzy, his stomach hurting as if he had been gutshot. He dropped to his knees.

"They're an evil I've been fighting for a very long time," the Raptor said, the flames from the burning trailer park reflecting off his black, metallic mask. "Evil beings who will stop at nothing to achieve their goals. . . ."

The Raptor looked at Lucas, his eyes burning with a mixture of anger and sadness.

"An evil I'm no longer sure I'm strong enough to fight."

And with those words, the Raptor began to cough. For the briefest of moments, the costumed warrior didn't appear quite so fearsome.

Lucas doubled over in agony. He felt as though he was dying.

"Why did they do this?" he gasped, on his hands and knees, looking around at the flaming remains of the trailer park. "Why did they have to kill everyone?"

"To hurt me," the Raptor said. "They believe that striking at the things I care for, the things I love, will weaken me all the more."

The Raptor coughed again, his body wracked with convulsions. Through pain-clouded eyes, Lucas watched the man drop to one knee beside him.

"They may have been right," the Raptor said, struggling to catch his breath. "I'm not sure I'm strong enough to take them on."

They were silent then, the only sound the crackling of the fire as it burned away the only home Lucas had ever known. And suddenly he knew what he was going to do. What he *must* do.

"Teach me," he said, his voice weak from hunger.

The Raptor looked at him. "Do you know what that means? What that truly means?"

Lucas slowly nodded. "There has to be someone . . . someone to stop them from hurting innocent people."

The pain grew worse and he hunched over, explosions of color expanding before his eyes.

"Hold on," the Raptor said, removing something from one of the many compartments that hung from his belt. "This should help."

The superhero held a hypodermic needle, and before Lucas could react, he plunged the needle into Lucas's arm. Instantly, relief flooded through Lucas, but his eyes grew incredibly heavy.

"Promise you'll teach me everything I need to know to hurt them," he said, reaching out to grip his father's arm. "Promise me."

"I promise," the Raptor said as Lucas surrendered to the embrace of darkness.

Lucas was dreaming.

In this dream, he left his bed, drawn by the delicious aroma of bacon cooking. He shuffled into the kitchen and found his mother standing at the stove, turning the sizzling meat in a frying pan.

Lucas didn't care for bacon that was too crispy, and he certainly didn't like his mother that way. He stared at her as she worked at the stove, her body black and still smoldering.

And suddenly he had to wonder, was it the bacon he smelled?

Or was it the burning body of his mother?

He came awake with a yelp.

He was lying in an enormous bed, his naked body

covered by cool silk sheets. Lucas looked around in a rush of panic. The room was huge, bigger than his and his mom's entire mobile home, and filled with big pieces of heavy wooden furniture.

And then it all came back to him.

He remembered his father, who he was.

Shifting on the bed, he felt a sting in his arm and looked to see that he was hooked up to an IV bag hanging on a bracket over his bed, dripping clear fluid into his vein. He reached over and carefully pulled the needle from the bend in his arm, dropping it onto his pillow. He maneuvered himself into a sitting position and threw his legs over the side of the big bed, letting his feet touch the floor.

He felt different.

Lucas studied his legs, arms, and stomach, not quite understanding what he was seeing. His body seemed harder, more muscular. It reminded him of some of his friends who spent way too much time at the gym.

He saw a mirror across the room and sprang off the bed toward it.

"Oh my God," he whispered, staring at his reflection. It was like he'd been given a whole new body. He'd always wanted to look this way, muscular and cut, but he'd never had the discipline.

Lucas quickly looked back at the bag of liquid that had been draining into his arm, wondering if there was a connection. He decided it was high time for some answers.

A bathrobe and a pair of sweatpants were slung over a wingback chair in the corner of the room. He quickly dressed and went to the closed door. He feared it might be locked, but it wasn't, and he turned the knob, stepping out of the room into a long, curving hallway.

"Hello?" he called out, his voice sounding strange in the silence.

He walked toward a staircase at the opposite end of the hall and peered over the banister. The house seemed to be enormous.

"Hello?" he called out again, but still got no response.

Lucas went down the stairs and found himself in a large foyer. The floor was marble, and the furniture looked antique. On a circular table in the center of the hall, he noticed a vase of dead flowers and a thick coating of dust. In fact, dust coated just about everything.

As if nobody lived here.

He walked over to the large wooden front door and opened it, stepping outside. The air was cool, and he pulled his bathrobe tighter around him as he turned around and took a look at where he'd ended up.

"Holy crap," he muttered, walking backward to try to fit the view in. He was outside a mansion; that was the only way to describe it. It reminded him of one of those old English manors he'd seen in movies about British royalty. The home was huge, with lush, green grounds on either side, and beyond them, thick woods.

His curiosity stoked, he went back inside, strolling from the dusty foyer into what appeared to be a parlor; it was hard to tell because the furniture in this room was covered with long white sheets.

Across the parlor was an open doorway, which led to a sunroom with glass doors looking out onto a patio.

Lucas was drawn to the view.

Swinging the glass doors open, he stepped outside, gazing out over more woods and a pristine blue lake to an almost dreamlike vision of a city barely visible through a heavy fog.

Seraph City, he guessed as a warm breeze flowed across the lake, dispersing some of the mist.

"An amazing view, isn't it?" asked a familiar voice behind him.

Lucas turned to see Clayton Hartwell wheeling a cart through the doorway onto the patio, cane tucked beneath one arm.

"Thought you might want some breakfast," he said.

Lucas had a million questions, but, enticed by the smell of the food, he decided they could wait. At once he felt an aching emptiness begin to form in the pit of his belly. Like somebody hypnotized, he walked to the glass-topped table, pulled out a chair, and sat down.

Hartwell lifted the metal covers from the various plates on the cart. "I've got scrambled eggs, cereal, toast, sausages, and grapefruit," he said. "Help yourself."

Within seconds, Lucas had filled a plate to overflowing and was eating as though it would be his last meal.

"How is it?" Hartwell asked, hanging his cane from the edge of the table as he sat down across from the boy. He was dressed in his usual dark attire, his white hair slicked back.

"Good," Lucas said through a mouthful of eggs and toast.

"It's been a while since I've cooked anything. I'm surprised it's edible," Hartwell said with a chuckle.

Lucas poured some orange juice from a glass carafe.

"You made this? Don't you have any maids or butlers or anything?"

"No, it's just me." His father smiled. "As my life grew more . . . complicated, I found myself having less to do with Clayton Hartwell and more to do with the Raptor. Eventually I thought it best to let the staff go, and I've been living here alone in the mansion's lower levels."

Lucas refilled his plate with even more food, then glanced at Hartwell sheepishly. "Sorry," he apologized. "I'm just really hungry."

"That's perfectly normal for your condition," Hartwell said.

"My condition?" Lucas asked before taking a bite of his third piece of toast. "Are you talking about my body?"

"I thought you would have noticed," Hartwell said.

Lucas nodded. "Well, I've never had muscles like this before."

"That's because the nanites in your blood weren't fully activated until now."

"Nanites?" Lucas repeated, his skin suddenly itchy.

"I guess I should probably start at the beginning." Hartwell poured a cup of coffee from a silver pot.

"Your mother and I were involved in a serious relationship, but one that became strained by my revealing to her that I was the Raptor." He poured a splash of milk into the dark liquid and stirred it with a silver spoon. "When she became pregnant, she left me." Hartwell sipped his coffee, staring out into space.

"And what does that have to do with these . . . nanites

you mentioned?" Lucas asked. He grabbed half a grapefruit and began to devour it.

"As she feared for her . . . our baby's safety, so did I." Hartwell paused as if considering his words before continuing. "And the last time we were together, unbeknownst to her, I injected her with the nanites—microscopic machines programmed to ensure the health of our unborn child."

"Microscopic machines?" Lucas asked incredulously.

Hartwell nodded. "It's why you didn't die during the trailer park attack."

It suddenly started to make sense to Lucas. "And why I didn't die when I got stabbed."

Hartwell looked at him, head cocked. "You were stabbed?"

"I'll tell you later. Go on," Lucas urged.

"The nanites were programmed to activate only when your life was in danger," Hartwell continued. "They would be undetectable until then."

"Is that what's making me so hungry?" Lucas asked, spearing four sausages with his fork and shaking them onto his plate.

"Exactly," Hartwell confirmed. "The nanites need fuel. If you didn't eat, they would be forced to consume muscle and body mass while trying to fix you."

Lucas gazed again at himself, at his new body. "They did this?"

"They did," Hartwell answered. "They were fully activated during the attack at the trailer park and have made you stronger than you've ever been before. The nanites have brought you as close to physical perfection as possible."

"I can't believe this," Lucas said. "It's all completely

crazy." He was staring at his hands, imagining tiny machines flowing through his blood like trucks speeding down a highway. "Where did they come from?"

"Scientists employed by Hartwell Technologies," his father explained. "I've utilized many aspects of their research in my war against crime. One of the earliest versions of their performance-enhancing drugs is even in my blood."

"Then how can you be dying?" Lucas asked point-blank. "If these drugs made you perfect . . . ?"

"The earliest versions of these drugs didn't work as well," the old man said. "My older system can't handle the strain anymore and is breaking down."

"Isn't there anything you can do?"

The old man nodded. "Yes, and I did it," he said. "I found you."

Nightmarish images of the trailer park massacre flashed through Lucas's mind, temporarily shutting down his appetite. "What about the park?" he asked.

"It's been more than two weeks since it happened," Hartwell said.

"Two weeks?" Lucas was shocked by the amount of time that had passed.

"While you were unconscious," Hartwell continued, "the authorities investigated the incident at the trailer park and determined that it was just a horrible accident. A faulty propane tank exploded, setting off a chain reaction that destroyed the park."

"An accident?" Lucas repeated in disbelief.

"Explanations like that help people hide from the reality of the world they actually live in," Hartwell explained.

"Is anyone looking for me?" Lucas asked. "Or do they figure I burned up with everybody else?"

"Sorry to say, but you're dead now," the older man said with finality. "To the outside world, Lucas Moore died in a terrible fire caused by a freak accident."

Lucas felt his eyes begin to well up with emotion. It wasn't every day that you were told you had died.

His father reached over from his chair and placed a powerful hand on his shoulder.

"I know how this feels," he said with a slight nod.

"What, did you die too?"

The man's expression became very serious. "In a way I did," he said. "It was very early in my career as the Raptor, and let's just say it changed my view of the world, and of the evil in it."

Now Lucas's curiosity was piqued. "What happened?" he asked.

"People died because of my carelessness," Hartwell said, pulling his hand from Lucas's shoulder. "Taken away in the flash and roar of an explosion. And on that day, the Raptor the world knew died as well . . . and a new Raptor was born."

Lucas could see that his father didn't want to talk about it anymore, that the memory was too painful. He recalled his own horrors—images of his attackers riding on their hovering vehicles, death rays cutting through the darkness. He felt himself grow angry.

"So you're saying that I died and have been reborn."

Hartwell nodded. "Yes, you have."

"That's good," Lucas said. "So when will I get a chance to go after the guys who killed my mother?"

Hartwell stood up from his chair, retrieving his cane. "You're not there yet," he said. "There's still a great amount of training you will need to undergo to prove to me that you're capable of taking on the mantle of the Raptor."

He slid the chair into the table.

"There's a chance you might never be ready," he added grimly.

"I'll be ready," Lucas said with an assured nod. "I've been reborn."

His father laughed as he turned.

"We'll see," he said, limping from the patio. "By the time I'm done with you, you'll probably be wishing you'd stayed dead."

The days became weeks, and the weeks flowed into months, but it seemed like years to Lucas as he came to truly understand his father's cryptic words.

At least ten times a day, when his body was screaming from exertion and his muscles burned and trembled as he forced them to their limits and beyond, a small part of him did wish he had died that fateful night at the trailer park.

But then he would remember his mother, and Mrs. Taylor, and even Fluffles, and somehow he would find within himself the ability to push his body that much further.

Someone had to avenge them.

And that someone was going to be him . . . if Hartwell ever finished with his damn training.

His schooling was relentless—multiple forms of hand-to-hand combat, military history, weapons training, advanced first aid. It just went on and on, until his brain was so crammed with information that he was sure nothing else could possibly fit.

But there was always something more to learn, always some new way to disarm an opponent or defuse an explosive device, so his training continued.

Lucas actually started to believe that his father was some sort of machine. In a world where costumed heroes existed, why not? Here was a man, in his mid to late fifties at the least, who was dying from some mysterious illness, who often needed a cane to get around, teaching Lucas relentlessly without any signs of growing tired. He couldn't possibly be human.

But a fire burned in the old man's eyes, and Lucas hoped that fire would one day—*one day*—burn in his own eyes.

So he went on with it.

And he would hear his father's oft-repeated words as he struggled to get through the latest lesson.

"You can have the most powerful weapon in the world at your disposal, but if you don't know how to use it, it's useless."

Lucas's body was that weapon, and this was how he was being trained to use it.

How he was being trained to become more than he was.

Trained to become the next Raptor.

The alarm clock began to chime, and Lucas let out a moan.

He felt as if he had just gone to bed, after a particularly grueling day that had dragged on into the early hours of morning.

Something has to be wrong, he thought, lifting his face from his pillow to squint at the clock across the room on his dresser.

5:00 a.m.

It couldn't be. How could that even be possible? He'd just closed his eyes what felt like five minutes before.

But he knew it wasn't wrong; the night had passed so quickly because he'd gone to bed only three hours earlier. Fearing his fate if he ignored the alarm, Lucas rolled onto his back and hauled his tired, aching carcass from the bed.

The one time he'd ignored the alarm and gone back to sleep had been a total nightmare. The training had been three times as grueling and had gone on through the night until the next morning, when it had started all over again.

He didn't want to chance a repeat of that.

Throwing on some sweats and a T-shirt, he left his room, heading down in the elevator to the gymnasium, in one of Hartwell Manor's many underground levels.

Lucas wondered what kind of abuse he was going to experience today. His entire body throbbed despite the body-repairing nanites running through his blood. He guessed there was only so much the tiny machines could do.

A growl like some kind of wild animal filled the elevator compartment, and he pressed a hand to his grumbling belly. He was starving again, as he always seemed to be these days, but he couldn't eat until the first round of training was done.

He wondered what it would be today—something physical, like an aikido refresher, or maybe a quiz on

Shakespeare's sonnets? He had no idea what Shakespeare had to do with becoming a superhero, but knew it wasn't wise to ask.

Roll with it had become his mantra these last few months.

Hartwell was the teacher, and Lucas was the student.

The elevator came to a stop, and the doors silently slid open on the gymnasium floor.

Usually his father would be there, impatiently waiting for him, but this morning only darkness greeted him. Lucas left the elevator, stepping out into the darkened gym, running his hand along the wall until he found the light switches. He flicked the switches up, only to find they didn't work.

"Huh," he said as he continued to stupidly push them up and down.

He heard a noise from somewhere across the gym, a door opening with a creak.

"Lights are busted," Lucas called out, expecting some sort of response.

None came.

"Hello?" he called out. "Are you in here? I said there's something wrong with the lights. Guess we're not gonna get to work out today."

He didn't hear a verbal response, but he did pick up the sound of heavy breathing from somewhere up ahead.

Lucas squinted, trying to see through the darkness. "Is that you?" he asked, catching sight of a moving shadow. "What's wrong? Is it silent-but-deadly day today or something?"

A roar like nothing he'd ever heard before filled the air

and was followed by the sound of pounding footfalls heading directly toward him.

Whatever it was, it was big. Lucas could feel the vibrations through the floor, and it was on him before he even had a chance to react.

It was a man—at least he thought it was a man—a big man who moved like a freight train. The figure growled, driving him down with arms the size of steel girders. Lucas took the full brunt of the attack, lifted off his feet and landing in the middle of the gymnasium floor.

Who let a giant gorilla into the building? he thought as he scrambled to his feet.

The mysterious figure roared again, charging at him through the darkness.

Lucas felt the first waves of panic as his attacker burst out of the shadows with an ear-piercing shriek. The creature snatched him up by the front of his T-shirt and slammed him viciously to the floor. The air exploded from Lucas's lungs in a wheezing blast, and colored lights blossomed in front of his eyes. He fought to keep from passing out.

As Lucas gasped for air the monster stood above him, lifting a bare foot with a grunt. Lucas knew he was preparing to bring it down and crush him.

He rolled out of the way just as the massive foot fell. The ground shook as it landed where his head had been.

His attacker roared in disapproval as Lucas sprang up.

A gigantic hand surged through the blackness and wrapped around his throat. Lucas gasped as the monster man began to squeeze.

He struggled uselessly to breathe. He felt his life start to slip away.

His attacker began to laugh, a horrible sound. Lucas didn't want it to be the last thing he heard before he died.

The right fighting technique came to him in a flash; it was an aikido move.

Lucas brought his hands up, grabbing hold of his attacker's wrist with one hand while applying just the right amount of pressure to the elbow with the other.

The monster man screamed out in pain as Lucas carried through, using his attacker's weight and size against him to drive him to the floor. It was as if all he had been taught was lining up inside his head.

The monster didn't stay down for long, rising to his feet with a growl.

But this time, Lucas was ready for him.

The key was to stay out of the monster's reach. His opponent was a brute, relying almost totally on strength and savagery. If he couldn't get to Lucas, Lucas couldn't be hurt.

Using speed and agility, Lucas kept away from the monster's clutches, zipping in when an opening presented itself to strike at sensitive areas on the monster's body.

It wasn't long before the giant was lurching about, his body stiff from multiple blows, and he began to slow down as the fight slowly drained from him.

Lucas couldn't have felt better.

This was where it all came together, all the long months and hours of training. This was what it was all for!

The monster was hurting, and his attacks became even more savage. Sloppy.

As Lucas circled him, keeping out of reach and deciding where to hit him next, the large man surprised him. Believing he was attacking to the right, Lucas dodged to the left, only to have the beast of a man change his direction suddenly and with a roar, snatch him up off the floor in a powerful bear hug.

The monster man roared with laughter, pleased by his cleverness, as he began to squeeze.

Lucas felt the first of his ribs snap. The pain was incredible. Even with the nanites inside him working overtime, he wasn't sure how much more of a beating he could take.

Glancing down, he looked into the hate-filled eyes of his attacker, more beast than man. The monster was smiling, his razor-sharp teeth almost glowing in the darkness of the gym. A rumbling laugh gurgled up as he began to squeeze even tighter.

Lucas squirmed in the monster's clutches. Suddenly remembering something he'd learned, not from his father but from the occasional brawl at the Hog Trough, he drew back his head and brought it forward with as much force as possible.

The top of his forehead connected with the bridge of the beast man's wide nose. There was a loud snap, and Lucas's face was spattered with something warm that had the acrid smell of metal.

And as the monster man cried out in pain, Lucas was able to pull his arms free. Then he threw them back and brought his hands together to savagely box his attacker's ears.

The monster bellowed, releasing Lucas to grab at the sides of his head.

Lucas delivered a snap kick to one of his enemy's knees.

His attacker crashed to the gym floor, hands still clutching his large, square head. Now at his level, Lucas drew back his arm, bringing the palm of his hand forward in a snap to the monster's lower jaw.

His attacker's head was driven backward, and the momentum carried his entire body to the floor, where he lay unconscious.

Lucas stood still for a moment, attempting to regulate his breathing the way he'd been taught and waiting to see if his adversary would get up again. But the beast man just lay there in a broken heap.

Lucas was aware of his body. It seemed he could actually feel the nanites working inside to heal him, to take away his pain.

His thoughts were in a jumble. He wondered where his father was, and whether this was one of the Raptor's enemies, who had somehow found his way to the manor to exact revenge. He decided he would find something to tie this monstrosity up, and then he would search for his father.

Starting toward one of the equipment closets, where he'd seen an old jump rope, Lucas suddenly found himself falling to the floor, a gigantic hand crushing his ankle.

The monster man was conscious again.

"Kill you," he growled, crawling atop Lucas.

Lucas tried to squirm away, but the monster grabbed hold, lifting him up off the floor and slamming him down.

This he repeated, again and again.

Each time Lucas hit the floor, the universe in all its glory appeared before his eyes, and he thought it would be the last thing he saw before it all went dark.

But Lucas decided he wasn't too keen on dying, especially today.

He allowed his body to go deceptively limp, flopping like a broken doll in the monster's clutches, and waited for his opportunity. He hoped it would be soon, because he wasn't sure how much more punishment his skull could take, repeatedly hitting the gym floor.

The monster had just pulled him close to see if he was still conscious when Lucas made his move.

He jammed a thumb into the monstrosity's eye, raking it from left to right.

His attacker cried out, releasing Lucas as he groped at his injured face.

Lucas didn't waste any time, climbing to his feet and quickly positioning himself behind his foe. He wrapped his arm around the beast's neck and started to pull back. The monster thrashed, attempting to get to his feet, but Lucas exerted every iota of his strength, forcing the monster to remain on his knees, while closing the grip on his throat.

Everything, no matter how big and strong, needed to breathe.

He felt his enemy's struggle grow weaker and knew that victory was only moments away. Lucas had to last.

The monster man struggled and gasped, but Lucas held on, tightening his grip.

The lights of the gymnasium suddenly came on, startling him, and he saw his father standing a few feet away, watching.

"That's it, Lucas," his father said, cheering him on. "Use what I've taught you."

His blood rushed in his ears, the thrumming of his heart like the roar of a powerful engine. The monster's struggles became pathetic, dwindling to practically nothing, and he knew he had won.

"His fate is in your hands now, boy," his father said to him. "It's up to you. Let him live, and the chance that he'll be back on the streets in no time, putting the lives of innocents at stake, is dropped squarely in your lap. Or you can tighten your grip for just a bit longer and . . ."

Lucas let the monster go, his large body dropping limply to the hardwood floor.

Breathing heavily, Lucas stared at his father. Hartwell was nodding, accepting his decision.

"The choice is yours," Hartwell said.

But Lucas could tell by the expression on his father's face that it wasn't the choice he would have made.

"What's going on?"

"You did quite well," Hartwell praised him. "A little slow at first, but then you started to utilize what you've been taught."

"That thing could have killed me," Lucas said, pointing to the unconscious behemoth lying on the floor.

"You're probably right," Hartwell said. "Something you should always be aware of when going into battle."

"Who the hell is he?"

"His name is Jackson Meeves. On the street they call him Bestial. He's a low-level supervillain with more strength than brains. The Raptor captured him the other night as he tried to knock over an all-night convenience store."

"You caught him and brought him here?" Lucas asked, confused.

Hartwell nodded. "I thought he'd be the perfect final exam."

"This was a *test*?" Lucas cried, pointing at the beast man.

"A final test before your real education begins," Hartwell replied. Lucas noticed that the older man had something slung over his shoulder. He tossed it to the boy.

"What do you mean by my 'real education'?" Lucas asked, catching what was thrown at him. It was a piece of clothing of some kind, and he held it up by the shoulders.

"It's time you understood what you're going to be fighting for," his father said.

It took a moment for Lucas to realize what he was looking at.

A costume.

7

"I feel like a dork," Lucas said, gazing down at himself in the dark, body-hugging outfit. He had yet to put on the mask.

"Do I look like a dork?" Hartwell asked. He was dressed in his own costume. They were in the back of a van, parked in the shadows of an alley in one of the worst sections of Seraph City. City dwellers referred to it as the War Zone. Here the popping sound of gunfire was as common as the roar of car engines and the screech of brakes.

"No," Lucas answered his father, watching as the older man slipped the Raptor's cowl over his head. "You actually look kind of scary."

"And that's how it's supposed to be," Hartwell stated.

Lucas looked down at himself, observing how the all-black outfit clung tightly to his every part. "I think the only person I'm going to be scaring is myself."

His father laughed as he stood and pushed open the van's back doors.

"You'll get used to it," the Raptor said, leaping from the back of the vehicle.

"I can't believe you're just going to leave this van here," Lucas said. He slipped his own mask over his head and joined his father. "Remember, this is the War Zone."

The Raptor stood in the darkness, looking toward the end of the alleyway, but Lucas sensed he was really looking at something else.

"It wasn't always this way," the older man said cryptically.

Then he seemed to snap out of his reverie and quickly turned to close the van doors.

"It'll be fine," the costumed hero said. "Not many go out after dark here, and those who do have higher criminal aspirations than stealing a van. Besides"—the Raptor touched a button on the wrist of one of his gauntlets and the vehicle's horn beeped twice—"I've got a security system."

Lucas chuckled. "And you think that'll work . . . around here?"

"I didn't say it was a conventional system," the costumed man said, spinning around suddenly and leaping up onto a rusted fire escape before starting to climb. "There's fifteen thousand volts waiting for anybody who touches it. That should be more than enough of a deterrent."

Lucas stepped back from the van cautiously.

"Are you coming?" his father called down to him. "Or are you going to stay with the van?"

Lucas gave their ride one more look before joining his father on the fire escape.

They climbed to the roof of the abandoned brick structure. From here they had a perfect view of the War Zone.

Lucas listened. He could hear voices screaming in argument, children crying, and the occasional gunshot. Too many gunshots.

"It's kind of nasty," Lucas said, looking down at the street below. The buildings were all run-down, made from brick stained black with the soot of pollution. Windows were broken, and garbage was strewn in doorways and on fire escapes. He couldn't believe that people actually lived inside the buildings. They all looked like something waiting to be torn down.

"I told you before, it wasn't always like this," the Raptor said. "This used to be a safe, working-class neighborhood, before the sickness set in."

"The sickness?" Lucas questioned.

A siren wailed somewhere in the distance, but he doubted it was coming here. From what his father had said earlier, law enforcement had pretty much abandoned the War Zone a very long time ago.

"Drugs, prostitution, guns, and gangs had an awful lot to do with its decline," the Raptor explained. "But good people once lived here . . . and still do. Good people who just want a chance at a good life."

The hero grew silent again as he watched the neighborhood.

"Some of us got that life, but others . . ."

He was gone in an instant, the costume enhancing his already powerful leap, allowing him to jump from one roof to the next.

Lucas followed, trying to keep up. He found it difficult to believe that this man was really dying.

Suddenly a great expanse loomed between the current building and the next, and Lucas slowed down, certain they were going to have to stop.

He almost cried out as his father bounded closer to the edge, sure he wouldn't make the jump. But the Raptor went over the side of the building, dropping down into the shadows between the buildings.

Lucas hurried to the edge of the roof. He seriously doubted the Raptor could be stopped by a mere seven-story drop, but he wasn't sure. Peering over the ledge, he searched for signs of his father.

Something surged up from the open expanse and Lucas stumbled backward. The Raptor flew above his head, glider wings unfurled beneath the arms of his costume.

Lucas wanted to applaud.

The Raptor then swooped down and plucked him up from where he stood, carrying him to the other roof.

"How come I can't do that?" Lucas asked as his father let him drop.

The Raptor landed, the opaque glider wings folding beneath his arms. "In time," he said. "Pretty soon you'll have all the bells and whistles too." He walked across the rooftop. "Come over here. I want to show you something."

Lucas followed, his footfalls crunching on the rough gravel surface.

"There's an example of why I do what I do," the Raptor said, pointing down to a little grocery store below them.

Lucas was surprised to see some activity there, people going into the store, others leaving with bags of groceries.

"It was owned by the Santarpo family for years, and now it's run by their kids," his father explained. "Despite the nasty turn in the neighborhood, they've stayed, confident that over time, things will get better."

Lucas watched the store with interest. An older man wearing an apron came outside and started to sweep.

"I know you're a billionaire and all, but did you happen to grow up here?"

"I did," the Raptor replied, a smile spreading across his face. "Hartwell Technologies began in a two-bedroom apartment right over . . ." He had started to point when the night was filled with the sound of screeching tires.

A car came around the corner below too fast, sliding sideways across the street as its wheels spun and smoked.

A gang of youths had just left a building at the other end of the street, three doors down from the grocery. They immediately reacted to the approach of the speeding car, each pulling a gun from a coat pocket.

"No," the Raptor said, eyes riveted to the scene.

The windows came down on the vehicle. Arms wielding automatic weapons appeared and began to open fire.

Lucas turned to ask his father what they should do, but he was alone.

The Raptor had already entered the fray.

* * *

The Raptor jumped as soon as he saw the windows on the speeding car go down.

He dove over the side of the building, glider wings unfurling long enough to slow his descent. The rival gang had already begun to return fire, explosions of thunder filling the streets.

It was supposed to be a drive-by; those riding in the car were planning on dealing death and driving away.

Something the Raptor wasn't going to allow.

He aimed the weaponry on his gauntlet. A blast of concentrated electricity arced across the street and struck one of the vehicle's front wheels. The tire exploded and the car careened out of control, speeding to the right, up onto the sidewalk and toward the market.

Toward Mr. Santarpo.

The older man stood frozen, broom still clutched in his {87} hands as the insanity unfolded around him.

The Raptor swore beneath his breath. How could he not have taken the life of an innocent into account?

He was running toward the car, attempting something—anything—to avert the coming disaster, but he knew it would be for naught. Nothing short of a miracle could stop that car from slamming into poor, innocent Mr. Santarpo.

Lucas noticed that the old man was still standing out in front of the grocery store. It was a disaster waiting to happen, and he knew he had to do something before the guy got hurt.

It was a long way down, but he didn't have the time to think about it.

Tensing the muscles in his legs, the boy jumped over the side of the building and dropped to the ground below. He landed in a roll, tumbling across the street as his father unleashed the weaponry of his costume, lighting up the night with a crackling bolt of man-made lightning.

It had disastrous results.

Lucas pushed himself to move as quickly as he could toward the sidewalk. From the corner of his eye, he saw the car careening toward the grocer. The man remained frozen in place, his fear making it impossible for him to move.

Lucas knew it was entirely up to him now. This man's life was in his hands.

He figured it was the nanites coursing through his body that made him move so much faster. He imagined the microscopic machines traveling through his blood, making his heart pump quicker, giving him the strength and stamina to spring off the sidewalk in mid-run and dive through the air like a missile.

He hoped he wouldn't hurt the man, but what choice did he have? It was either be struck by a ton of speeding metal or be tackled by a teenager.

Lucas thought he knew which one the man would choose as he connected with the grocer's midsection, his momentum carrying them both out of the path of the hurtling vehicle.

As they tumbled, Lucas used his own body to shield the old man from the worst of the roll. The shriek of twisting metal and shattering glass filled the air as the car crashed through the front of the grocery store.

Lying atop him, Lucas looked down into the dazed and confused face of the older man. He had scratches and cuts on his face and arms, and probably some serious bruises everywhere else, but as far as Lucas could tell, he had come through in one piece.

"Are you all right?" Lucas asked.

"Better than I would have been," the man replied in a trembling voice.

Lucas helped the grocer stand up and brought him toward the damaged storefront.

"I would have been killed," the man said as he stared at the twisted wreckage of the car. "You saved me. . . . I would have been killed for sure."

Lucas didn't know what to say.

"I guess so," he said, doubting that was the right thing. He would need to ask his father for some pointers on the proper way to respond in situations like this.

Then he heard something. He looked toward the wreckage and saw that several gang members had managed to force open the doors of the wrecked car and were crawling out onto the sidewalk.

To say he was shocked by what he saw was an understatement. Their faces were covered in heavy green makeup, apparently in an attempt to make them look like walking corpses, and he realized who the criminals might be.

A supervillain called the Zombie wore elaborate, Hollywood-quality prosthetics to make his rivals in crime believe he was a walking dead man. Lucas remembered his father talking about how even the normal, everyday criminals were being inspired by supervillainy. It didn't take a rocket scientist to figure out that these guys were members of the Zombie fan club.

And even after all they'd been through, their clothes torn and bloody, they still managed to hold on to their guns.

"Get inside," Lucas ordered the grocer, giving him a shove toward the store entrance. Then he turned back toward the car. Gunfire was erupting again as the two gangs came face to face.

He was about to move when he saw something land in the street between them. Lucas knew what it was, even though its movements were a blur. It was as if a small twister had set down in the center of the city street, first attacking the Zombies—the roar of their guns abruptly cut off by their own screams—and then going at the others.

The second gang stood about as much chance against the costumed figure as the first.

And Lucas understood why it was smart to be afraid of the Raptor.

The Raptor had taken both sides out, but he wasn't stopping there.

The men of the two gangs lay beaten and bloody in the city street, but the crime fighter wanted more. More blood. More punishment. He wanted them to know the full extent of the pain they'd caused.

Lucas didn't know what to do. At this point he wasn't sure if his father was even there. It was as if his father had stepped back and something . . . *inhuman* had taken over.

The Raptor walked among the unconscious and moaning, lifting their squealing bodies up from where they lay and shaking them in his fury.

"Is that all you have?" he growled to one in particular. The man's leg was twisted and bent, and Lucas was sure it was broken.

"My leg!" the man shrieked, feet dangling in the air. "Please don't. . . ."

"You're lucky I don't break the other one," the Raptor said, mercilessly tossing the man aside like a child tossing away an unwanted toy.

"Who's next?" he snarled.

Those who were still conscious shied away, not wanting to make eye contact with the monster. Lucas couldn't blame them. At this moment, he too was afraid of his father.

Who is this man really?

A shot rang out, and Lucas watched in horror as the Raptor went down on one knee.

Lucas saw the shooter—a Zombie gang member no older than he was—lying on the ground, smoking pistol in hand.

The Raptor brought a hand to his head, rubbing the area where the bullet had struck. Earlier that week his father had talked about the importance of lightweight body armor and how even the cowls they wore were reinforced for their protection.

As the Raptor rose, the shooter tried to get away. He managed to climb to his feet, still holding his gun, and began to hobble away.

He didn't stand a chance.

"I love it when they run," Lucas heard the Raptor say.

The Raptor was on him in a heartbeat, like a falcon pouncing on a rabbit.

Lucas stepped from the front of the store, debating what to do. The other gang members were down, either completely out of it or too scared to move. In the distance he could hear the howl of police sirens. Were they on their way here?

It wouldn't be good to be here if they were.

A horrible scream suddenly filled the night. Lucas watched, horrified, as the Raptor crushed the gun and the hand that held it. He melded the two together in a bloody ball of broken bones, metal, and skin.

"You think you're scary?" the Raptor asked, with a disturbing laugh. "Let me tell you something. You're not."

The man was hurt—badly hurt—and Lucas was wasn't sure how far his father was going to go.

He saw the night light up in the Raptor's hand, sparks of electricity dancing from his fingertips. Slowly the costumed hero brought his electrified gauntlet closer to the man, who now struggled in his clutches. *He's going to kill him*, Lucas realized as the wailing sirens drew closer. Superheroes did not kill; it was common knowledge. They could injure, disable, rough up—anything to keep the bad guys from committing their destruction. But killing crossed the line. A line that, it now seemed, Lucas's father was willing to leap over.

The gang member was crying, his makeup-covered face illuminated by the glow of the lethal sparks jumping from the Raptor's gloved fingertips.

"*This* is scary," the Raptor growled as the glove moved

closer. The man closed his eyes, tears streaming down his face, washing away some of the smeared green makeup as he prepared for an inevitable death.

And the Raptor was smiling.

Lucas couldn't watch anymore. This was too much. He stepped in and grabbed his father's wrist.

"You don't want to do that," he said in his strongest voice.

The Raptor turned his gaze to him, and Lucas felt his blood freeze.

"It's exactly what I want to do," the Raptor answered, trying to pull the still-crackling glove out of Lucas's grip.

Lucas held fast. "The police are close," he told the man. He didn't know what to believe anymore. Was this truly his father?

The Raptor seemed to recognize the truth of Lucas's {93 words. "They would have killed each other, with no account given to the innocents around them," he growled, still holding the man up with one hand. He gave the guy a good shake, and the Zombie gangbanger moaned. His hand looked awful, like something out of a horror movie, dangling uselessly at his side, only this was real, not a special effect. Lucas wondered if doctors would be able to save it.

"I know that," Lucas said. He tried to make his voice sound as calm as possible. "But you stopped them . . . him . . . and now we should leave it up to the proper authorities."

Something in the Raptor's expression changed. Was that his father now looking back at him through the red lenses of the hero's cowl?

"Put him down and let's go," Lucas urged again.

The police were even closer now, and from the sounds of it, they'd brought the whole force.

"We've really got to go," Lucas said, giving his father's arm a tug. "The police will be swarming this place in seconds."

His father nodded slowly, turning his attention to the mewling man still held aloft in his grasp.

"Next time, punk," the Raptor snarled, letting the wannabe supervillain drop to the ground. The shooter curled up into a tight ball, clutching his injured hand to his chest.

The Raptor then turned to Lucas, and for a moment the boy had no idea what might happen next. "Are . . . are you all right?" Lucas stammered.

The costumed hero turned, lifting his arms and activating his costume's flight capabilities.

"I stopped being all right a long time ago," he replied coldly.

Then he jumped into the night sky, soaring above the carnage.

8

It was a cool autumn night in Seraph City, a sharp wind blowing off the Atlantic giving a hint of the harsh winter that would arrive all too soon.

Illuminated by a hunter's moon, the lithe, costumed figure of Lucas Moore darted across a rooftop, preparing to leap to the next one.

"Oh, crap," he muttered beneath his breath, coming to a screeching halt.

"What is it?" Hartwell asked through a tiny receiver built into the black mask Lucas wore.

"Nothing," Lucas answered.

"You wouldn't have said 'oh, crap' if there wasn't something."

"It's just that . . . they're a lot farther apart than I

thought," Lucas admitted, looking from one roof across to the next.

"You shouldn't have any problem with the jump," Hartwell said dryly. "Your nanite-enhanced leg strength, plus the augmentation provided by the costume's exoskeleton, should allow you to make the distance with very little effort."

"You think?" Lucas asked, still not convinced.

"Lucas, I designed the costume. I know full well what it and the nanites in your blood are capable of. Trust me."

It had been a month since he'd been given the more sophisticated costume—his "supersuit," as he liked to call it, much to his father's distaste. Hartwell didn't appreciate his calling such a complicated piece of hardware such a cartoonish name.

But Lucas thought it was perfect.

Lucas had gone through another extensive training period so that he could fully appreciate all the capabilities of his new costume. According to his father, this suit had been designed to improve his already-nanite-enhanced body, making him *better* than perfect. In it he would be unstoppable; at least, that was what his father was telling him.

Lucas had to admit, it was a rush to feel this strong.

He walked away from the building's edge and turned around. "Probably going to need a running start," he said to himself, forgetting that the old man could hear.

"Not necessarily," Hartwell answered in his ear. "But if you think it will help."

Taking a few quick breaths—the smell of his sweat mixing with the chemical-plastic smell of his mask—he started to run toward the building ledge.

Before reaching the end of the rooftop, he tensed the muscles in his legs, springing off with some pretty incredible results.

Lucas soared through the air on his own power.

Hartwell had brought him to Seraph proper for this exercise in a small helicopter designed for stealth. The craft was much smaller than the average chopper and was equipped with technology that rendered it nearly silent and practically invisible.

From a secret helipad at the back of Hartwell Manor, they had flown to the city, dropping Lucas off atop one of the city's many tall office buildings. Jumping down from the craft to the roof, Lucas hadn't even heard the stealth craft leave.

But now he was flying without the help of a high-tech helicopter. This was all him, his strength increased by the exoskeleton built into his costume, of course.

He started to descend, the rooftop of the next building coming up fast, and he braced himself for impact. Barely avoiding an air-conditioning unit on the roof, he landed in a crouch, his momentum causing him to tumble toward the building's edge.

"And how did we do?" his father asked from his command center back at Hartwell Manor.

"Good," Lucas answered, not feeling the need to share everything. "It was good."

He was going to need to work on his landings.

"Excellent," Hartwell responded in his ear. "I need you to make your way south toward the Kessler Building."

Lucas placed a hand against the side of his mask and

pushed gently. A small computer mapping system was projected in front of his eyes.

"Got it," he said, leaping from that rooftop down onto another with growing confidence.

He left the mapping system up to help guide him to the Kessler. Seraph was about a hundred times the size of Perdition, and he needed all the help he could get.

Jumping from rooftop to rooftop on nightly patrols, he guessed that eventually he would get to know the place. He couldn't help being in awe of Seraph. He had never been to any place larger than Phoenix, so this was like visiting another planet.

The buildings grew significantly smaller as he neared the Kessler, in one of the older sections of the city. He'd reached an area bustling with new construction. Out of the corner of his eye, he noticed a banner hanging from one of the skeletal new buildings bearing the name of one of Hartwell's many companies.

"Putting up some new buildings?" he asked casually. He jumped down to the shadows, moving across the construction site, practicing not being noticed.

"Yes," his father answered. "Please proceed to . . ."

Something caught Lucas's attention and he stopped to stare.

"What's this?" he asked aloud.

He was standing before a statue—a monument, really. It was a statue of the Raptor. A statue in honor of his father.

Lucas examined it more closely. He read that it had been erected by the city as thanks for what the Raptor had done to save lives in this very spot over twenty years ago.

He thought of his father's story about the explosion that had changed his life. The explosion that had killed one Raptor and allowed another to be born.

"Lucas?" his father called to him.

"I'm looking at a statue of you," he said.

"Oh, that," his father said coldly. "A monument to my failure."

"It's pretty awesome," the boy said. The statue was bronze and depicted the Raptor—wearing an older design of his costume—standing with his head bowed. There were bronze representations of a firefighter and a police officer standing on either side of the superhero. The plaque read, IN HONOR OF THOSE WHO RISK THEIR LIVES SO THAT OTHERS MAY SAFELY LIVE.

"Is this where it happened?" Lucas asked, looking around. There was no sign of how it had once been.

"Yes," his father answered. "Now I think it's time for you to move along."

Lucas was about to ask more about that night but decided against it. His father seemed very uncomfortable talking about the incident. Lucas made a mental note to do some research. After all, if he was going to assume the mantle of the Raptor, he would need to know every possible detail.

Lucas left the construction site, climbing the side of a nearby office building to return to the rooftops. He was getting better at leaping, no longer imagining himself splattered on the ground beneath the towering city structures. This was what it was all about, he thought. Little by little, he was learning everything that would allow him to become the kind of hero Seraph needed.

His thoughts flashed back briefly to the night in the War Zone. Later, when Lucas had questioned Hartwell about whether or not he would have killed the Zombie thug, his father had claimed he never would have done such a thing. It had all been part of Lucas's training, he had told him, to see how he would react in that particular situation.

Lucas wasn't exactly sure he believed that. What he'd seen that night had scared him a bit, but it had also moved him to make a promise to himself. No matter how hard it got, or how desperate the situation, he would never take a life. He wasn't sure what had pushed his father so far that night that he had been willing to kill. He chose to believe it was stress, a momentary impulse. He chose to believe his father was a good man.

Crouching on the roof of a hotel, Lucas spotted his destination.

"I see it," he said.

"Good," Hartwell answered. "I want you to find your way inside."

"Are you going to tell me what I'm doing tonight?" Lucas asked, dropping down to an alleyway from the roof of the hotel. He barely felt the impact, his legs and the mechanisms in the suit absorbing the shock with ease.

"Street intel has provided me with information about the current location of the Science Club," Hartwell explained.

"The Science Club?" Lucas questioned, darting down the alleyway. "They certainly don't sound like much."

"The Science Club is a band of renegade scientists

responsible for providing high-tech weaponry to criminals around the world," Hartwell said.

"Interesting," Lucas muttered as he sprang up from the alley, using the claws built into his gloves to scale the wall like some giant insect. "I always wondered where the super-villains got their stuff." He clambered over the side of the abandoned office building and onto the roof.

The map in his face mask told him the Kessler Building was right across from his current location. He figured the easiest way inside the old building was through the roof.

He reached up to the other side of his mask and tapped alongside his eyes. Telescopic lenses were activated, giving him a good view of the rooftop. He saw a skylight and figured that would probably be the easiest way to get inside.

"I'm getting ready to jump across," Lucas said, walking back to get a good running start. "And then I'll see what I can do about closing down this Science Club for good."

A thrill of excitement went through him as he crossed the rooftop. This would be his first physical confrontation since the incident in the War Zone.

"Lucas," his father called, interrupting his thoughts.

He stopped to listen. "I'm here."

"There's something more you might want to know about the Science Club."

"Okay, shoot."

"I believe they're the individuals who provided the weaponry and vehicles to the ones who attacked the trailer park," he said.

Lucas felt a jolt like electricity course through his body,

as if he'd accidentally taken hold of a live wire. He remained silent, fixated on the building across from the rooftop.

"Are you still there?" Hartwell asked.

"I am," he answered coldly.

"The information from the sensors in your suit suggests there might be something wrong."

"Wrong?" Lucas asked, starting to run across the roof at top speed before leaping out into space. "What could possibly be wrong?"

Lucas touched down silently; he was getting better at this. Scanning the rooftop, he saw nothing out of the ordinary and carefully crossed to the skylight.

"I'm approaching the skylight," he whispered for only his father to hear.

"Careful now," Hartwell cautioned. "The Science Club is far more dangerous than you could even hope to imagine."

Lucas reached the skylight and peered down through the bird droppings and thick glass at an elaborate warehouse space below.

"It looks kind of like a factory," he said, watching as men clad in colorful jumpsuits moved from one machine to another. "These are the guys who made the weapons that killed my mother? They look like a bunch of geeks."

Lucas heard a scuffling sound on the rooftop behind him and spun around to face it.

"Oh, crap," he said, not believing his eyes. "Where the hell did that come from?"

"What is it, Lucas?" Hartwell asked.

Lucas was about to tell him that there was a robot with

machine guns for arms standing across from him, but he didn't have the chance.

The robot opened fire. Multiple rounds from both weapons drove Lucas backward toward the skylight. He put up his hands, attempting to block some of the bullets, and silently thanked his father for finding the special bulletproof material his costume was woven from.

Not that he couldn't feel the shots. They were sort of like hornet stings, only about ten times more painful.

Another robot rose up from a hidden compartment in the rooftop and also began to fire at Lucas.

"Lucas!" Hartwell screamed in his ear. "Report! What is your status?"

Lucas wanted to answer, but it was too much. It was like being caught in a storm of pain. He was driven farther backward until he had nowhere else to go.

The heel of one of his boots struck the frame of the skylight, throwing him off balance. No matter how hard he tried to regain his balance, he couldn't. He found himself falling backward, the full brunt of his weight landing on the skylight, shattering the thick glass as he fell through to the warehouse space below.

At least I got away from the robots, he thought as he fell, just before hitting a table covered in machine parts that collapsed under his weight.

Stunned by the impact, Lucas managed to push himself up. Alarms began blaring inside the vast space, and the Science Club members ran around wildly.

"Lucas!" Hartwell screamed again, startling him.

"I fell through the skylight," Lucas said, slipping on the glass beneath his feet.

"You fell?" Hartwell asked.

"I know, I suck, anything else?"

"So they know you're there?"

He watched the uniformed men scurrying around, many of them with machinery clutched lovingly in their arms.

"Oh yeah," Lucas said.

"Get out of there . . . now!" Hartwell ordered.

"What? You don't want me to do anything?"

"If their security has been breached, they're going to defend themselves."

Lucas was about to argue that there didn't seem to be much going on when the armored security team came around a corner. They were each holding a weapon that looked like a high-tech cannon, and he decided that maybe it wouldn't be such a good idea to be shot with those.

"Halt, or we'll shoot!" one of the men said in a voice that sounded like he was talking through a speaker at a drive-through.

Lucas scanned the warehouse for an escape route and found a door on the other side of the space. He bolted for it as the armored men continued to order him to stop.

He reached the door and pulled.

Locked! Just his luck; he should have figured.

He was about to flex his muscles and knock it down when he was hit by a bus.

It wasn't an actual bus, of course, but it felt like one. He was zapped by one of the high-tech cannons the security guys were carrying.

Lucas was thrown into the wall by the intensity of the blast. His father's plaintive cries were gone from his ear, replaced with a high-pitched squeal, as the communications device built into his headpiece ceased to function.

Through the roar of white noise, he could just about make out the sounds of the Science Club security squad coming closer, their armored boots clicking on the warehouse floor. He struggled to stand but was having a great deal of difficulty. The suit felt heavy, stiff, and he sensed that more than the communications functions had been damaged.

He looked through the cracked lenses of his face mask for a different way out.

Another of the cannons fired and he was lifted off his feet. The blast picked him up, hurling him backward and into the body of a machine that hummed with power. Some sort of generator, Lucas imagined as he was showered in a spray of sparks and fire.

Grabbing on to the burning machine, he fought to stand while a tiny, nagging voice in the back of his head told him over and over again that he wasn't ready for this.

That he would probably never be ready for something like this.

Because he was going to die.

"No," he said, dispelling the sudden memory of his mother's blackened body. After all he had been through, after all he had learned, he wasn't about to let it end this way.

Exerting every muscle, he climbed to his feet. The nanites in his blood must have been working overtime to keep him alive, because he suddenly felt ravenous. But the four-course meal he craved would have to wait. The Science Clubs' goons were at him again, and he could just about make out through his damaged mask what it was they were saying.

"Finish him off," one of the security team said.

"Who is he?" asked another.

"Probably just another wannabe," someone with a bit of an accent contributed.

"We'll get a bonus for this for sure," said another.

They all laughed, probably thinking about how they would spend their bonus money.

That made Lucas even madder.

There wasn't much time for him to waste. He had to do something right away or he was going to end up as a stain on one of the walls. He considered throwing himself at the sentries but decided that feeling the way he did, they probably would kick his butt, then shoot him dead.

That was when he remembered one of his many instruction sessions and one of the emergency functions his father had described.

What was it again?

His father had referred to it as a "last resort."

An EMP emitter, installed as an emergency deterrent. From what Lucas could understand, a tiny device was built into his weapons system that would allow him to emit a powerful electromagnetic pulse—just like nuclear bombs did—that would shut down most high-tech machinery.

Lucas couldn't think of a better situation in which to use it.

Swaying unsteadily on his feet, he watched as one of the soldiers aimed his gun.

"Say hello to my little friend," the guy said, doing one of the worst imitations of Al Pacino in *Scarface* Lucas had ever heard.

The guy deserved the EMP for that alone.

Just as he was about to be shot, Lucas raised his arm, using his other hand to find the button beneath the heavy fabric of his costume and push it.

At first he thought that it, too, had been broken by the blast from the cannons, but then the emitter came alive with a high-pitched whine and an electromagnetic pulse surged from the tips of his gloved fingers, throwing the security team backward with squawks of surprise.

He wasn't going to get another opportunity like this, so he put everything he had into a race across the warehouse toward the door that had been locked before. Lucky for him, after he'd been blasted, the cannon fire had also torn the heavy metal door from its hinges, providing him with an escape route.

Climbing over the twisted metal of the door, Lucas was glad he'd paid enough attention during training to remember how to activate the EMP emitter. He hung on to the metal railing and stumbled down the steps. He was having a hard time standing, and the exertion of moving the damaged costume was exhausting.

But what choice did he have?

His thoughts drifted to his father and what he was doing to help him out here. A part of him wondered whether the old man was really doing anything. Lucas imagined Hartwell sitting at the mansion, waiting for him to make it back alive, the whole incident chalked up as an excellent training opportunity.

Lucas made it to the first-floor level and threw himself at a set of chained double doors. At least he had enough left in him to snap the chains, and he spilled out onto the trash-strewn docking area.

Not sure whether or not he was being chased, Lucas forced himself around the corner of the building, out of the yellowish glare of the streetlights. He hoped to use the shadows of the back alleys to make his way someplace safe, where he could catch his breath and figure out what he should do next.

That was when he darted into the street and was suddenly bathed in the headlights of an oncoming van. He was too stunned to react. The van hit him head-on, sending him through the air backward to the street.

And as he lay there fighting to stay awake, his entire body numb, he heard his mother's voice whispering in his ear.

Always look both ways before crossing the street.

Truer words were never spoken.

Clayton Hartwell again checked the instruments of the control panel to make sure the problem wasn't on his end.

All he could hear was a grating static hiss.

"Dammit," he said beneath his breath, stroking his chin and moving the swivel chair nervously from side to side.

It had been close to thirty minutes since he'd lost contact with Lucas.

His eyes darted to the digital clock above the control panel, watching as another minute ticked past. He knew what he should be doing—sitting back patiently, waiting to see how the boy would react—but at this stage he wasn't even sure the boy was still alive.

The Science Club could be quite deadly, given the opportunity.

Reaching out, he raised the volume on the static, straining to hear if there was anything behind it. But the signal was shot; there was nothing transmitting from the source.

That was when he made up his mind.

Clayton Hartwell rose from his chair, leaving his cane leaning against the side of the control panel. He walked from the communications chamber into a much larger room and approached a metal door with a number pad in its frame.

The older man punched in a code and stood before the door as it slowly opened.

It was a room filled with Raptor costumes, from the prototype of the very first suit to the latest armored and cybernetically enhanced model.

He decided to go with one of the less flashy designs, but one of his personal favorites. It was the one he had been wearing when he revealed his true identity to the boy.

He reached for the costume, ready to suit up.

It was time for the Raptor to get involved.

This time there were no dreams, only deep, cold darkness.

But there was a light, barely visible at first, like a single star in the night sky growing brighter by the second.

Lucas realized that this light . . . this star . . . pulsed with each beat of his heart. He found himself drawn to it, as if pulled by its gravity. But the closer he got to the throbbing light, the more uncomfortable he became.

He wanted to stop and retreat to the safety of the cold shadows, where the pain could not reach him, but the star had other plans, refusing to let him go.

And eventually he gave in, allowing himself to be pulled within the body of the star.

He tried to keep his eyes open, but it was just too bright. He tried to lift his hands to shield his vision but found he could not. His hands were bound—handcuffed—and it wasn't a star that floated above his head. It was only a lamp.

He was lying on a small cot, hands and feet bound together.

"Where am I?" he croaked. He lay on his side, looking around at the cramped space.

Somebody was across from him. A teenage girl, dressed in a baggy sweatshirt and jeans. She was typing on a computer.

She looked briefly over her shoulder at him, her horn-rimmed glasses slipping down her nose.

"He's awake!" she called out, then turned back to the computer and continued her work.

Lucas tried to maneuver himself around to glimpse the person she was talking to, but couldn't.

"Who are you?" he called out, nearly certain now he was a prisoner of the Science Club, but the girl just ignored him.

The suit's strength enhancers were probably damaged, but this didn't prevent him from trying to break free of the handcuffs that bound him; he did have nanites in his blood. With a grunt, he yanked on the chain. Excruciating pain shot through his body and Lucas let out a scream, falling back breathlessly on the bed.

The girl turned in her chair and watched him.

Is that a look of concern on her face? he wondered. *Why would the Science Club give a rat's behind if I hurt myself?*

His thoughts were interrupted by the sound of footsteps and he turned his head to see who was coming.

It was a man who walked with crutches, his legs looking almost useless as he struggled to stand before Lucas. One half of his face was badly scarred.

He simply stood over Lucas, leaning on his crutches, staring.

"What did you do to me?" Lucas asked finally.

The man smiled and shook his head. "We haven't done anything. It's the nanites that are causing the problem."

Lucas was surprised. *How can this guy know about the nanites?*

"They've used up all the biological fuel in your system to heal you from your run-in with the Science Club."

"And the van," the girl added.

The man rolled his eyes. "And getting hit by the van," he repeated. "So the little mechanical bugs have started to look for other food . . . like muscle and bone. I imagine it can get pretty painful."

"If you're not from the Science Club, who are you?" Lucas managed to ask. "Some other villain looking for revenge against the Raptor?"

The man laughed, looking over at the girl sitting at the computer. She was smiling as well, and Lucas noticed how cute she was.

Bad timing or what?

"No, we're nothing like that," the man said. "Believe it or not, we're the good guys."

Lucas just stared at the man, not believing a word.

The girl got up from her chair and walked out of view.

"If you're the good guys," he said, watching her go, "then why am I handcuffed?"

"Only as a precaution," the crippled man said. He reached into his shirt pocket and produced a key. "We weren't sure how you'd react once you came to."

He leaned in, first undoing Lucas's wrists and then his ankles.

Part of Lucas wanted to lash out and fight his way free, but another considered that maybe these guys really didn't mean him any harm.

The girl returned with a plate of sandwiches, and Lucas felt his stomach lurch and grumble in anticipation. He sat upright on the cot, his only thought at the moment of filling his belly.

He had to feed the nanites.

"Here ya go," the girl said, handing him the tray.

Lucas hesitated, staring at the food. His body was telling him to eat, but . . .

"What's wrong?" the girl asked. "Not into PB&J?"

"No, it's just that . . ."

The girl laughed. "You're afraid we did something to them, right?" She helped herself to a random half of a sandwich from the tray and took a big bite. "Better?" she asked {113 through a mouthful of bread, peanut butter, and jelly.

More at ease, he took the tray from her and snatched up a sandwich. In two bites it was gone and he was moving on to another, eating so fast he could barely taste them.

The handicapped man pulled the computer chair over so that he could sit down across from Lucas, while the girl leaned against the wall with a smile. "Hungry much?" she asked, wiping a stray bit of jelly from the corner of her mouth.

"It's no joke," the man said. "When the nanites need fuel, they can be pretty aggressive."

Lucas slowed down just long enough to ask a question.

"How do you know so much about the nanites?"

The man looked to the girl, and she nodded.

"Now's as good a time as any, I guess," he said. "Does the

name Nicolas Putnam mean anything to you?" He stared intently at Lucas, waiting for his response.

Lucas was eating another half of sandwich as he shook his head. "Is that you?" he asked through a mouthful.

The man nodded. "I can't believe he didn't mention me," he muttered.

"Who?"

"Hartwell," Putnam snarled. "The Raptor."

Lucas decided to play dumb. "I don't have any idea what—"

"Cut the crap. I know all about Clayton Hartwell and his other identity. I used to be his sidekick," Putnam said with pride. "I used to be Talon."

Lucas's eyes widened in surprise. "*Talon?* You were actually Talon?"

Putnam nodded. "I certainly was."

"But I thought you were dead." Lucas vaguely remembered the stories about the Raptor and Talon and how something really bad had happened to the team, leaving only the Raptor alive.

Putnam snarled. "He probably wishes I was, but no such luck."

"And I'm Katie," the girl said with a quick wave.

"Hi," Lucas said, returning the wave before turning back to Putnam. "I don't get it. Why would he want you dead?"

The man's eyes became very dark. "Isn't that what a murderer does?" he asked. "Wish people dead?"

"What are you talking about?" Lucas asked, starting to feel uncomfortable. "Are you talking about my . . . about Hartwell?" He caught himself.

"Don't worry, I know all about him being your father," Putnam said. "And yeah, that's exactly who I'm talking about."

Lucas set the half-empty tray of sandwiches down on the cot beside him. "I don't like where this is going. If I were you, I'd explain myself really quick."

"He killed my father," Katie blurted out.

Lucas felt as though he'd been doused with freezing water. He could see the emotion in her eyes, the hurt on her face, but before he had a chance to question her more, a series of alarms began to blare.

"It's too late for this now," Putnam said, glancing over at the computer.

Katie went to the screen, leaning in to the keyboard. "It's him," she said, looking back to them.

"I figured we'd have only so much time," Putnam said. "The whole business with him sending you into the Science Club's hideout provided us with the perfect opportunity to meet you. I wasn't about to look a gift horse in the mouth."

"You knew I was going to be there?" Lucas asked. "What, did you follow me or something?"

"Or something," Putnam said, straining to lift himself out of the chair. "We keep an eye on whatever Hartwell is doing."

Katie was still at the computer, her fingers flying over the keys. "He's homing in on a signal still coming from the costume," she said. "I think we've got to drop our guest right here, now, before it's too late."

Putnam grabbed Lucas by the arm and hauled him to his feet.

"If you value your life, I don't recommend you mention this little meeting," he said.

"Are you threatening me?" Lucas asked, feeling a spark of anger.

Putnam shook his head. "Not at all," he said, escorting Lucas down the cramped hall until they reached a door.

Up until this point, Lucas had believed he was inside a building of some kind, but he suddenly realized he was actually inside an RV.

"I just think you'd be smart to keep your mouth shut until you've heard all the facts," the man said. He leaned over and pulled on the latch, and the door swung open.

"And what if I don't?" Lucas asked, stepping outside.

The RV was parked on the side of a dirt road, not too far from the waterfront. Lucas could smell the ocean in the air.

"Then I can't be held responsible for what he does," Putnam said, ready to slam the door on the buslike vehicle. "Just give me a little time, and I'll find a chance for us to talk again."

"And when will that be?" Lucas asked.

"I'll be in touch," the man said.

Katie suddenly appeared in the doorway, holding his damaged mask in her hands. She bounded down the steps to hand it to him.

"Don't forget this. And don't let him see this," she added, handing him a folded piece of paper.

"I don't—" Lucas began.

"We gotta go, girl," Putnam said, and she turned away and jumped into the RV. Lucas could still hear the sound of the alarms blaring inside.

"All I'm asking is for you to trust us," Putnam said before he closed the door.

A moment later, the tires spun out in the dirt as the RV drove quickly away, heading back toward the city.

Lucas watched the vehicle until it was out of sight; then he turned his attention to the folded piece of paper in his hand. He unfolded it, his curiosity getting the better of him.

On the paper were nine names.

He wasn't familiar with any of them.

Lucas flinched, suddenly bathed in a blinding light from above. Shielding his eyes against the glare, he looked to the sky to see his father's stealth copter silently hovering over his head.

Just like the whole conversation he'd just had with Nicolas Putnam and Katie, he hadn't seen it coming.

The ride back to Hartwell Manor was filled with questions: the ones from his father and the ones bouncing around inside his own head.

Is it possible? Lucas asked himself as the craft made its descent toward their sprawling home. *Is Clayton Hartwell a murderer?*

He chanced a look at the man as Hartwell dropped the chopper to the landing square at the back of the manor. He had to admit, he'd been a little surprised to see his father in full costume.

"Something wrong?" Hartwell asked as they touched down with a gentle bump.

"No," Lucas responded. "Just surprised to see you all dressed up is all."

"Didn't know what I might be up against," the older man said, climbing from the craft. "Let's get down to the nest and check you out."

Lucas climbed stiffly from the passenger's side. He was amazed at how much his body still ached, even after the sandwiches. The Science Club must've really done a job on him.

"I told you I was fine," he said. "I just need a hot shower and a good night's sleep."

"That will come later," Hartwell said, stepping into the elevator. "I'm going to run a complete diagnostic on you, as well as on the costume, and then you're going to tell me exactly what happened, beat by beat."

Lucas leaned against the elevator wall with a sigh. "It wasn't embarrassing enough, now you want me to relive it?"

"That's how we learn," Hartwell said, pulling his own mask off as the doors to the elevator opened onto his elaborate workstation.

Lucas followed. He was finding it difficult to put one foot in front of the other.

"Take the costume off and get up on the examination table," Hartwell ordered. He went to one of the control panels and flicked a few switches, activating the tools he would use on Lucas.

Lucas did as he was told, but waited until his father wasn't looking to remove the folded piece of paper Katie had given him from inside his boot. There was a bathrobe hanging from a hook nearby and he put it on, sliding the paper into the pocket.

Hartwell turned from the instrument panel. "So, shall we begin?"

The tests went on for hours. Lucas swore there wasn't a part of him that didn't get scanned or poked. He lay on the table, having great difficulty keeping his eyes open as his father went over screen after screen of data.

"From the looks of this," Hartwell said, startling him awake, "you're lucky to be alive right now."

I don't know if I'd call it lucky, the way I feel, Lucas thought.

"Your nanites were seriously damaged in the attack. They actually had to repair themselves before they could repair you," Hartwell explained gravely.

"That's probably why I feel like I got hit by a bus," Lucas said, remembering that, in fact, he had been hit by a van.

"I'm surprised you're not feeling worse," Hartwell said, wheeling his chair over from the computer screens to sit beside the examination table. "Where did you go after getting out of the Kessler Building?"

Lucas shrugged. "I just ran," he lied. "I wasn't sure I could survive another blast from one of their guns."

"So you just ran until I found you?" Hartwell asked.

"I think I might've passed out for a few seconds here and there, but yeah."

Hartwell nodded and stood, placing a strong hand on Lucas's shoulder. "You did well tonight," he said.

Lucas smiled. "How come I get the idea you're lying through your teeth?"

His father laughed. "Not at all," he said. "I'm just glad to see you in one piece. For a while there, I thought you were dead."

He went back to the computer to check the diagnostics

on the costume, which had been hooked up to a series of sensors.

Lucas wanted to tell him who he had met, but Nicolas Putnam's words echoed through his mind, rendering him mute.

All I'm asking is for you to trust us.

"I'm probably going to be pulling an all-nighter down here," Hartwell said, turning from his work. "Why don't you go get something to eat and hit the sack? We'll see how you're doing in the morning."

Much relieved, Lucas jumped down from the table and padded across the cold floor of the underground lab to the elevator. He pushed the button, and as the door slid open, he stuck his hands into the pocket of his robe. The folded paper from Katie was still there.

"Clayton," he called out.

His father turned toward him. "Yes, Lucas?"

Lucas closed his hand around the mysterious list.

He killed my father, he heard the cute girl say again, each word dipped in pain.

"Thanks for coming for me tonight," he said.

"You're welcome." Hartwell turned back to his work. "Good night."

"Good night," Lucas responded as the elevator door closed and the car began its ascent back up to the manor house.

Good night, Lucas thought wryly. With all he had to think about, he wondered if he would ever have one of those again.

10

His sleep that night was marred by bizarre dreams. He was back on the streets of the War Zone, but all the buildings were burning, and his father—fully costumed—stood staring at the neighborhood engulfed in fire.

"It wasn't always like this," Lucas heard his father say, before the Raptor leapt into the air.

A voice he could barely make out whispered in his ear, and he looked to see the girl—Katie—standing beside him.

Her eyes were fixed on the sight of his father—of the Raptor—circling the sky above the flames.

"What did you say?" he asked.

"He killed my father," she said, her voice louder as she began to cry tears of blood.

The air was suddenly filled with the sounds of screaming,

and Lucas saw that his father had come down to the street, fighting a gang that attacked him.

There was something different about him now. He seemed larger, the black and red Raptor's colors he wore looking less like a costume and more like his actual skin.

The gang had dropped to their knees, covering their heads in submission. But that didn't stop the Raptor. He attacked with abandon, picking up the surrendering gang-bangers and tearing them limb from limb.

The victims screamed as the Raptor laughed, moving from one to the other without a sign of mercy.

"You don't want to do this!" Lucas found himself screaming, running toward the ominous figure.

The Raptor whirled on him with a snarl, eyes like two burning coals floating in the darkness. He was holding bloody, dripping pieces of one of the gang members in large, clawed hands.

"It's time for you to wake up, Lucas," the monstrous version of the Raptor growled, its eyes burning brighter.

"Wake up."

Lucas awoke bathed in warm sunlight. The sudden exposure made him squirm, sending him scrambling beneath the covers like a vampire.

"What's going on?" he grumbled, his voice rough from sleep. His heart was still racing as he remembered his dream. His nightmare.

"I'm going to be gone for most of the day," Hartwell said, pinning back the curtains, allowing the sun's full effect to flood the bedroom. "And I want to be sure you're up and around."

Lucas slowly emerged from beneath the sheet and blanket. His father was dressed in a tailored black suit and was normal size again, nothing like the monster in his dream.

"Where are you off to?" Lucas asked, pushing himself up in the bed.

"Every once in a while I have to go into the city and show my face to the board of directors," Hartwell explained.

He didn't look at all pleased, and Lucas was sure the man would have prefered to be back in the lower levels of the manor, in the nest, working on some new kind of gadget.

"I like to remind them I'm still alive," the man added.

Hartwell leaned on his cherrywood cane, and Lucas noticed he looked a bit paler this morning.

"Are you feeling all right?" the boy asked, pictures of a {123 brutish Hartwell flashing before his eyes.

"I'm good," the older man said gruffly, turning on his heels and limping toward the door. "Our activity last night has taken a bit more from me than expected. I'll be fine."

Lucas threw back the covers and climbed from the bed.

"There's plenty to keep you busy while I'm gone," Hartwell said in the doorway. "I've set up a computer tutorial that will tell you about all the catalogued supervillains in the world. I'd like you to read up on them . . . get to know them . . . their strengths and weaknesses. You never know when you might run into one."

Lucas shook his head. "You've catalogued all the known supervillains?"

"Do you find something strange about that?"

The boy walked stiffly to the chair in the corner and retrieved his robe. "No, it's just that sometimes I wonder how you have time to fight crime with all your research and cataloguing."

"It hasn't been an easy life," the older man said. "I made a lot of sacrifices. And I guess you could say I'm paying for them now."

The room became deathly quiet, and Lucas felt awkward.

"I'll see you sometime tonight," Hartwell said, quickly turning to leave.

Lucas sat down heavily on the edge of his bed. The previous night's activities and the memories of his nightmare flooded into his mind. What was he going to do?

Putnam had asked for time to prove he was telling the truth. Should Lucas give it to him? What should he do until then? The questions gave him a headache, but Lucas really didn't see that there was much of a choice.

He stood up, deciding that the best thing he could do was to have some breakfast and feed his nanites. Then maybe he could start that tutorial on supervillains his father had left for him.

He put his hands into his pockets as he padded toward the door, and found the paper Katie had given him.

Again, he read the nine names. They still meant nothing to him.

He left the bedroom and went down to the kitchen for something to eat, already knowing what he would do after that.

* * *

Four bowls of cereal and two large glasses of juice later, Lucas found himself down in the lower levels of the manor, in the Raptor's nest.

He still felt uneasy down there, as if he didn't belong.

His costume had been laid out on a worktable, and it looked as though his father had already made some repairs to it. Lucas picked up the black mask; the cracked lenses had been replaced.

He'd be back to training again in no time.

Crossing the lab, he approached one of the smaller computer setups and booted it up. He'd surfed the Web a few times on these computers while waiting for his father to finish his own work, so he knew there was Internet access along with all the crime-fighting functions.

He sat down in the chair and took the list of names from his pocket, typing the first into a search engine.

Thomas Stanley.

He hit Enter and waited. There were a lot of Thomas Stanleys out there, involved with all sorts of things. He found one who had given a speech about advances in water purification, and another who had just been accepted into a high-profile California legal firm. Nothing out of the ordinary that he could see.

Bored with Mr. Stanley, he tried the next name.

Sheila Walker.

It was pretty much the same—multiple Sheila Walkers doing multiple things across the country. Hooray for Sheila Walker.

Lucas scrolled down the list, reading the descriptions of the various Sheila Walker Web sites. He found a Sheila

Walker who had been killed in a motor vehicle accident not too long ago. *That sucks*, he thought, and a morbid curiosity made him click on the story. It really did suck; she was a year younger than him.

Lucas punched in the next name.

Scott Wallace.

Lucas sighed. All kinds of people floating around out there named Scott Wallace. But then something caught his eye.

Leaning closer, he scrolled down to see that a Scott Wallace had died as well. The story was from another newspaper archive, and this particular Scott Wallace had died in a mysterious house fire.

He'd been right around the same age as Lucas.

The boy's heartbeat did a little jump. He quickly went to the next name.

Marc DiPietro.

Marc DiPietro the Elvis impersonator; Marc DiPietro with a blog about his love for pirate films. And strangely enough, Marc DiPietro who died while hiking late last summer.

Lucas's heart began to race even faster as a picture began to come into focus. A nasty picture.

He went back to Thomas Stanley and scrolled through page after page until he found it.

Death.

On page seven of twelve, Thomas Stanley, only twenty-one years old, had passed away quite suddenly of heart failure.

He went to the next name on the list.

Tyler Devin.

A Tyler Devin had died while vacationing in Florida. Although he'd been captain of the swim team in high school, he appeared to have drowned.

And that was how it went for the remaining four names—all of them dead, all of them only a few years older or younger than Lucas. Was this what Katie and Putnam had wanted him to discover? And if so, for what reason?

Lucas's thoughts raced, and then his mouth went dry.

What if this has something to do with my father?

Lucas quickly erased his Web history before signing off and shutting down the computer.

He picked up the crumpled piece of paper and read the names again. It wasn't a list of strangers anymore; the names had gained an ominous new meaning.

Lucas didn't know what to do. The supervillain tutorial was what he should have been doing, but he knew he wouldn't be able to concentrate. He stood up and began to pace.

Thomas Stanley. Sheila Walker. Scott Wallace . . .

Lucas wanted to shut his brain off, but he couldn't stop thinking about it.

"Lucas Moore." A tiny voice suddenly interrupted his troubled thoughts.

Now he was really beginning to think he was losing his mind. He listened for the sound of his name again.

"Lucas Moore, can you hear me?"

"Hello?" he asked, walking in a circle, trying to pinpoint the location of the voice. He knew that all his senses had been enhanced by the nanites in his bloodstream, and that included his hearing.

"Lucas Moore . . . calling Lucas Moore."

The voice was coming from somewhere across the room. He moved in that direction.

"Hello?" he called out again.

"Lucas?" the tiny voice squeaked. "Is that you?"

It was coming from the vicinity of the workstation where his father had been making the repairs to his costume.

"Are you here?" Lucas asked, approaching the table.

"Lucas, it's me . . . Putnam," said the voice, and finally Lucas realized it was coming from the communications system built into his mask. His father must have repaired that as well.

"Putnam?" he asked, picking up the mask and speaking into it.

"Yes, hello, can you hear me all right?"

"Took a minute to find where your voice was coming from," Lucas said. "How are you doing this? I thought this system was exclusive to Hartwell."

Lucas put the cowl on over his head. In his ears he heard the man laugh.

"I got a chance to study the system in your mask while you were unconscious," he explained. "Figured it might come in handy if I needed to get in touch with you."

"Does this have anything to do with the list?" Lucas asked.

"The list?"

"The names Katie gave to me," Lucas answered.

He could hear Putman speaking to someone in the background. His voice sounded tense, suddenly upset.

"Hey!" Lucas called out. "Where'd you go?"

"Lucas, have you done anything with that list?"

"I did a search online," he answered. "I wasn't sure what I was looking for, but I found something sort of scary. Each of the names . . . they all died in accidents."

There was a deathly silence on the other end, and a cold finger of dread ran up his spine.

"Was that it?" Lucas asked. "Was that what you were hoping I'd find? What does it mean? Because right now—"

"You need to get out of there," Putnam said firmly.

"What are you talking about?" Lucas asked, trying to keep calm.

"You need to come to me," Putnam stated. "You need to come to me, and I will explain everything."

{129

"No," Lucas answered, anger growing from his frustration. "No, I will not come to you." He started to pace, his voice growing louder. "I don't even know who you people are, for God's sake."

"And you know who Hartwell is?" Putnam asked bluntly. "A man suddenly walks into your life, says 'Hey, I'm your father—and oh yeah, by the way, I'm a superhero,' and that's perfectly easy for you to accept? Come on, Lucas."

"He's proven to me who he is," Lucas said, wanting desperately to remove the cowl and throw it across the room so he wouldn't have to listen anymore.

But he didn't.

"And who's that? The Raptor? The hero of Seraph City?" Putnam asked.

"Yes, he's a hero," Lucas argued. "I've been hearing about him for as long as I can remember. . . . They build statues to him and everything."

"We saw what he did to that gang member last night," Putnam said.

"I don't know what you're—"

"Somebody in one of the apartments filmed it with their cell phone. He looked as though he wanted to kill him," Putnam went on. "But you stopped him."

"He was just trying to scare him," Lucas said, remembering how frightened he had been.

"Do you really believe that, Lucas?" Putnam asked. "If you do, we can end this here. You'll never hear from me again."

"He's a superhero," Lucas replied, certain what he was saying was true.

But is it? He remembered the horrific dream, and the reality that had spawned it.

"He would never—"

"Goodbye, Lucas," Putnam said.

"Wait," Lucas said suddenly. "Tell me about the list."

"For that, you have to come to me."

Lucas didn't know what to say. He felt himself being sucked down into the darkness, deeper and deeper. But what if that was where the answers were?

"Will you do that, Lucas? Will you come to me and let me tell you everything?" Putnam asked.

Lucas had to know the truth.

He stopped fighting and allowed himself to be drawn into the depths.

"How do I find you?"

* * *

Lucas had actually learned to hotwire a car before he could even drive.

His mom had always said that hanging around with the wrong crowd would bring him nothing but trouble, but if he hadn't, he wouldn't have been able to do what he was doing now in the front seat of his father's vintage Ford Mustang.

The man seems to love his Mustangs.

Lying across the seat, head bent beneath the steering column, he managed to get at the ignition wires and twist them together. The car's powerful engine turned over with a roar and then idled to a purr.

"Sorry, Mom," Lucas said beneath his breath, knowing how horrified she would have been.

He backed out, careful not to scratch any of the other fifty vehicles parked in the underground garage. He drove up a winding concrete ramp, but he was forced to stop before a closed metal door.

"C'mon, c'mon," he said, flipping down the sun visor. "Yes!" he exclaimed when he found the garage door opener clipped to the visor. He pushed the button, and the heavy door began to slowly rise.

This is it, he thought, waiting for the door. *My last chance to forget about Putnam and the names on that list.*

The garage door was fully open, but Lucas sat behind the wheel for a moment, listening to the engine hum and thinking about his options. Part of him wanted to call it all off, to go back inside and begin the supervillain tutorial; but there was another part of him, one that was starving for answers, hungrier even than the nanites flowing through his blood.

Lucas stepped on the gas, the tires squealing as he peeled out of the garage on his way to answers.

There was no turning back now.

He was surprised that Putnam had just given him an address.

Lucas had half expected to be picked up in an unmarked car, blindfolded, and driven to some supersecret location.

He was to find a place called Seraphim Way. Using the car's GPS system, he punched in the address and followed the directions that appeared on the small computer screen attached to the dashboard.

The Mustang felt very different from his pickup truck. The closest he had ever come to driving anything this fast was when he had needed to pull a vehicle into the garage for work or park it when he was done.

This car was something else. He was amazed by its response, a tap of the gas taking him from the speed limit to over in the blink of an eye. Lucas reminded himself to be careful; he didn't need to be pulled over for speeding in a car he had pretty much stolen. He slowed down, still managing to enjoy the experience of driving the fine vehicle. He wanted to get to Putnam's as soon as possible, but he knew not to risk it.

The answers would still be there.

From a winding two-lane road, he was directed to an exit that would bring him onto the highway going north, and he stepped on the gas, merging with the oncoming traffic.

As he drove, Lucas studied the city around him. There was something both thrilling and frightening about the place. It was a strange mixture of old and new architecture, buildings of brick, concrete, and wood mingling with towering structures of steel and glass.

It was as if two cities—one from the past and another from the future—had been crammed together to form a single place.

He could see why his mother had been sad about leaving here, and why his father had chosen to protect it so fiercely.

He wanted to know the Angel City better. To learn all her secrets.

The highway eventually took him to the outskirts of Seraph, to a lonely country road that wound its way through a heavily wooded area.

Eventually he passed a sign that read EDEN STATE PARK, and he realized he was getting close.

At a barely visible entrance, he banged a sharp right and {133 carefully drove the sports car down an uneven dirt road. According to the GPS, Seraphim Way would be at the end of this rocky stretch.

The car bumped along. Lucas tried to steer around the most obvious dips and craters, but he found it impossible to avoid them completely. If Hartwell was going to be pissed at him for taking one of his cars, he would have a stroke for sure after seeing what the vehicle's frame looked like after this excursion.

After a sharp bend, the road got a little bit better, and Lucas suddenly found himself coming to a stop in front of a high metal gate.

"Great," he muttered, getting out of the car to see if he would be able to pass.

The double wrought-iron gate wasn't locked or chained, so he was able to push it open.

Getting back into the car, he drove through the passage, up the roadway, and around a bend, which was where he saw it.

Lucas knew he had arrived.

It looked as though at one time it had been a house, or an old mansion really. Not quite as big as Hartwell Manor, but still plenty huge to Lucas.

He drove up to the front of the building and stopped. The place looked like hell. A small island of overgrown weeds punctuated the circular drive, and in the midst of it, Lucas saw something. He left the car and went to it. It was a rotting wooden sign.

Reaching down, he hauled it up, and brushing away the dirt and bugs, he read what it said.

THE HANNIFORD PSYCHIATRIC FACILITY.

A *mental hospital*, he thought, letting the sign fall back to where it had probably lain for years. He wondered if he should take the sign as an omen of bad things to come.

He left the circle and approached the building. It was a mess—windows boarded up, shingles fallen away to reveal rotting tar paper beneath. From the looks of it, nobody had been here for a very long time.

Had Putnam been playing with him? Making him jump through hoops like some trained puppy, just to see if he could be trusted?

"Maybe I wrote down the address wrong," Lucas muttered, staring at the forbidding structure. It reminded him of a place out of one of the slasher movies he and his mother used to watch when he was still too young to hang out at the Trough.

"*I wouldn't go in there if you paid me,*" he remembered her saying as they showed a building or house very much like this one.

Lucas smiled as he approached, doing the very thing he and his mother used to complain about.

Why did the main characters always act so freakin' stupid?

It was the need for answers, he would tell her now, speaking from experience. *The need to know . . . It makes you do stupid things.*

He walked up the steps, the ancient wood moaning and creaking, and onto the large front porch.

Lucas could just imagine the former residents of the Hanniford, sitting in chairs, lined up in a row, getting some fresh air and sunshine.

The large double doors seemed to beckon to him. He gripped the glass knob and tried to turn it. It refused to move, and Lucas let out an exasperated sigh.

It must've all been a game, he thought, walking to the edge of the porch. He was about to go back to the car and return to the manor when he heard the sound from behind him.

Lucas turned to see that one of the double doors had opened. A damp, musty odor wafted out from inside.

"Hello?" he called out, cautiously sticking his head through the doorway.

The inside was as depressing as the outside.

The building was just a shell, some random pieces of moldering furniture strewn around the entryway and what looked like a reception area over to the left.

He entered, blinking as his eyes adjusted to the gloom. Muted sunshine found its way through the dust-, dirt- and grime-encrusted windows.

He walked farther into the foyer, searching for something to tell him he was in the right place.

The door slammed behind him and he jumped.

"Glad you could make it," said a disembodied voice he immediately recognized as Nicolas Putnam's. "Hang a right and head on down the first staircase to your left."

"Where are you?" Lucas asked.

"You'll see soon enough," Putnam said.

Lucas walked down the dark corridor, found the staircase, and started down.

Putnam's voice followed him, seemingly coming from the walls.

"Keep going until you reach the bottom," he told him.

Lucas obeyed, heading down into the darkness. He was surprised at how well he could see, but figured it was the nanites doing their job.

At the bottom of the steps he saw that he was in some sort of basement work area, probably a laundry room. "Now what?" he called out.

"Step over to the door," Putnam's voice told him.

A faint red light illuminated a barely noticeable closet door at the far end of the large room. He walked toward it.

"Sorry for keeping you waiting outside," Putman said as the old closet door, its surface covered in peeling white paint, swung open to reveal a more impressive-looking metal door.

It reminded Lucas of the doors he'd seen on bank vaults.

"Had to be sure that you were alone," Putnam went on.

The door began to hum. Lucas could hear the muffled metallic clicking and clanking sounds as the locking mechanism disengaged.

"That you hadn't shared our discussion with Hartwell."

The door slid open to reveal Putnam, leaning on his crutches, in the middle of a large, well-lit room.

"What makes you think I didn't?" Lucas asked, stepping inside.

The room was a dirtier version of Hartwell's nest: computers and various pieces of unrecognizable technology lying around; multiple projects at different stages of completion.

"I'm a good judge," Putnam said. "You want to know what this is all about . . . what it's *really* all about?"

The heavy metal door closed behind Lucas with a hiss. {137}

"Come in, and I promise to make everything clear," Putnam said.

"What is this place?" Lucas asked.

"The Hanniford Psychiatric Facility," Putnam began. "If you were crazy or had a problem with an addictive substance, this was the place for you . . . until 1975, when it was shut down for tax evasion."

"Do you own it?" Lucas asked.

Putnam shrugged. "We borrow it. It's the perfect location for our supersecret research lab." The man waggled his eyebrows as Lucas followed him into the work area.

"This looks like a workshop," Lucas said

"That's exactly what it is," Putnam answered. "This is how I support my extracurricular activities. I design security and surveillance systems for big businesses, and for anybody else who can afford them."

"Which is how you've been able to keep an eye on me," Lucas added.

"Exactly," Putnam responded with a smile and a nod.

"So if you've got this business, why are you hiding in an abandoned hospital?" Lucas asked.

"Because I feel safer staying out of sight," Putnam replied.

"Who are you afraid of?" Lucas asked. "Hartwell . . . the Raptor?"

"Let's just say Mr. Hartwell wouldn't approve of what my observations of his activities over the last twenty or so years have revealed."

They reached a workstation with two seats. Putnam gestured for Lucas to sit down.

"I think I'll stand," Lucas said, crossing his arms. He looked around, wondering where Katie might be.

"Suit yourself," the older man said as he leaned his crutches against the station and lowered his disabled body with a grunt. "Don't ever get old," he said as Lucas looked his way. "Or have sixty percent of the bones in your body broken in an explosion rigged by supervillains."

"Is that what happened to you?" Lucas asked, his curiosity piqued. "Is that why you stopped being Talon?"

The older man nodded. "Pretty much," he said. "Hartwell and I . . . excuse me, *the Raptor* and I had been tracking a group of villains that had decided to team up. They called themselves the Terribles."

Putnam paused a moment, as if he had to prepare himself for what he was about to say.

"They were responsible for a number of robberies where some innocents had been hurt, and that just made Hartwell insane. He'd had enough. He used everything at his disposal to track these guys down and bring them to justice."

A can of soda sat on the counter and Putnam reached for it. Lucas noticed the burn scars on his hand.

Putman took a pull from the can, and continued. "The Raptor and Talon became real pains in the ass out there on the streets. We utilized every street source we could find to get our information. After we were done with them, the lowlifes of Seraph City were pretty happy to give us the location of the Terribles' hideout."

Putnam chuckled, bringing his hand up to touch the disfigured portion of his face.

"And I'm sorry to say they paid the price," he said, his voice growing soft and quiet. "We were so damned cocky, we didn't realize they were playing us."

"Playing you?" Lucas asked, leaning back against a counter. "Who, the Terribles?"

"Yep. It was a trap," Putnam explained. "They led us right to their door—an unfinished convention center downtown."

"And that was where you got hurt?"

"That was where a lot of people got hurt," the older man said. "Killed, in fact. The Terribles had captured our key informants and rigged the entire building to explode once we were inside."

Putnam reached for his can of soda again, and Lucas noticed how badly his hand was shaking.

Lucas saw movement from the corner of his eye and watched as Katie strolled by, talking to someone on a cell phone. She took notice of him and waved before continuing on, still talking as she disappeared into another part of the workshop space.

"So the Raptor was hurt too?" Lucas asked.

"Yeah, but not as badly as me. He pulled me from the wreckage, removed my tattered costume, and brought me to the closest hospital, telling the emergency room physicians I was an innocent bystander who had been caught in the blast."

"So nobody knew who you were."

"Nobody knew I was Talon," he said. "And after a while, Hartwell seemed to forget as well."

"What do you mean?"

"Being the rich philanthropist and friend to Seraph City, Hartwell volunteered to pay for all my medical expenses. That was the last I saw of him."

"But you were his partner," Lucas said.

"I was, but after that incident, it was like I didn't exist anymore. As if what happened had changed all the rules, turning him into a completely different person."

Putnam paused.

"It was as if whatever humanity he'd had was destroyed in the explosion. What left the inferno was some kind of cold, calculating machine."

The words were chilling, but Lucas needed more. He had to know why Putnam believed this.

"Nick," Katie said, coming into the area.

Lucas immediately straightened up, standing taller.

"Hate to interrupt, but Fabonio is insisting he speak with the system's designer." She held the phone out to Putnam.

The man sighed, pushing himself up from the seat and gathering his crutches.

"I'll be back as soon as I can," he said, placing the phone beneath his chin and hobbling out of sight.

"Mr. Fabonio?" Putnam asked the person on the other end. "Good day to you, sir. This is Robert Larrange."

He was soon out of earshot.

"Robert Larrange?" Lucas asked, turning to Katie.

"One of Nick's many aliases," she said with a pretty smile.

Lucas half expected her to take off, leaving him alone until Putnam came back, but she stayed.

"I guess he was hurt pretty badly," Lucas said finally.

Katie nodded. "Physically, as well as mentally," she said. "When the Raptor abandoned him, it kind of messed him up more than the explosion did. Even after his wounds and bones had healed as well as they were going to, he still had some issues."

She really is pretty hot, Lucas thought, struggling to concentrate on her words.

"He tried to contact Hartwell to find out what had happened, but every attempt went unanswered."

"So what did he do?"

Katie shrugged. "I think he just sort of disappeared. He had money saved, and he took it all out and went off the grid so that nobody could find him. Being the Raptor's partner had taught him some pretty amazing skills, so it wasn't hard for him to drop off the face of the earth."

"Did Hartwell notice?" Lucas asked. "Did he even try to find him?"

The girl shook her head. "It wasn't part of his new mission," she explained. "Hartwell was all about the big mission . . . about wiping out evil for good."

There was a question that Lucas wanted to ask, but he didn't know how to go about it. He didn't want to sound like an insensitive jerk, but he had to know.

"You said he . . . the Raptor . . . he . . . ?"

"Killed my father?" Katie asked casually.

She leaned against the opposite side of the counter, crossing her ankles. Lucas noticed she was wearing red Converse sneakers and some pretty crazy striped socks.

"He did," she said, her voice sounding small. "Matter of fact, that was how I first met Nicolas. My dad was one of the original Terribles."

Lucas nodded, not sure how to react when a cute girl let you know that her dad was a murderous supervillain.

"He called himself the Frightener. He was a chemist and had developed this gas that caused people to experience their deepest fears."

"Sounds . . . sort of cool," Lucas said carefully.

"Yeah, but he was a jerk. I hadn't seen him in years. He'd left the country with the other Terribles not too long after I was born, I guess, but when he showed up dead, he actually had me listed on a piece of paper in his wallet as his next of kin." She stared at her sneakers for a bit. "Yep, a real piece of work, but even a supervillain doesn't deserve what happened to him. I was always under the impression that the good guys weren't supposed to do stuff like that, y'know?"

Lucas nodded, sharing in her emotion.

"I was fifteen, hadn't seen him in years, and I was the one who got the call to go and identify the body. Can you believe it? If it wasn't for some old pictures my mom had hanging around, I wouldn't even have known what he looked like," she said angrily.

"And you think my dad . . . Hartwell was responsible?"

"I know he was," she said. "It took him quite a few years, but the Raptor was taking down each member of the Terribles. They must've decided it was safe to come back from wherever they were hiding. Wrong. The week after he offed my dad he hung this guy called the Blade Master by his neck over the Seraph City Freeway." She shook her head. "Not nice at all."

{143

Lucas was about to ask her how she knew it was his father, but Putnam returned, handing Katie her phone. "Thanks, hon," he said as she took it from him.

"I was just telling Lucas how we met," she said, checking her phone to see if she had any messages.

"Nice," the former Talon said. "I'd heard about what happened to the Frightener and wanted to see for myself. You know how it is with those supervillains—they're never as dead as you think they are."

"He was dead all right," Katie said, still looking at her phone.

Putnam continued. "I ran into her at the morgue. We were the only ones there."

"My mom had passed away the year before," Katie added.

"Right then I didn't have anybody in the world . . . not even a lousy supervillain for a dad."

"She thought I might've been one of her father's partners . . . y'know, another bad guy, but I found myself opening up to her. We struck up a conversation, realized we had similar goals, and here we are."

"We've been buddies since," Katie said with that really pretty smile. "We both had something in common with the Raptor, and we formed a partnership."

Putman smiled in her general direction. "I felt I needed to keep an eye on her so she didn't follow in her father's footsteps," he said with a laugh.

"Yeah, right, like I know anything about chemistry," she added with a giggle.

"But she did know a thing or two about computers," he said. "It wasn't long before we were designing some of the top surveillance systems in the country and making a bundle."

"All tax-free," she chirped, and then laughed.

Lucas's head was spinning. "Let's back up," he said. "My father, as the Raptor, killed your father, who was a supervillain?"

Katie looked him squarely in the eye. "Slammed him against an alley wall so hard that it broke his neck. It was not a very spectacular, supervillainy way to go."

"And he killed other members of the Terribles as well," Putnam added.

Lucas tried again to process the info. They were telling him his father had hurt some people . . . *killed* some people, but they were bad guys. They were supervillains who had hurt Talon, as well as some innocent people in Seraph City.

But was that enough to justify murder?

"And he hasn't stopped there. He's killed others since," Putnam said.

Lucas wanted to dismiss everything they were saying. It just wasn't possible. Yeah, his father had lost it a bit the other night, but who wouldn't after years of trying to clean up Seraph City? And besides, where was the proof? Two complete strangers stood in front of him, spouting what could very well be lies.

Hell, they could be villains themselves, Lucas thought. He shook his head. "He's a superhero. He doesn't murder people. I—I'm not so sure I'm buying this."

"Should I show him the latest?" Katie asked.

"Might as well," Putnam answered.

Katie turned around to face one of the computers on the desk and opened a file for Lucas to see.

"What's this supposed to be?" He leaned closer to the screen.

"It doesn't look familiar?" Putnam asked.

It was a crime scene photo—a large body dumped in the middle of an overgrown lot.

"I still don't—" Lucas began.

"Look closely," Putnam instructed.

Katie hit another key and a close-up shot of the crime victim appeared. Lucas gasped. The last time he'd seen the supervillain Bestial, the monster man had been lying unconscious on the floor of Hartwell Manor.

"He's dead?" Lucas asked, unable to tear his gaze away.

"Murdered and dumped in an abandoned lot," Putnam said. "Forensics says he died from a massive electrical shock."

"He was . . . he was my final exam," Lucas said, staring at the villain's blank expression, frozen in death.

"Did you kill him, Lucas?" Putnam asked flat out.

He felt both of them staring, their eyes burning into him.

"*No,*" Lucas answered vehemently, shaking his head from side to side.

No, but his father had wanted him to.

"I—I just beat him in a fight. I have no idea what happened to him after."

Putnam tapped the screen with a finger. "This is what happened," the man said. "Bestial served your father's purpose, and then your father was done with him."

Lucas didn't quite understand it, but suddenly he was overcome with a sense of responsibility. "I feel like it's my fault," he said.

Putnam gripped his shoulder and squeezed. "It's not," he reassured him. "But you need to listen to what we're trying to tell you."

"I don't understand," Lucas began. The world he had just recently come to know was beginning to crumble. "He's a hero. . . . How could he do this?"

"Your father doesn't know it, but I've been watching him. He's desperate now. The years of strength-enhancing drugs and steroids, along with the physical wear and tear on his body, have had a lasting effect on him. The Raptor isn't the same anymore, and Hartwell can't accept that. He's doing everything in his power to correct the situation."

Lucas swallowed, not liking where all this had gone, and where it was sure to go.

"I learned that Hartwell Technologies had started to do extensive research into nanite technology, with specific applications aimed at healing the human body," Putnam continued.

Katie cleared the screen of Bestial's corpse and called up a search engine. "While Nick was attempting to figure out what our scary superhero was doing with that technology, the gossip columns were filled with all sorts of stories about the eligible multibillionaire bachelor Clayton Hartwell and his numerous one-night stands."

She pulled up some files from gossip newspapers twenty years old and scrolled through picture after picture of his father, much younger. A different woman was on his arm in each picture.

"Wait!" Lucas yelped when he saw someone he recognized.

His mother. It appeared, from the picture, that she and Hartwell had gone to the theater together.

His mother loved the theater. Especially musicals.

"You look like her," Katie said before changing the screen.

"Believe it or not, all of this ties together," Putnam explained.

Lucas felt sick to his stomach. "And I'm sure you're going to explain it all to me," he said, closing his eyes, preparing for the worst . . . if it could possibly get any worse.

"All the women you just saw with Hartwell . . . with your father," Putnam said. "They all became pregnant with his children."

"All of them?" Lucas asked.

Putnam slowly nodded.

"And they all left Seraph before their children were born," Katie contributed. "There are rumors floating around that some were paid to leave, if you catch my drift."

"My mother knew about Hartwell . . . who he actually was. She told me she left to protect me."

"Which was probably the case," Putnam responded. "But each of them left Seraph and had their babies."

"Jump ahead twenty or so years," Katie said. Her fingers were again flying over the keyboard. A yellow file folder appeared, and she brought the mouse arrow up to click it open.

Multiple yearbook photographs of smiling young adults appeared.

"And here they are, ladies and gentlemen," the girl said, stepping back and watching Lucas carefully.

There were nine photos of young men and women.

And there had been nine names on the list Katie had given him.

"These are the people from the list," Lucas said, his voice a nervous whisper.

"Bingo," Putnam said. "And each and every one of these handsome kids is dead."

"All except one," Katie said. "One of the kids has managed to survive longer than all the others."

She did something with the mouse and the nine pictures disappeared, replaced by one.

The photo was of Lucas, taken for the high school newspaper over a year ago, just before he dropped out.

"You're the only one of his children left," Putnam said.

"I can't believe this," Lucas blurted out. "Why does it have to be him?" he demanded. "Couldn't it be one of his enemies . . . one of the Raptor's enemies? That's what he told me . . . and . . ."

"And you believed him," Putnam teased.

"Flight plans were filed with the FCC that show Hartwell took his private jet to all the victims' locations prior to these so-called accidents," she explained.

Lucas's legs felt like rubber, and he was finding it difficult to catch his breath. He squatted down, holding his head in his hands.

"I can't believe this," he said. "I don't want to believe this. Why? Why would a hero murder his own children?"

He looked up at them, hoping for something that would somehow ease the fever now wracking his brain.

"It wasn't just the children," Putnam said as Katie nodded seriously. "In some instances the entire family was wiped out."

"But why?" Lucas demanded. "Why would he do this?"

Putnam shrugged. "That's something we've never really been able to figure out. They've all died . . . except for you."

Lucas was about to tell the man he didn't understand when Katie's phone started ringing.

She took it from her sweatshirt pocket and looked at the screen.

"Who is it?" Putnam asked.

She shrugged, opening the phone. "Larrange Scientific," she answered in her most professional voice.

Lucas slowly stood, his stomach doing backflips. He

thought he might be sick, until he glanced at Katie. The color was draining from her face, and her expression was one of utter shock.

"What's wrong?" Putnam asked, reaching for the phone. "Who is it?"

She broke the connection, appearing dazed.

"It was *him*," she said, on the verge of panic.

"Hartwell?" Putnam asked.

She shook her head slowly.

"He said he was the Raptor."

11

One Hour, Thirteen Minutes, and Twenty-five Seconds Ago

Clayton Hartwell sat at the head of a long mahogany conference table. The upper management of Hartwell Tech sat at attention on either side.

They were always on their best behavior when he decided to pay them a visit. Hypocrites. He was sure they would just as soon see him hurry up and die so that the company could be turned over to the board of directors and run in a way they saw fit.

Forbes magazine said that Hartwell Technologies could be one of the biggest tech companies on the planet, bigger even than Microsoft, but its focus was too broad. It had its fingers in everything rather than focusing on a few particular areas. The company made millions, but these people wanted billions. Hartwell had never been concerned about the money, as long as he had what he needed to take care of the city.

After all, what was money when you had the safety of every man, woman, and child in Seraph City to worry about?

Hartwell swiveled in his chair ever so slightly as Timothy Cole, the head of development, droned on and on about something Hartwell probably wouldn't have found interesting even if he hadn't been so distracted. His gaze traveled to the floor-to-ceiling windows that made up two walls of the conference room. He could see Seraph City sprawled out below him.

Crimes were being committed while he sat, trapped at the table, pretending to be something he really wasn't.

Murder. Rape. Arson. Robbery. Child abuse. The offenses went on and on.

He would have loved to tell them that Clayton Hartwell had indeed passed away twenty years ago. Back then, he had been Clayton Hartwell, the man who had become the hero known as the Raptor. He'd even found a sidekick, someone who shared his love of the city, someone he could train to pick up some of the slack in his duties to the Angel City.

Crime was on the rise, too much for the Raptor to handle alone.

Talon was his answer.

Staring out the window, he tried to find the location where it had happened, where Clayton Hartwell had died and the Raptor alone had crawled from the ashes.

He remembered the sound of thunder as the explosives

detonated and the building fell down around their ears. The fact that Talon had survived was a blessing, but it had shown Clayton how it needed to be.

No longer would he put others at risk. It was up to him, the Raptor, to do everything in his power to see his city protected. And to ensure there would always be a Raptor watching out for them.

He had taken the time to see to Talon's care, before making the break completely.

It was a whole new world now—one Clayton Hartwell was no longer strong enough to protect.

Hartwell would be the mask now.

Long live the Raptor.

"Sir?" he heard a voice call to him.

Hartwell looked away from the window to see Cole and the others staring at him.

He had no idea what they had been discussing, but he was about to bluff his way through when his cell phone began to ring.

The first notes of Beethoven's Fifth Symphony began playing, and he felt a slight chill run up and down his spine. He had programmed different rings into his cell phone to indicate certain things. This one told him there was Internet activity at the computer back at the nest.

"Excuse me a moment," he said, turning his chair completely around to look at the phone screen.

His fingers moved across the small keyboard, instructing the handheld device to show him what information Lucas had accessed.

He imagined it was probably something of little

importance—YouTube or whatever else the kids were looking at these days—but he needed to know for sure. Hartwell saw that a search engine had been used, and then he saw the names Lucas had been researching.

His jaw dropped. This was far from harmless.

"Something's come up," Hartwell said as he quickly stood. "I'm afraid I need to leave."

"But there are acquisition contracts that need to be signed. . . ."

"What part of *I need to leave* don't you understand?" Hartwell barked, feeling his patience ebb. The Raptor did not care to be questioned in any way.

Cole immediately backed down. Everyone else looked through their papers or out the window, anywhere but at him.

"Have anything that needs to be signed messengered to the manor, and I'll take care of it as expediently as I can."

He left his chair at the head of the table and walked to the door, holding his cane by his side.

There wasn't even a hint of a limp.

Behind the wheel of his modified Lamborghini, Hartwell tore from the underground parking garage of the Hartwell Technologies building, heading for home.

He removed the phone from the inside pocket of his jacket and placed it in a docking bay on the car's dashboard.

"Call home," he instructed the phone, while the images called up in the Web search his son had done scrolled by in a separate window on the side.

He drove through the city streets with amazing precision,

avoiding red lights with the help of a special mechanism similar to the fire department controls that halted traffic-signal changes until the fire engines had passed.

The phone at the manor rang and rang, but nobody picked up.

"Dammit," Hartwell cursed, reaching out to press one of the buttons on the phone. "Override phone. Patch me to PA home system."

He waited a moment, saying a silent prayer that the boy had been in the bathroom, or napping, and hadn't heard the phone.

"Lucas," he called out, imagining his voice being broadcast into every room of the manor. "Lucas, it's me. Are you there? I believe we need to discuss something. Please pick up the closest phone."

He waited, a ball of dread hardening in his stomach.

"Lucas?" he tried again. "Please, I know you're probably confused by what you've found, but I can explain."

Hartwell's thoughts had already begun to dissect the situation. *Where did the boy get the idea to search for those specific names?*

Either Lucas had chosen not to communicate with him, or worse, he was gone.

Hartwell came to a screeching halt in front of the main entrance to his home and barreled through the front doors. "Lucas?" he called out, walking through the empty corridors, sticking his head into the equally empty rooms. The boy was nowhere to be found. Hartwell bounded up the stairs. He practically ran down the corridor and flung open the door to his son's room.

"Lucas," he said, bursting in and looking around. He went to the closet to find that the boy's clothes were still there.

There was only one other place he could imagine the boy might be.

He descended the stairs two at a time and headed to the elevator that would take him down into the nest.

But if he is in the nest, wouldn't he have heard my call? he wondered as the elevator began its descent.

Maybe Lucas was choosing not to respond, wanting to figure out answers on his own before confronting Hartwell with what he had found. That was a possibility.

Hartwell left the elevator as soon as the doors began to open.

"Lucas!" he called out, but no one answered. He was alone.

Hartwell stood in the center of his lab, looking for any sign indicating where the boy might have gone. His eyes touched upon an area in the ceiling where a camera was hidden.

"Computer active," he said aloud, and all the systems in the lab immediately activated at the sound of his voice. "Security systems review," he ordered as he turned toward one of the monitors.

The image of Lucas sitting before the computer screen appeared.

"Advance recording," Hartwell instructed the voice-sensitive system.

The digital recording moved ahead, until he saw the boy

complete his search, shut down the computer, and then stand still in the middle of the lab.

Hartwell's curiosity was piqued. It appeared the boy was listening to something.

"Volume up," he instructed the system.

Vertical bars appeared at the bottom of the monitor, showing the volume rising.

And then Hartwell heard what Lucas had been hearing. A tiny voice calling out his name.

Lucas left the vantage point of that particular camera, but another hidden in the ceiling of the lab switched on to continue the surveillance. This one showed the boy near the worktable where Hartwell had been repairing his costume.

"Lucas, it's me . . . Putnam," said the tiny voice.

The cold hand of dread that had been gripping Hartwell's heart slowly began to squeeze.

Putnam.

Nicolas Putnam.

Talon.

"No," Hartwell snarled at the screen, feeling his resolve beginning to disintegrate. "Don't do this."

Lucas had put on the cowl, making it difficult for Hartwell to hear what Putnam was telling him.

"Does this have anything to do with the list?" he heard Lucas ask the voice.

"Damn you!" Hartwell raged. "You're going to ruin everything."

"Each of the names," Lucas said to Hartwell's former partner. "They all died in accidents."

Hartwell experienced a sudden wave of calm.

The Raptor had fully emerged. Cold, hard, calculating; it was he who would handle this delicate situation. The bird of prey watched the boy on the screen as he listened to the voice inside his helmet.

"How do I find you?" Lucas asked, and the Raptor knew what had to be done.

In the digital video, the boy removed his mask and left the lab.

The Raptor stared at the screen for quite some time, formulating his plan. There was a part of him that looked at this situation as dire, that knew nothing good could possibly come from it, yet there was still a spark of damnable humanity that didn't want to believe it.

This one had shown such promise. He hated to think of Lucas having to go the way of all the others.

The failures.

Disturbing images flashed before his mind's eye, images of those that had failed the tests sprung on them. He hated to think of them as anything more than test subjects. It made things much, much easier to handle.

Hartwell stalked across the lab toward the special cabinet where he stored his weapons systems and armor. He decided to give the boy a chance as he punched in the code that would open the cabinet's wonders to him. The doors slid apart with a welcoming hiss, and he strode inside.

He'd always known that Putnam could be a problem, that he could come so close to perfection and have it all come crashing down around him.

It was enough to make anyone a little crazy.

Now Putnam was attempting to turn the boy against him.

The Raptor knew that the former Talon would not give up without a fight, so he would have to wear his most powerful costume. At the far back of the cabinet, the Raptor stealth armor hung by thick chains, like some sort of mechanical shell waiting to be infused with life. Hartwell removed his clothes and stood before the fearsome visage of the shiny black and scarlet armor. Slowly and purposefully, he began to clothe himself in the new skin that would define his true self.

A fearsome bird of prey on the hunt.

A raptor.

He hoped it wasn't too late for the boy, that he hadn't somehow been corrupted by his former partner's poisonous words.

But if that were the case, he would do what was necessary.

He would put the boy down, as he had the others.

And start the process all over again.

Putnam leaned against the counter. He raised a trembling hand, passing it over the smooth side, then the scarred side of his face.

"I was afraid it might come to this," he said with a sigh, closing his eyes.

"How did he find us?" Lucas asked, panic growing in his voice.

Putnam shrugged. "He might have stuck some kind of a bug under your skin while you were sleeping, or it could be something as simple as a tracking signal coming from the car you used to get here."

"Under my skin?" Lucas asked, rubbing his hands over his arms. "Would he do that?"

Putnam laughed. "This is the guy who's been killing his own children. To him, sticking some kind of tracking device under your skin is like giving you a piece of candy."

Katie had moved to her workstation, and her fingers were clicking across the keyboard. "I'm activating all the security systems."

"Good," Putnam acknowledged, although he didn't sound convinced it would be much help.

"You don't seem all that concerned," Lucas said. "If he's as . . . as crazy as you're saying . . ."

Putnam nodded. "I think he is," he said. "And if I'm right, there isn't anything that's going to keep him from getting to us."

"GPS says that he's less than five miles away," Katie announced.

"Maybe we can talk to him," Lucas suggested. "Maybe there's a reason for all this that you . . . we don't even realize. Maybe it's not as bad as it looks."

Putnam looked as if he felt sorry for the boy. "I know what you're doing," he said. "I did the same thing not all that long ago. No matter what I discovered—no matter what he had done to me—I still wanted to believe in him."

"Less than two miles out," Katie said.

Putnam grabbed his crutches and hobbled from the work area, the boy at his heels.

"But you still haven't answered the major question. Why

would he do this?" Lucas asked. "There has to be something. . . ."

Putnam led the boy to a darkened area of the work space.

"You want to know what I think it's about?" Putnam asked, flicking a wall switch.

A single bulb illuminated a glass display case.

"It's about that." He pointed to the costume behind the glass. Over the years he had worked on it, trying to improve it so that if the time ever came, he could wear it again. . . .

Lucas stood before the case, staring.

"It's about never being able to live up to the expectations of what he believed being a hero was all about."

The boy said nothing.

"Those he killed . . . his children . . . maybe they didn't live up to his expectations either."

Lucas turned his head slowly to look at Putnam. *Could it be true?* he wondered. *Could the others have disappointed the Raptor somehow and paid the price with their lives?* With a chilling realization, Lucas wondered how close he might've come to letting the old superhero down.

How close he might've come to really dying this time.

"I survived," he said.

And Putnam nodded ever so slowly. "You did," he agreed.

"He's here!" Katie announced, her voice cracking.

"Let's see how you do now."

12

The sirens were deafening.

Lucas stood with Putnam and Katie, their eyes glued to the flat-screen monitor on her desk.

"Here's hoping our security systems hold him back," Putnam said, watching the screen intently.

"And then what?" Lucas asked.

"I haven't thought that far ahead yet," Putnam said.

"That certainly inspires confidence." Katie's voice was no louder than a whisper.

The Raptor had touched down in front of the facility, the microjets built into his flight boots slowing his descent with powerful bursts of air that kicked up roiling clouds of dust, hiding him from their cameras.

Video cameras were everywhere, and Putnam reached

out to activate them all, individual screens breaking down the single image on the monitor into multiples.

Still, all they could see was dust.

And then the armored figure emerged.

"Holy crap," Putnam said. "He's wearing the battle suit."

"I've never seen that one before," Lucas said, his stomach growing increasingly uneasy. It was as if Hartwell was wearing the superhero-costume equivalent of a tank—dark, sleek, and deadly.

"It's not something he uses all that often," Putnam explained. "He must be figuring he's going to be up against some heavy artillery."

Putnam moved them aside so he could sit down in the chair. He punched some sort of code into the keyboard, overriding the automated security defense systems.

He was in the driver's seat now.

"Let's not disappoint him."

The dust was settling, and the Raptor scanned the grounds, using the vision-enhancing lenses in his mask, looking for signs of life.

The first thing he noticed was the Mustang.

All the cars in his vast collection were equipped with an antitheft device that emitted a signal that could be traced by most police forces. It hadn't been any trouble at all to follow the signal using the combat suit's advanced tracking systems.

No sign of Lucas, though. He turned his attention back to the abandoned medical facility.

He remembered this place as he started toward the stairs,

a place for the wealthy to recover from the stresses of the world. He didn't remember hearing that it had been closed, but then again, would he have even cared? This had been a place for the weak-minded, for those broken by the ferocity of a changing world.

The Raptor had his own way of dealing with such things.

A tripod-mounted machine gun rose up from a section of lawn to the right of him.

The Raptor spun toward the movement, ready to react as the high-powered weapon opened fire.

The gun roared, a seemingly endless supply of 50-caliber shells striking his armored body and driving him back.

The weapon paused momentarily as its systems reloaded. That was all the Raptor needed.

He sprang at the machine gun, grabbing hold of the firing mechanism before it could begin to spray its deadly projectiles again. The exoskeleton within the costume whined with exertion as it enhanced his strength. He ripped the heavy gun away from the tripod in a flurry of sparks and hissing electrical cables.

"You're going to need to do better than that, old friend," the Raptor snarled, throwing the machine gun through the front entrance.

"He's in!" Katie announced.

"No kidding," Putnam grumbled, working furiously on the keyboard while staring at the multiple screens.

Lucas gazed in fascination at the armored figure now standing in the entryway.

"Maybe we should leave?" he suggested, considering

what his father might do to them. He was less concerned for his own safety than he was for that of Katie and Putnam.

"A little too late for that," the former Talon said. "If we were going to abandon ship, we should have done it right after we got the call that he was on the way."

He punched some more keys. "Don't worry, we still have a few tricks up our sleeves."

Lucas didn't respond, but he was certain it was going to take a lot more than tricks to get them out of this one.

It was going to take a miracle.

More guns waited for the Raptor inside.

From trapdoors hidden in the once-beautiful hardwood floors, new weapons emerged.

The diagnostic system built into his cowl's eyepieces attempted to determine what type of weaponry it was but could find no match in its extensive library.

It appeared that his former partner had been busy, designing something that hadn't been seen or catalogued by anyone.

Interesting.

The guns began to spray him with a thick white liquid, and he immediately knew what he was in for.

Activating his boot jets, he tried to get above the four nozzles, which continued to spray him, but it wasn't long before the vents in his boots became clogged with the quick-drying material and he dropped heavily to the floor.

The fluid was a liquid polymer, a kind of glue. He had read that something like this was currently being developed for crowd control, as a way of managing angry mobs. The liquid was to be sprayed, covering the perpetrators, encasing them in a quickly drying and expanding cocoon.

Which was exactly what was happening to him.

The Raptor became stuck to the floor, his upper body encased in the expanding foam. He could hear the servomotors built into the armored exoskeleton straining to break free of the sticky encasement, but with no luck.

The nozzles of the guns continued to spray him, covering him in layers of the fast-drying polymer prison.

Lying there, glued to the floor of the hospital corridor, he could just imagine his enemies laughing.

Let them laugh, the Raptor thought as he began to reroute power through the armored suit. *Let them think they've won.*

It will just make their defeat all the sweeter.

"Boo-yah!" Putman yelled as he pumped his fist in the air. "I knew that would be the one," he said.

Lucas leaned toward the screen, as did Katie. The two were very close, and he could feel the heat coming off her flushed cheeks.

"Think that'll hold him?" Lucas asked.

"Sure it will," Putnam said confidently, leaning back in the office chair, throwing his hands behind his head. "That stuff is designed to incapacitate an entire mob. I doubt he's that strong, even wearing the armor. . . . Probably pretty close, but not close enough."

Putnam smiled as he stared at the screen. "I've got you right where I want you," he said, a nervous hand coming up to rub at his chin. "But now what do I do with you?"

That was a good question.

"What *do* you do with him?" Lucas asked.

The man seemed to be thinking. "First off, we've got to get him out of that costume . . . and then we turn him over to the police."

"The police?" Lucas asked. "You can't treat him like a criminal! He's the Raptor, for God's sake!"

"He broke the law just like any other criminal," Katie said.

"But—"

"No buts," Putnam said. "He's gone over the line, and he has to pay for his crimes. He may have forgotten what it means to uphold the law and to play by the rules, but I haven't."

"This doesn't feel right," Lucas said.

"He's a murderer, Lucas," Putnam said fiercely. "He's crossed over that line, and as soon as you accept this, you'll be better off."

Lucas felt as though he might throw up.

The alarm siren that had been pealing since the Raptor's attack fell silent.

Putnam leaned forward in his chair and studied the keyboard again. "Now what keys do I push to release the somnolence gas?" he asked, looking to Katie.

"Hold the Control key and then three Zs," she prompted.

"Cute," Putnam said, preparing to release the sleep gas on the upper level.

Another alarm began to ring, stopping him.

"Oh no." Putnam rolled his chair closer to the monitor. "You sneaky son of a bitch," he hissed.

The sprinklers had come alive, streams of water raining

down on the Raptor's frozen form on the floor above, and on them in the basement.

"What's happening?" Lucas asked, cringing as the cold water poured over him.

"Aarrrrrrgh!" Putnam cried, typing in another code to shut down the flow of water before the delicate electronics in the basement lab could be damaged.

He didn't answer Lucas's question, but the boy got a sense that something was most definitely up as he stared at the screen and his supposedly incapacitated father.

The white foam that restrained him was smoking now.

"Do you see this?" Lucas asked.

Katie, blond hair matted to her head, glasses covered in water drops, moved in for a closer look. She took off her glasses, searching for a dry spot on her sweatshirt to clean them.

"He's burning the foam!" she yelled at Putnam.

"It's what I figured once that heat sensor went off," he said. "The clever SOB figured out the foam was flammable and somehow raised the external temperature of the armor until it caused the foam to combust."

The entryway of the upper floor caught fire as the foam ignited into a thick, oily smoke and hot orange flame.

"Not good," Putnam grumbled. "Not good at all."

The flames continued to spread, the smoke becoming thicker, and soon they lost sight of the villainous hero.

The cameras positioned in the upper levels were malfunctioning. It seemed the combination of heat, smoke, and water was too much for them.

"Dammit," Putnam barked.

A sudden sound froze them all in place.

Lucas was pretty sure it had come from above, and looked up as jagged cracks appeared in the ceiling. Pieces of plaster began to rain down to the floor.

"Get to the safe room!" Putnam ordered, pushing himself out of the chair and grabbing at his crutches. "Go on. There's no sense in all of us having our butts handed to us. I'll make up something . . . tell him the two of you took off when we figured out he was on his way."

"I'm not going to leave you," Katie said.

"You don't have a choice," Putnam said, pushing past them on his way toward a chained metal supply cage in the corner of the basement workshop. "Go. You don't have much time."

The ceiling was beginning to crumble, huge chunks of plaster falling.

"What the hell is he doing?" Lucas asked, leaping out of the way as a boulder-sized piece of ceiling narrowly missed him.

Putnam had opened the door to the cage and was now inside, searching for something.

"I'm not going to tell you again," the man said, finding what he was looking for and limping out of the cage.

Lucas wasn't sure he'd ever seen a gun so big.

It was like the end of the world had arrived.

Lucas leapt for cover as a huge section of the floor above, and probably even the one above that, crashed down through the ceiling into the basement.

Putnam's work space had started to fill with smoke, the

multiple levels of debris that had fallen through the ceiling continuing to furiously burn. Lucas grabbed Katie's arm, pulling her away from the fire.

And that was when he noticed something moving in the rubble.

The armored figure rose up out of the fire, shrugging off the sections of burning roof and floor as if they were nothing.

"Hello, Lucas," the Raptor said, his voice sounding cold and metallic from within the metal cowl. "I've come to bring you home."

Nicolas Putnam wasn't afraid of death; he'd faced that beast once and lived to tell the tale.

With watering eyes and his lungs filling with smoke, the man lurched painfully toward his friends, high-powered weapon clutched beneath his arm.

He heard the Raptor speak in a robotic voice. It was almost as if any sign of Hartwell's humanity had gone away completely.

"Get the hell back!" Putnam bellowed, placing himself between Katie, Lucas, and the heavily armored Raptor.

He aimed the gun at his former mentor, marveling at the technology that had gone into the armor's upgrades. *It's a real shame when somebody with that much genius loses his mind.*

"Nicolas," the Raptor said, "I never wanted to believe you were capable of falling so far."

"You should talk," Putnam said, keeping the pulse rifle aimed at the man. "We know all about what you've been doing . . . your children, and what you did to them."

The Raptor slowly shook his helmeted head from side to

side. "You don't understand a thing." He fell silent, the smoke swirling around him, the dancing fire reflecting off the armor's smooth metallic surfaces. "I know how it must look," he offered.

Lucas moved around Putnam, desperate for a reason to believe in his father again. "Tell them you didn't do it," Lucas cried. "Tell them all of this is just a mistake!"

The Raptor lowered his head. "Sacrifices had to be made," he said, his voice echoing eerily, as if from somewhere down a very long tunnel. "It was all for the greater good."

He made a sudden movement, and Putnam reacted. He shoved Lucas back and opened fire with his weapon.

The pulse rifle had been designed to take out armored vehicles. He figured it should have some effect against the Raptor's defenses. The multiple blasts struck the superhero's chest plate, and he stumbled awkwardly backward, toward a pile of burning rubble.

"Go," Putman ordered, momentarily taking his eyes from his target.

That was all the time the Raptor needed. He was suddenly there, ripping the gun from Putnam's hands and hurling it away.

"I never wanted it to be like this," the Raptor said, wrapping a powerful hand around Putnam's throat. "Do you think if there was any other way, I wouldn't have tried?"

Unable to breathe, Putnam witnessed an amazing fireworks display as silent, colorful explosions blossomed before his eyes.

From somewhere very far away, he heard Lucas's voice.

"Leave him alone!"

And suddenly he was able to breathe again, even though he was falling backward to the floor. But Katie was there—sweet, wonderful Katie—dragging his useless body away as he gulped greedily at the smoky air.

Through the shifting haze he saw that it was Lucas who had saved him, defiantly standing up to his father.

The poor kid didn't have a chance.

Lucas grabbed hold of the armor, trying to drive his father back.

The Raptor's battle suit was still hot, and he could feel the flesh on the palms of his hands begin to blister.

It was almost as if his father didn't want to fight back, allowing himself to be pushed backward. "I don't know what they've told you," he began. "But give me a chance to explain. . . . Everything is so complicated."

"Complicated?" Lucas yelled. "Since when is *murder* so damn complicated?"

He was seeing red. He let go of his father and lashed out, his fist connecting with the front of the Raptor's mask. He was going wild, his nanite-enhanced strength allowing him to hold his own against the armored adversary.

"Why did they have to die? Did they somehow disappoint you?"

Lucas threw a left and then a right, leaving dents and bloody smears across the front of the Raptor's cowl.

"Not live up to your expectations?"

He was drawing back, ready to send another blow into

his father's face, when the Raptor moved and caught Lucas by the wrist.

"If only it were that simple," the Raptor said.

Lucas struggled to break free, feeling the bones in his wrist snap with the exertion. He cried out as an armored hand swatted him across the face, leaving the taste of copper in his mouth.

"I thought you were going to be the one," the Raptor continued. "But it looks as though I was sadly mistaken."

Lucas spat a bloody wad onto the Raptor's face mask. "That's what I think of your mistake," he said defiantly.

If Lucas thought the first slap was bad, the blow that followed was like nothing he'd experienced before. It sent him flying through the air, into the glass display case holding the former Talon's costume, shattering it on impact.

As he lay there, gathering the strength to get up, he closed his bleeding fingers around the heavy fabric of the superhero costume beneath him.

And had an idea of how they might survive this.

Nicolas didn't have the strength to stand, and there was no way Katie could carry him.

He hissed at her to run, but she refused to listen.

This man had become like a father to her, replacing the one who had filled her life with nothing but disappointment and sadness. This man had looked beyond her past, seeing the person she really was and the promise of her future. And she wasn't about to leave him on the floor to die alone.

She watched in horror as the Raptor swatted Lucas

across the room like a bug, and her hopes that he would be their saving grace quickly went to zero.

The Raptor then turned his monstrous attentions their way, making the hair on the back of her neck prickle.

Nicolas squirmed, trying to roll onto his stomach to retrieve the pulse weapon from where it had fallen. Katie knew he didn't have the strength and decided it was up to her. She reached out, grabbing the weapon with both hands. She hated violence, and the powerful weapon felt completely wrong in her arms, but if it would give them a chance at survival, she was willing to make the sacrifice.

Silently, she pointed the weapon, trying to aim for the damaged areas of the Raptor's face mask, hoping a blast from a pulse rifle to those areas would do some real damage.

The Raptor froze, his cold eyes studying her through the lenses of the mask. "You disgust me, Nicolas," he snarled at Putnam. "Bringing a child into this?"

"I'm no child, and we're in this together," Katie barked, doing her best to keep the tremble of fear from her voice. "Ever since you murdered the Frightener."

"The Frightener," the armored hero repeated. "Yes, I should have seen. . . . You have the same eyes. . . . You're his daughter, aren't you?"

"Smart as a whip *and* a murderer," she said, still pointing the weapon. "All the trappings of a real nasty supervillain."

"Little witch," the Raptor growled, springing at her.

Katie stumbled backward, firing the weapon wildly, blasting another hole in the already damaged ceiling.

The Raptor's hand shot out before she could fire again. He grabbed the pulse rifle, bending the barrel before roughly yanking it from her hands and throwing it to the floor, useless.

Nicolas managed to climb to his knees, struggling to put himself between the girl and the Raptor's rage.

"Nick, get back!" Katie screamed.

"I won't—I won't let you hurt her," he said to the Raptor, his voice raspy and coarse.

"I wish it had never come to this, but . . . ," the Raptor began, reaching out a clawed, metal-gloved hand toward Putnam.

And then Katie noticed movement behind the Raptor. Something darted through the smoke, jumping across the rubble-strewn floor.

The Raptor must have noticed the change in her expression and began to turn, but he was too slow.

Lucas, wearing the old Talon costume, was coming up right behind him.

13

Lucas remembered his pain when his father had struck him, and tried to give back better than he'd gotten.

He figured the only way they were going to survive this encounter was if one of them had the strength to go up against the Raptor. The obvious choice was Lucas, but without the enhancements of a supersuit, he wasn't going to last five minutes against his father.

He liked to think fate had something to do with where his father had tossed him. Shucking his own clothes and getting into the costume, he had hoped the old Talon outfit was still operational, or this would end up being one of the shortest superbattles ever fought.

As soon as he'd slipped the cowl over his head, he could feel the mechanics in the costume come alive. The suit felt heavier and was more difficult to move in than his own, but he would just have to get used to it. It was certainly better than nothing.

Through the thick lenses in the face mask, Lucas saw what was about to happen. He leapt across the basement and landed right behind the Raptor with hardly a sound.

Lucas noticed the expression of surprise on Katie's face and saw his father begin to turn. He drew back his fist and sent it rocketing forward with as much power as he could put into it. The blow connected with the Raptor's chin, knocking him back and across the basement into a small kitchen area.

"Nice," Lucas said, flexing the fingers of his gauntlet.

He checked to see if Putnam and Katie were all right. Nicolas stared at him with wide eyes, perhaps seeing a bit of his former self standing there.

"Hope you don't mind," Lucas said, on the verge of an apology.

Putnam shook his head. "Not at all."

"You look good," Katie said with a smile before turning to see where the Raptor had ended up. He had collapsed a section of wall and was now rising.

"But it isn't over," she added.

"Keep at him," Putnam said, pulling himself to his feet, leaning on a broken piece of countertop. "Don't give him time to catch his breath. Remember, he's sick, and the suit can only enhance what he already has."

"Right," Lucas said.

He started to run, activating the costume's flight capabilities. He was thankful the suit worked pretty much the same as the one back at the manor, as the jets in the soles of the boots ignited with a flash, doubling his momentum.

Lucas collided with his father, propelling them both backward. The two of them crashed into the already damaged wall with tremendous force. He heard his father grunt with the impact, and then the Raptor's body went limp, sliding to the floor as Lucas stepped back.

The boy was elated and turned to give his friends a thumbs-up, but no sooner had he done that than he saw Putnam's eyes bug and Katie let loose with a shriek.

Lucas turned back just in time to realize what a stupid mistake he'd made. His father was completely awake and pointing a piece of wrist weaponry that whirred and lit up as it prepared to fire at him.

Lucas's brain told his body to move, but it wasn't fast enough.

The Raptor fired a single concussive blast. *It's like being hit with a battering ram*, Lucas thought as his feet left the ground. *No, strike that. It's like being hit with twenty battering rams at exactly the same time.*

The force was so great that it picked Lucas up, launching him through an undamaged—until then—section of the basement ceiling and into the ceiling of the level above.

He fell to the floor of the first level and lay there unmoving; even with the protection of the costume, he was finding it difficult to catch his breath. Everything hurt, and the supersuit was making strange noises. The less advanced technology must have been damaged by that last blast, and Lucas wasn't sure how much longer the outfit would be able to protect him. But he couldn't worry about that now. He had to keep Putnam and Katie safe.

He pushed himself to his feet, and then he heard the sound. It was like the roar of a fighter plane, muffled at first, but reaching full screeching crescendo as the Raptor exploded up through the floor in a cloud of plaster dust and splintered wood.

"I'm surprised you're still conscious," the Raptor bellowed over the roar of his boot jets.

Lucas could see that his father was getting ready to strike again. He ignited his own boosters and launched himself at the man, remembering his touch football days, which seemed a thousand years ago. He tucked his head low and plowed his shoulder into his opponent, driving him upward.

Locked in struggle, the two costumed combatants flew about the room, smashing into walls, turning plaster to white powder.

There was a sudden buzz and then a crackle inside his mask, and Lucas feared that something was about to go wrong. But then Putnam's voice shouted over the static.

"Lucas? Are you there, Lucas?"

Temporarily distracted by the voice in his ears, Lucas let his father get the upper hand. The Raptor managed to get behind the boy and wrapped an arm around his throat, squeezing.

"Busy right now," Lucas managed. The bracing built into the neck of the costume was affording him some protection, but he didn't know for how long.

Lifting his legs, he directed a concentrated blast from his

boot rockets that sent them both hurtling across the empty room toward a window that was boarded up. The wood shattered as the two slammed into it, sending them outside, up into the sky above the hospital.

"Are you all right?" Putnam asked. "What was that?"

"Being choked," Lucas gasped. The braces were starting to buckle, and the pressure on his neck increased.

He bent forward, directing their flight back toward the building. Just as they were about to strike the front of the structure, he spun himself around, allowing his father to take the brunt of the blow. A section of the outside wall shattered on impact, raining debris on the courtyard below, but still the Raptor hung on.

"Listen to me," Putnam shouted. "I think I got a pretty good look at the Raptor's armor."

Lucas tried to focus, but somebody was dropping a curtain over his eyes.

"There are chinks in its design," Putnam said. "Reach behind you and use the claws on the gauntlet to find a space between the armored pieces. Force them apart. This'll give you access to some pretty sensitive internal workings."

Lucas was choking. He tried to move his head around, fighting to release some of the pressure bearing down on his neck.

"Don't make this so hard," he heard his father say, his voice cold, robotic. "Let the inevitable happen. You were the closest to perfection, but sadly not perfect enough."

Screw that, a voice screamed inside Lucas's brain. He drove the clawed fingers of his gauntlet back into the belly of the Raptor's armor. Frantically he searched for a break between it and the chest plate, but it was becoming harder and harder to remain in the waking world.

His father must have sensed what he was up to and intensified his hold, trying to bend Lucas backward to hasten his death.

"Your life signs are going crazy!" Putnam's voice suddenly screamed in Lucas's ears. His voice sounded more and more distant as it began to grow dark.

Lucas knew he was dying and had almost resigned himself to his fate when the pointed tips of his gloved fingers found what they had been probing for. Using the last of his strength, he dug his claws into the space between the two segments of his father's body armor. There was little resistance, and his father immediately began to struggle.

The Raptor's grip loosened, and Lucas took in a revitalizing gulp of air. His claws tore through a thick layer of protective mesh, finding a web of wires beneath. With a powerful yank, he tore them free in an explosion of sparks.

He heard the Raptor yell and was immediately propelled away from his armored adversary. Lucas touched down in a stumble, falling to his knees as static erupted in his ears.

"Life signs are better," Putnam said. "How we doin', Lucas?"

Lucas looked up and felt his heart leap into his throat as he spied the Raptor, dropping out of the sky directly at him.

He didn't even have a chance to get out of the way.

The Raptor fell on him with such force that they skidded across the blacktop driveway, stopping only when they hit the overgrown grass island that surrounded a dry concrete fountain.

"Did you honestly believe you could hurt me?" his father raged, raining blow after blow into Lucas's masked face.

The face mask was taking the brunt of the blows, but Lucas knew it was only a matter of time before it would break and his face would be shattered. His arms flailed as he strained to get out from beneath his foe, and his hands brushed against something hard and unyielding behind his head. The fountain. Lucas reached up and back, grabbing hold and using every ounce of his remaining strength to bring the concrete decoration toppling forward onto the Raptor.

The concrete crumbled as it struck the armored superhero. Stunned, the Raptor fell to the side.

Leaping up, Lucas snatched up a large section of the broken fountain, spun around, and let it fly toward the Raptor, who was just climbing out from beneath the rubble. The concrete connected with devastating force, breaking away a piece of the damaged face mask to reveal his sweating and wild-eyed father beneath.

"That's right," the man said, his fevered eyes twinkling. "Show me what you've got."

The Raptor charged, and Lucas braced himself as the two of them collided.

"Show me that I was right about you," the older man growled, swinging wildly at the boy.

Lucas dodged to the right and left, evading his father's blows.

"Right about me?" Lucas asked, his anger the only thing keeping him on his feet. He moved aside as a punch flew by his mask. Seeing his opportunity, he took it, driving his own fist into the exposed flesh of his father's face.

The Raptor's head flew violently backward, and he fell into the high grass and weeds.

"Tell me," Lucas demanded as he stood over his father. "Tell me why they had to die."

"You know why," the Raptor said. Slowly, he climbed to his feet, swaying a bit as he stood. "I'm dying, and the city needs someone to protect her."

Lucas shook his head. "That's not good enough. That's not good enough to justify murder."

His father lifted a gloved hand to his damaged face. The entire right side had started to blacken and swell. "It wasn't murder," he said. "They just failed to pass the test I presented them with."

"Test?" Lucas shrieked, stomping forward and pushing his father.

The man staggered back but did not attack.

"Yes, a test," the Raptor explained. "I hoped that at least one of my children would be strong enough to carry on my legacy. But to do that, they had to be tested."

Lucas felt as though he was suffocating. He ripped the mask from his face.

"So what was my test?" he asked, already knowing the answer, but hoping—praying—it wasn't true. He threw his mask to the rubble-strewn ground. "It wasn't the Science Club, was it?"

Hartwell nodded. "Oh, it was. . . . They were most definitely responsible for the attack on your home, and for the death of your mother."

Lucas couldn't help himself, lashing out again at the old man and knocking him to the ground.

"You told them where I lived . . . where to find me. Their attack—their attack was my test."

Hartwell slowly nodded, thick black blood oozing from his swollen lips. "Yes," he said simply. "I was hoping you'd never have to know about that. You survived everything I tossed at you that day. The men I hired to attack the trailer park had strict orders to kill you if they could, but you survived, son."

He paused, staring intently. "You passed the test."

The words echoed through Lucas's mind, reverberating over and over, but still he could not believe them.

"You killed my mother . . . to test me?"

"You refused my other offers," the Raptor explained. "What did you expect me to do? You didn't realize how important this was to the city. I had to give you an incentive. . . . I had to show you the depths of the evil that is out there . . . show you why somebody like me"—he paused and pointed to Lucas—"somebody like *you* is needed."

From the mask on the ground came the sound of Putnam's voice. "Lucas? Are you all right? Are you there?"

But Lucas wasn't hearing anything other than the roar of blood in his ears.

"My mother died so you could get me to do what you wanted," Lucas said through gritted teeth, reaching down to grab his father by the armored shoulders.

The Raptor struggled weakly, but Lucas could tell that the fight had gone out of him.

"You had her killed to show me about evil?" Lucas screamed, shaking him. "I could have learned all I need to know about evil just by looking in your eyes!"

The rage had gotten the better of him. He didn't even re-alize what he was going to do until he was doing it. Straining the servomotors of his exoskeleton, he picked his father up and tossed him toward the Mustang parked in front of the hospital.

The Raptor hit the car with the force of a freight train, windshield and windows exploding in a shower of glass as the vehicle bent around the armored man.

Lucas took deep breaths, trying to calm himself. He stared at the still shape of his father, caught within the twisted embrace of the vehicle, and oddly enough, he began to fear he might have killed him.

That he too might have crossed that terrible line.

The Raptor stirred with a grunt, and Lucas breathed a small sigh of relief.

"You realize I'll need to deduct the cost of the Mustang from your allowance," the Raptor quipped.

The metal of the car screeched and groaned as his father tried to extricate himself from the vehicle's twisted hold.

Too late, Lucas noticed the puddle that had started to form beneath the ruptured gas tank. As the Raptor moved, light flashed and sparks sprayed from beneath his damaged chest plate, and suddenly the gasoline ignited into a sea of fire.

"*No!*" Lucas screamed, bounding across the courtyard to-ward the growing conflagration.

But a tiny voice inside his head told him to let the man burn.

A voice that sounded an awful lot like his father's.

* * *

Lucas darted into the flames, his eyes scanning the blackened, twisted metal for a sign of his fallen father. The air had become superheated, searing his lungs and scorching the exposed flesh of his face.

He found the man lying on his stomach. He'd managed to free himself but was now surrounded by burning puddles of gasoline.

Shielding his face, Lucas jumped over the burning lakes of gas and knelt beside his father, carefully turning him over. The Raptor's face was burned, but his body appeared to have been protected by his armor.

"I'm going to get you out of here," Lucas said, preparing to lift the man into his arms.

"No," the Raptor protested, suddenly conscious.

Lucas leaned back, staring in confusion.

"Let me die," the Raptor said, waving the boy away.

"Is that what you would do?" Lucas asked coldly.

The Raptor stared with one eye, the other swollen shut. "The strong survive and the weak—"

"Shut the hell up," Lucas said, and yanked him up from the ground. He hung his father's arms over his shoulders and tensed the muscles in his legs, praying that the Talon exoskeleton had enough juice left to carry both of them.

Lucas leapt, the powerful jump taking him over the lake of fire to the courtyard beyond. He touched down in a crouch and let his father slide from his grasp to the ground.

The Raptor lay there, his body wracked by powerful coughs.

"Do you need to go to the hospital?" Lucas asked, kneeling beside him again.

The man shook his head. "Must finish . . . must finish the test," he gasped.

Lucas didn't understand. "Finish the test?" he asked, grabbing hold of his father's arm in a steely grip. "What are you talking about?"

Putnam and Katie had come from the building, and he looked to them for possible answers. But they seemed to be as much in the dark as he was.

"Should have let me die," the Raptor whispered. "It would have been over then."

The man rolled over onto his side, his fingers probing at a band around his wrist.

"Watch him," Putnam warned.

Lucas reached out and grabbed his father's arm, but not before he had managed to punch a numbered code into a small keypad.

"What have you done?"

"You're still not quite ready," the Raptor said. "Mercy lives in your heart." He shook his head sadly. "For this city to survive, you must have none."

The mechanism around his wrist began to emit a series of blips and beeps.

"What did you do?" Lucas demanded again, squeezing his father's wrist so tightly that the metal of the man's gauntlet began to bend.

The Raptor winced in pain but did not try to pull away. "I've begun the final test," he said. "To show you what happens in these new and terrible times when you show your enemies compassion."

Lucas felt a chill go down his spine. If this man could kill his own children to achieve his twisted goals, what else was he capable of?

"Tell me!" he shrieked, yanking the man up from the ground and shaking him.

"I've activated a small-yield nuclear device," the man said sleepily, fighting to keep his eyes from shutting.

"Oh my God," Katie gasped.

Lucas shook him again. "Stay awake!" he commanded. "Why would you do this?" He was getting tired of asking the madman the same question over and over again. *Why? Why? Why?*

The Raptor smiled, his teeth stained pink with blood. "You had your chance, boy," he said, and started to laugh. "It could have all been over if you'd let me die. Now you still have something to prove. Show me you've got what it takes to keep *her* safe. It's out there someplace . . . hidden in the Angel City, and will detonate in . . ."

He thought for a moment, the unswollen eye beginning to close.

"Less than thirty minutes . . . unless you can stop it."

Lucas dropped his father's body to the ground and turned to the others.

"What are we gonna do?" he asked, panic on the rise.

They were all silent, but a look of steely determination came over Putnam's face.

"We're going to stop it," Putnam said. "Or die trying."

Lucas was retrieving his face mask when the new sounds began.

"What now?" he asked, exasperated, turning to see Katie

and Putnam stepping back as his father's body began to rise from the ground on twin jets of fire.

"Must be some kind of escape command," Putnam said, shielding his eyes as he watched the Raptor arc into the sky. "Must've been activated once the final test was started."

"The jerk is probably being flown to safety," Katie said with a snarl.

"I'll go after him," Lucas said, slipping on his mask and preparing to activate his own flight capabilities.

"There's no time," Putnam said. "If we're going to save Seraph City, you're going to need to get there pretty damn fast."

"This is pointless. Once I get there, what do I do?" he asked, frustrated. "I haven't any idea where he could have hidden a bomb."

"So, what, then?" Katie spoke up. "We're just going to stand here and wait for it to detonate? I don't think so."

"But—" Lucas began.

"Get into the air," Putnam said, awkwardly turning and heading back to the abandoned hospital with Katie's help. "I'll man the command center and use some of the diagnostic instruments built into the suit. Maybe we'll get lucky."

Lucas watched them go, pretty sure he'd never felt quite so useless in his life.

Katie turned to look at him. "What are you waiting for?" she asked, gesturing wildly toward the sky. "Go . . . fly!"

He activated his boot jets and rocketed into the sky in the direction of Seraph City. He was thinking about all the people who lived there, going about their day-to-day existences, never realizing the fate that was so close to befalling them.

Putnam was right. He had to do something, anything, to keep his father's plan from being carried out.

It wasn't long before he was over the city, and a crackling in his ears told him Putnam was checking in.

"I'm over the capitol building right now," Lucas said. "Any chance this might be the place?"

"Too political," Putnam said. "He's trying to make a statement about weakness . . . about the consequences of weakness."

Lucas angled away from the golden dome of the capitol and flew toward the financial district. Using the magnifiers built into the eyepieces of his face mask, he scanned the crowds milling about the streets below.

"I'm over downtown. If he wanted to cause the most casualties, this would be the place," Lucas informed his copilot.

"It's a possibility," Putnam said. "But I still don't see it relating to his point."

"Aren't there any instruments built into this suit that might help locate this thing?" Lucas asked. "It is a nuclear bomb, right? Maybe there's radiation leaking from it or something?"

"I've got all the scanners running, but so far there's nothing. He's probably got this bad boy shielded up pretty good just for that reason. Remember, this is a test. He wants us to be able to figure this out, but he isn't going to make it easy. The clues are there; we just have to pull them all together."

Lucas zoomed by the window of St. Sebastian's Hospital. A small child was sitting in a wheelchair by the window, and he caught the excited expression on her face as she spotted him.

That was what it was all about, the whole hero thing, and why he couldn't let them—the citizens of Seraph City—down.

It was what his father had been trying to show him in his own, twisted way—the hope that heroes brought to others. The responsibility they had to protect the weak.

When did it all go wrong for him? Lucas wondered. *When did the message become so distorted?*

And then he recalled something Putnam had said. Something Lucas had found incredibly sad.

It was about the trap set by the Terribles.

"It was as if what had happened changed all the rules for him, turning him into a completely different person," Putnam had said. *"It was as if he'd been turned into some kind of cold, calculating machine."*

And suddenly it clicked. Lucas stopped flying as he tried to gather his thoughts. [191]

"What's going on, Lucas?" Putnam asked. "Is everything all right? Should I run a diagnostic?"

"Shut up a minute, would you?" the boy said. "I'm trying to think."

"Well, think fast, because we've got less than twelve minutes to go before Seraph City is swallowed up by a mushroom cloud."

"When did it all change for him?" Lucas asked, his boot jets blazing, holding him steady in the air.

"Who, Hartwell?" Putnam asked.

"He wasn't always this way," Lucas continued. "What changed him?"

"After the business with the Terribles . . . after their trap was sprung and all those people who depended on him to protect them died."

"Right," Lucas said.

"Are we going someplace with this?" Putnam questioned.

Lucas continued to hover, trying to follow the thread of his thoughts. "He told me that on that day, he felt he had died—that everything that made him human was taken away in the flash and roar of an explosion."

And then Lucas knew.

"The memorial," Lucas said.

"The memorial . . . ," Putnam began. "Oh, crap, you might be right."

Lucas started to angle his body toward the memorial where the old convention center had once stood. He heard the growl of an engine and the hiss of spinning rotor blades, and a police helicopter was suddenly in front of him.

An officer was leaning out of the passenger seat, a bull-horn at his lips. "Drop to the street immediately. If you do not comply, we will . . ."

"Is that the police?" Putnam asked.

"Yeah," Lucas replied.

"Well, get the hell out of there. You don't have time for their nonsense," the older man ordered.

Lucas did as he was told, giving the cop a little wave as he spun himself away and took off with a blast of his rockets.

"Hartwell really seemed put off by the statue," Lucas recalled. "Said it was a memorial to his failure."

He flew above the building zone, activating the retro-rockets in his boots to begin his descent. Landing, he ran toward the small plaza where the monument stood.

"All right, I'm here," he said, looking around, trying to keep his growing panic at bay.

Construction workers from the nearby sites had seen him land and were slowly making their way toward him.

"Oh, crap, I'm getting an audience," Lucas said as the workers approached.

"Ignore them. We haven't much time," Putnam said. "Check out the statue. Look for signs that it might have been tampered with."

Lucas walked around the statue, carefully examining it.

"Hey," he heard one of the workers yell. "You supposed to be Talon or something?"

"Please step back," Lucas said, trying to keep his voice authoritative.

"What's going on?" another asked. "Something wrong with the statue?"

Lucas ignored the question, turning on the magnifiers in the lenses of his mask.

"Anything?" Putnam asked.

"Nothing," Lucas answered, his hopes starting to wane. "How much longer?"

"Five minutes."

"Hey, superhero guy!" another of the construction guys called out. "I told them to be extra careful when they were moving it last week, so it's the city's fault if they've fouled it up somehow."

Little bells went off inside Lucas's head. "The city moved the statue?" he asked.

The worker nodded. "Yeah, they wanted to make the base more secure or somethin'."

"Did you hear that?" Lucas asked Putnam as he knelt down near the base.

"Like music to my ears," Putnam replied. "What do you see?"

"Looks like fresh concrete around the base," Lucas answered.

"You realize you're going to have to move it," Putnam said.

Lucas had figured as much. He glanced quickly at his audience. There wasn't any time for subtlety. Exerting his full strength, enhanced by the exoskeleton, Lucas pushed on the statue with all his might.

Bolts popped and concrete cracked as the bronze statue toppled onto its back.

The construction workers went wild, screaming at him, running toward him as angry words spewed from their mouths.

"Get back!" Lucas screamed, and thankfully, between the costume and the sound of his voice, he was just scary enough to get the reaction he needed.

"Anything?" Putnam asked.

Lucas looked down into the hole that had been left in the base. At first all he could see was broken concrete, but as he moved aside some pieces of stone, he saw it—a black box.

"Think I've got it," he said, carefully lifting the box from the hole.

"If you don't, we're screwed," Putnam reminded him. "We've got two—make that one minute, fifty-eight seconds remaining."

Lucas tried to ignore the words as he gingerly placed the

box on the ground before him and pulled back the lid. His heart skipped a beat as he gazed at a small nuclear explosive. He'd had no idea they could be built this small.

One minute and forty-six seconds, the digital clock on the face of the device informed him.

"What next?" Lucas asked, far more calmly than he had ever dreamed possible.

The crowd was moving closer again, and he screamed at them to keep back.

"Hey, look at the device again, will you?" Putnam shouted in his ear. "I'm trying to figure out how to disarm it."

Lucas could hear Katie in the background saying "crap" over and over again. "What's going on?" he asked.

"There's not enough time," Putnam began. "I don't know how to—"

Lucas didn't wait for him to finish. Pure instinct kicked in. He snatched up the box and leapt into the air, his boot jets igniting with a roar, propelling him upward on plumes of smoke and flame.

"Lucas, what are you doing?" Putnam demanded.

"The only thing I can do," Lucas answered. "I have to get this thing as far away from the city as possible."

"Lucas, you know that armor isn't strong enough to—"

"I'm not stupid," Lucas said as he felt the air growing colder. It was becoming harder to breath.

He held the box out before him, watching the timer clicking down.

Thirteen . . . twelve . . . eleven . . .

He couldn't decide if this was the bravest thing he'd ever done, or the stupidest.

Ten . . . nine . . . eight . . . seven . . .

He gripped the box, pulling back his arm, preparing to give it everything he had . . . *the costume had* . . . to toss the explosive as far away as possible, out of the atmosphere, if he could.

The numbers ticked down in his mind's eye.

Six . . . five . . . four . . . three . . .

Lucas threw the box high into the sky and gunned the rockets in his boots as he spun away, hoping to outrun the shock wave that could very well pummel him senseless.

Two . . . one . . . zero . . .

He pressed his arms to his chest and descended in a free fall, like a bullet shot from a gun, waiting for the explosion.

An explosion that never came.

He considered that he might have counted wrong, but he'd seen the clock. It was impossible that he'd been that far off in his calculations.

He fired his retros, slowing his descent, and brought himself to an upright position, scanning the open sky for signs of impending doom.

"Lucas?" Putnam called out tentatively.

"Yeah, I'm here."

"What happened?"

"There wasn't any explosion," Lucas said.

"The bomb was a dud?"

Lucas's voice was grave. "I don't really know what it was."

14

Lucas dropped from the sky, his descent kicking up dirt and dry leaves as he touched down in the driveway in front of Hartwell Manor.

"I still don't think this is a good idea," Putnam said in his ear.

"I don't care what you think right now," Lucas retorted, walking up the marble steps to the front door.

"The fight with the Raptor did some serious damage to that battle suit. You're functioning at only forty-three percent efficiency."

"Better than nothing," Lucas said, lifting his leg to kick at the heavy wooden doors.

The doors flew from their hinges and sailed through the

foyer, bouncing noisily off the walls. Lucas knew this would be where he would find him. His father.

His enemy.

"That was subtle," Putnam commented.

"Shut up." Lucas stalked through the house to the elevator that would take him down to the lab.

"How close are you?" he asked Putnam as he pushed the button, somewhat startled when the doors slid open to grant him access.

"Should be there shortly," Putnam answered.

Lucas stepped into the elevator, looking around, expecting some kind of trap to be sprung. But nothing happened as the doors closed and the elevator began its descent to one of the manor's lower levels.

Down there was where Hartwell really lived. The upper floors of the mansion were just a mask, like the mask of humanity his father wore to hide what he had become.

The elevator came to a stop, and Lucas braced himself. The doors parted and he tensed, holding his breath, but again nothing happened.

Cautiously, he stepped out.

Clayton Hartwell was slumped in his chair before the multiple computer screens. His Raptor armor was in pieces on the floor around him, and he sat nearly naked in his underwear and a bathrobe.

It appeared the man was sleeping.

Lucas moved closer and saw Hartwell jump as the heavy footfalls awakened him with a start.

Hartwell turned, then smiled. One side of his face was

badly burned and it looked incredibly painful. Slowly raising his hands, he started to clap.

"What's that for?" Lucas asked.

"You've succeeded," Hartwell said, his hands dropping back limply to his lap. "You passed with flying colors."

"The bomb was a fake."

"Oh no," the old man said feebly. "It was very much the real thing."

"But it didn't go off," Lucas retorted.

"Because I shut it down," Hartwell said. "You achieved what you were supposed to. You found the bomb."

It felt like a hand of ice closing around Lucas's heart.

"But—but what if I hadn't . . . ?"

Hartwell sighed, leaning his head wearily back in his chair. "Then Seraph would have been destroyed . . . all its evil finally purged from the earth."

The man seemed to drift off before speaking again.

"For a while there, I must admit, I had my doubts, but deep down . . . deep down I knew you were the one."

Lucas felt the anger coming back, the anger that could very easily cause him to do something he would most assuredly regret later.

"You would have murdered all those people . . . all those people you were supposed to be protecting?"

Hartwell's eyes snapped open, and Lucas stepped back from their intensity.

"It would have been too late for them," Hartwell snarled. "Without me . . . without somebody to protect them . . . the evil would have won, and I wasn't about to let that happen."

He began to cough, and Lucas suddenly realized how fragile the man had become outside his costume. His skin was pale, almost glowing in the faint light of the nest, and he looked as though he might shatter if the violent coughing continued.

"Time is running out," Hartwell wheezed. "My body is degenerating far faster than I anticipated. Decades of strength-enhancing drugs are finally taking their toll."

"If only you could hear yourself," Lucas told him. "I think they've also made you completely insane."

Hartwell's eyes opened wide and he pushed himself up in his seat. "I did what had to be done!" he yelled. "I knew I would never be strong enough, and only the strongest will survive what is coming."

His expression started to soften, a smile gradually forming on his sickly features.

"The strongest is you," the old man said. "The city will never be denied its protector . . . its Raptor. You've earned that title."

"No," Lucas said, shaking his head. "I don't want it. The name is dirty now! It's covered in too much blood."

Hartwell sadly nodded. "You're right," he said. "Too much blood indeed."

With some exertion, he turned the chair toward one of the computers, trembling hands reaching out for the keyboard.

"I'm not going to fight you anymore," Lucas said. "It's over."

His fingers poised above the keys, Hartwell glanced over his shoulder at him. "So true," he said as he quickly typed.

"It's done."

* * *

Silently Lucas cursed himself for once again letting his father get the best of him.

He fully expected clouds of poisonous gas to fill the Raptor's nest, a shrieking alarm bell warning of imminent self-destruction. A pack of robot dogs trying to tear him apart would have been interesting as well.

But only a faint hum came from one of the many computer modems, and then nothing but the usual nest noises.

He was about to ask his father what he had just done when the cavalry arrived.

Or at least Putnam and Katie.

Putnam, using his crutches, didn't look all that bad, considering what he'd been through that afternoon. Katie, for her part, was holding a nasty-looking pistol that would have put the blasters in *Star Wars* to shame.

"Where is he?" she asked as they joined Lucas.

"He's over there." Lucas motioned toward the monitors. "Don't worry, I think he's pretty much harmless now . . . but he did just do something on the computer."

"Oh, great," Putnam said, moving around the boy. "What insanity are you responsible for now, Clayton?"

Lucas noticed that the old man had retrieved one of his armored gauntlets and was now wearing the heavy glove.

"Nothing to concern you, my friend," Hartwell told him. "Just making sure the recipient of my legacy will have all he needs to continue the battle, now and into the future."

He swiveled in his chair toward the multiple monitors. "It's all his," he said. "To the only surviving heir of the Hartwell empire . . . He owns everything."

Lucas felt as though he'd been kicked.

"No way," he said.

Standing beside him, Katie looked as stunned as he did.

"I—I don't want it."

"But you'll need it to face your future," Hartwell said. He seemed to be getting weaker, his breath coming in short gasps.

"You keep talking about my future," Lucas said.

"It . . . it is something . . . you will need to . . . face on your own." The older man struggled with his words. "It's too late for me now," Hartwell said, slowly starting to raise his gloved hand.

Putnam moved back, not sure what the old man was up to.

"Just want . . . want you to know how sorry I am . . . it all turned out this way . . . ," he said. "And how proud I am . . .

to have been . . . your father."

Hartwell grabbed his own throat with the heavy metal gauntlet.

"What are you—" Putnam began.

"Time to go" were Hartwell's last words as he activated the weapon built into the glove, unleashing the full effects of a concussive-force blast at very close range.

Ending his life by his own hand.

They found an old sheet in a corner of the workshop to cover the body.

Lucas was still in a state of shock.

He was sitting with Katie at the back of the nest while Putnam busied himself trying to figure out what Hartwell had done on the computer.

"Are you all right?" she asked softly.

"Yeah." He had removed the Talon helmet and was holding it in his hands. "I never wanted to be a superhero," he explained. "I doubt that anybody coming out of high school decides this is what they want to do with the rest of their lives, y'know?"

She nodded.

"The only reason I put the costume on was to get even with the guys who killed my mother."

"And you've done that . . . kind of," Katie said with a shrug.

"Yeah, I have," he answered. He was still staring at the helmet. It was damaged, some of the black paint scraped away.

"Now what?" he asked, looking at her.

The girl shrugged. "I guess that's up to you."

Putnam came over, swinging his body forward on his crutches.

"It appears he's been planning this for quite some time," the man said. "By entering that command into the system, he got the ball rolling. Everything has been signed over to you as his last living heir."

Lucas was still in shock.

"Congratulations," Putnam said. "You're probably worth billions."

Lucas's eyes were drawn to the sheet-draped figure still in the office chair across the way. "What are we going to do with him?" he asked.

Putnam looked toward the body as well. "That's been taken care of too. We're to bring the body to his room and wait for a funeral home to come and pick him up."

"Isn't how he died going to cause some problems?" Katie asked curiously.

"Like I said, it's all been taken care of. The medical examiner has already signed off, and the funeral home is extremely discreet. The undertakers will take it from here." Putnam shook his head in disbelief. "It appears he thought of everything."

They were silent then, each of them alone with their own thoughts.

"So, Lucas," Putnam finally said. "It would be a real shame to see all this . . . technology go to waste." He gazed around at the crowded nest, which was overflowing with machines. "What are your plans?" he asked. "Are you going to leave crime fighting behind you, or are you seriously considering taking up the mantle?"

Lucas stood and set the Talon helmet down on a crate of machine parts. Without a word, he turned away and headed for the elevator.

He stopped as the doors opened to admit him, and turned.

"If you're interested, I'm going to need a new costume," he said, and glanced down at himself.

"This one's looking a little rough."

epilogue

Four Months Later

Lucas was tempted to drink the champagne.

How many fancy crystal glasses of the stuff had he been offered, only to leave them scattered, untouched, around the various dining establishments and rooftop parties?

Lucas Moore was Seraph City's newest celebrity, the previously unknown heir to the Hartwell fortune. Clayton Hartwell had been one of the city's most fascinating individuals, and while most people were very sad to hear of his passing, they now had someone new to occupy their thoughts.

Tonight was a party in honor of Lucas—*another* party in his honor. It was the third this week. He had to wonder if the wealthy had anything to do with their time other than plan parties.

A man approached with two glasses of golden liquid and ice. He offered one to Lucas. "A real pleasure to meet you, Lucas," he said with a smile. His skin was perfectly tanned, his hair stylishly messy. "We're very sorry for your loss."

Lucas smiled sadly and shook the man's hand.

"Thank you," he said. How many times had he uttered

those same words in the last four months? How many hands had he shaken, and how many cheeks had he kissed?

Too many.

"All right, you might want to pay attention to this one," Nicolas Putnam said in his ear.

Lucas was wearing a small, nearly invisible communications device that Putnam had just recently perfected. It was something Hartwell Technologies was planning to put on the market by the end of the year, but until then, Lucas was giving it a test run.

He was also wearing special contact lenses with built-in microcameras that allowed one of his tech specialists back home at the nest to see exactly what he was seeing.

"This is Stephen Oxford, and his company, Ox-Tech, is currently under suspicion for secretly selling biological-weapons technology to the highest bidder. Needless to say, the buyers aren't the nicest of people," Putnam finished.

Lucas was still smiling falsely and shaking the man's hand.

"You should come by the marina," Oxford said to him. "We'll take the yacht out for a spin, make a day of it."

"That would be awesome," Lucas lied.

The man left. Lucas watched him go, pretending to drink from the glass of scotch.

"What a scumbag," Lucas muttered so only Putnam could hear.

"Welcome to the world of movers and shakers, my son," the former sidekick commented. "These are the sharks you will be swimming with for a long time to come."

"Great," Lucas sighed, already tired of the whole party scene.

He set his latest untouched drink down on a table. He glanced around to find that others had seen he was standing alone and were starting to make their way toward him, like predators zeroing in on their prey.

"I hate this," he said, preparing for more mind-numbing conversation with the city's supposed elite.

"Then you might want to consider getting out of there," Putnam commented.

Lucas's heart did a little flutter. "Why, what's up?" he said, already moving toward the nearest exit.

"Just eavesdropped on a police call to a convenience store on Madison. Looks like we've got an armed robbery that's escalated into a hostage situation."

Lucas smiled and waved at the predators as he ducked out the rooftop door and headed for the stairs and the lobby of the swanky hotel.

"Does Katie know?" he asked, strolling past the security desk and through the revolving doors.

"On her way," Putnam said.

Lucas had just reached the curb when the shiny black limousine pulled up. The window on the front passenger's side came down with a mechanical whine.

"Need a ride, mister?" Katie called out.

Lucas couldn't help smiling as he opened the rear passenger door and climbed into the spacious backseat.

"How was the party?" she asked as she pulled the limo into traffic.

"Same as all the others," he said. "They blend together after a while."

He removed the tiny earpiece and stuck it in his shirt pocket. There was a metal carrying case on the seat beside him, and he opened it. Lucas felt a tingle of excitement, as he always did these days when he looked at its contents.

"That's hot off the presses," Katie said. "Nicolas and I just put the finishing touches on it this afternoon."

"Cool," Lucas said, reaching inside the case.

"I guess things are getting pretty tense over on Madison," Katie said, leaning her head back slightly to speak to him through the open rectangular window between the driver and passenger areas of the limo.

"Then we should probably hurry," he said, starting to un-button his shirt. He could see she was still watching him in the rearview mirror.

"I'll never get used to seeing that," she said.

"What, me taking my clothes off?" Lucas asked.

"No, watching a real-life superhero appear before my eyes."

"Now you're just trying to embarrass me," he said, reaching out to close the partition.

"Party pooper," Katie said, her voice now coming over the speaker system in the backseat.

Lucas was amazed at how good he'd gotten at this—getting undressed and putting on his costume in the backseat of a moving limousine.

"How close are we?" he asked, putting on the last touches of the new outfit.

"Not close enough, I'm afraid," Katie said. "We've got some serious traffic issues."

"Then find someplace discreet to park so I can get there under my own power," Lucas ordered as he slid on his gauntlets.

Using her amazing memory of the Seraph street layout, and a GPS that would make NASA jealous, Katie found a side alley that would provide him with the cover he needed.

"This is good," he said, peering through the one-way glass of the backseat into the deserted alleyway.

In full costume, he emerged from the car. He was just about to slip his cowl on when the driver's-side window came down.

"Chinese and a movie tonight?" Katie asked.

"Sounds good," he said.

She smiled at him then, and he felt the chill of excite- {209 ment, matched only by the way he felt when wearing the costume.

"I'll pick the movie this time," he said, bending down to give her a quick kiss on the lips before pulling the mask over his face.

"Let me guess," Katie said. "It'll be something with a lot of action."

"Am I that predictable?" he asked, feeling the awesome tingle of power flowing through his body as the suit's neuro-sensors enhanced his strength.

Before she could answer, he leapt up into the air, his boot jets kicking in to propel him into the sky and over the city.

On the way to save the day.

* * *

"It's the Shop-Quick on Madison." Putnam's voice filled him in.

"Got it," Lucas said, landing in a trash-strewn alley behind the convenience store.

Clinging to the shadows, he found the rear door of the store and prepared to act. Putnam continued to feed him information through the communications system in his cowl.

"We've got four hostages and three gunmen inside, with the police out front. As of five minutes ago, they were still waiting for the hostage negotiator to arrive."

Lucas approached the door, peering through the window into the back of the store.

"I'm going to move fast," he said.

"You're going in, then?" Putnam asked curiously.

"Yeah, this needs to end before the situation gets any worse."

"So what's your plan?"

"I'm going in under cover of darkness," Lucas explained.

"EMP?" Putnam asked, referring to the electromagnetic pulse emitter built into the costume. Once it was activated, it would shut down all the power in the vicinity for at least an hour.

But Lucas needed only a few seconds.

"You read my mind," he said, turning on the infrared lenses in his face mask while getting ready to set off the emitter.

"It's showtime," he said, depressing the button on his wrist.

The air shimmered briefly as the wave of electromagnetic force emanated from his body, and the entire neighborhood around him went black.

He tore the locked door from its hinges with ease and made his way toward the front of the convenience store.

Lucas had to work with surgical precision. He needed to strike hard and fast so that nobody would get hurt.

When he looked through the lenses of his mask, it was as bright as day, and he saw exactly what he needed to do.

The thieves were in a panic, screaming at the top of their lungs that they would hurt the hostages if anybody tried to take them.

Lucas wasn't about to give them that chance.

He saw them right away—three men with guns, two with handguns and one with a shotgun. The four hostages were lying on the floor at their feet. The gunmen had their weapons pointed at their frightened captives as the leader screamed a warning to the police outside, blaming them for the sudden darkness.

It was scenes like this that made Lucas sick to his stomach, and that made him realize that what he did—the role he had chosen—was a complete necessity.

He grabbed one of the men by the back of the shirt, yanking him backward so he became airborne, sailing through the store to hit the wall just beside the doorway to the back room.

By the sound of the impact, Lucas didn't figure he'd be much of a threat anytime soon.

The remaining two thugs barely had time to react.

Lucas darted in, ripping the pistol from one criminal's hand. The man shrieked like a little girl, going quiet only after Lucas drove his fist solidly into his face, knocking him out cold.

The hostages desperately tried to run to safety, but their panic put their lives at risk.

The last of the criminals, a bald-headed man with a cobra tattooed on the side of his face, immediately raised his shotgun and prepared to fire into the escaping prisoners.

"No!" Lucas screamed, leaping into the air to place himself between the shotgun blast and the captives.

The gun belched fiery thunder, and multiple pellets peppered his chest and lower body.

"I got you!" the man shrieked as he pumped another round into his weapon and readied to fire once again.

Lucas had just about enough of this.

The costume he wore was bulletproof, but that didn't mean the flesh beneath wasn't bruised by the force of the gunfire.

Springing to his feet, he reached out, grabbed the gun, and tossed it across the store.

Lucas could see the sudden terror fill the man's eyes as he emerged from the darkness to bear down on him. With his eyes glowing red from the infrared lenses in the mask and his sleek costume the color of darkness and blood, Lucas could just imagine what he looked like to the frightened man.

Cobra Face tried to run, but Lucas moved much too quickly, grabbing him by the front of his T-shirt and pulling him close.

Lucas almost started to laugh as he heard the man pathetically whimper.

"Who . . . what are you?" the man asked as Lucas leaned in closer to him.

This was the part he loved—letting them know who they were dealing with.

Raising one of his gloved hands, he showed the man the razor-sharp claws extending from his fingertips, hoping to scare the crap out of him.

"I'm the Red Talon," Lucas said, savoring the way the name rolled off his tongue. "And Seraph City is under my protection."

She's mine now, this Angel City, Lucas thought.

And he would do everything in his power to show her.

To show her what it truly meant to be a hero.

THE END?

THIS BOOK BELONGS TO

Harry Potter

shared by Ron Weasley
  because his fell apart

why don't you buy a new one then?

write on your own book
            Hermione

you bought all those dungbombs
on Saturday, you could have
bought a new book instead

  Dungbombs rule

WITH THANKS

J. K. Rowling, Comic Relief U. K., and Scholastic Inc.
would like to thank the following individuals and organizations
for their generous contributions in this endeavor:

HarperCollins Publishers
Command Web Offset
Quebecor World (USA Corp.)
R. R. Donnelley & Sons
Alliance Forest Product Inc.
Digicon Imaging, Inc.
J. M. Wechter & Associates, Inc.
Rose Printing Company
ICG/Holliston
Lehigh Press, Inc.
The Display Connection Inc.
Universal Printing Company
JY International Inc., Sales Division of LeeFung-Asco Printers
Berryville Graphics
Von Hoffmann
Leo Pacific Pier
Four Lakes Colorgraphics Inc.
Schneider National Inc.
Combined Express, Inc.
Fey Publishing
Delta Corrugated Paper Products Corporation
Webcrafters Inc.
Yellow Corporation

◊

And of course, the publisher would especially like to thank
J. K. Rowling for creating this book and so generously
giving all her royalties from it to Comic Relief.

FANTASTIC BEASTS
AND WHERE TO FIND THEM

NEWT SCAMANDER

Special edition with a foreword by
ALBUS DUMBLEDORE

Arthur A. Levine Books
AN IMPRINT OF SCHOLASTIC PRESS

in association with

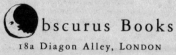

bscurus Books

18a Diagon Alley, LONDON

you die
Weasley

a _ _ _ _ _ a n _ _ l a

g ø ý d e
ŗ ø j e k b

o	x	x
o	o	x
		x

Harry
loves
~~Moaning~~
~~Myrtle~~

Scholastic Inc.'s net proceeds from the sale of this book will go to Comic Relief U. K.'s Harry's Books fund. J. K. Rowling is donating all royalties to which she would be entitled. The purchase of this book is not tax deductible. Comic Relief may be contacted at: Comic Relief, 5th Floor, Albert Embankment, London SEI 77P, England (www.comicrelief.com). Comic Relief in the United Kingdom is not affiliated with the organization of the same name in the United States.

ISBN 0-439-29501-7
Library of Congress Cataloging-in-Publication Data Available
12 11 10 9 8 7 6 5 4 3 2 1   1/0 2/0 3/0 4/0 5/0
Printed in the U. S. A.
First American edition, February 2001

CONTENTS

= CHUDLEY CANNONS =
write a decent team in
my book for a change
Weasley

ABOUT THE AUTHOR

nice name

NEWTON ("NEWT") Artemis Fido Scamander was
born in 1897. His interest in fabulous beasts was
encouraged by his mother, who was an enthusiastic
breeder of fancy Hippogriffs. Upon graduation from Hogwarts
School of Witchcraft and Wizardry, Mr. Scamander joined the
Ministry of Magic in the Department for the Regulation and
Control of Magical Creatures. After two years at the Office for
House-Elf Relocation, years he describes as "tedious in the
extreme," he was transferred to the Beast Division, where his
prodigious knowledge of bizarre magical animals ensured his
rapid promotion.

Although almost solely responsible for the creation of the
Werewolf Register in 1947, he says he is proudest of the Ban on
Experimental Breeding, passed in 1965, which effectively
prevented the creation of new and untameable monsters within
Britain. Mr. Scamander's work with the Dragon Research and
Restraint Bureau led to many research trips abroad, during which
he collected information for his worldwide best-seller *Fantastic
Beasts and Where to Find Them*, now in its fifty-second edition.

Newt Scamander was awarded the Order of Merlin, Second
Class, in 1979 in recognition of his services to the study of
magical beasts, Magizoology. Now retired, he lives in Dorset with
his wife Porpentina and their pet Kneazles: Hoppy, Milly, and
Mauler.

FOREWORD

I WAS DEEPLY HONOURED when Newt Scamander asked me to write the foreword for this very special edition of *Fantastic Beasts and Where to Find Them*. Newt's masterpiece has been an approved textbook at Hogwarts School of Witchcraft and Wizardry ever since its publication and must take a substantial amount of credit for our students' consistently high results in Care of Magical Creatures examinations – yet it is not a book to be confined to the classroom. No wizarding household is complete without a copy of *Fantastic Beasts*, well thumbed by the generations who have riffled its pages in search of the best way to rid the lawn of Horklumps, interpret the mournful cries of the Augurey, or cure their pet Puffskein of drinking out of the toilet.

This edition, however, has a loftier purpose than the instruction of the wizarding community. For the first time in the history of the noble publishing house of Obscurus, one of its titles is to be made available to Muggles.

The work of Comic Relief U. K. (which, funnily enough, has nothing to do with the American organization of the same name) in fighting some of the worst forms of human suffering is well known in the Muggle world, so it is to my fellow wizards that I now address myself. Know, then, that we are not alone in recognizing the curative power of laughter, that Muggles are familiar with it too, and that they have harnessed this gift in a most imaginative way, using it to raise funds with which to help save and better lives – a brand of magic to which we all aspire. Comic Relief U. K. has raised over 250 million dollars since 1985 (that's also 174 million pounds, or thirty-four million, eight hundred and seventy-two Galleons, fourteen Sickles, and seven Knuts).

It is now the wizarding world's privilege to help Comic Relief in their endeavour. You hold in your hands a duplicate of Harry Potter's own copy of *Fantastic Beasts*, complete with his and his friends' informative notes in the margins. Although Harry seemed a trifle reluctant to allow this book to be reprinted in its present form, our friends at Comic Relief feel that his small additions will add to the entertaining tone of the book. Mr. Newt Scamander, long since resigned to the relentless graffitiing of his masterpiece, has agreed.

This edition of *Fantastic Beasts* will be sold at Flourish and Blotts as well as in Muggle bookshops. Everyone involved in getting this book to you, from the author to the publisher, to the paper suppliers, printers, binders, and booksellers, contributed their time, energy and materials free or at a reduced cost, making it possible for proceeds from the sale of this book to go to a fund set up in Harry Potter's name by Comic Relief U. K. and J. K. Rowling. This fund was designed specifically to help children in need throughout the world. Wizards wishing to make additional donations should do so through Gringotts Wizarding Bank (ask for Griphook.)

All that remains is for me to warn anyone who has read this far without purchasing the book that it carries a Thief's Curse. I would like to take this opportunity to reassure Muggle purchasers that the amusing creatures described hereafter are fictional and cannot hurt you. To wizards, I say merely: *Draco dormiens nunquam titillandus.*

Albus Dumbledore

INTRODUCTION

ABOUT THIS BOOK

*F*antastic *Beasts and Where to Find Them* represents the fruit of many years' travel and research. I look back across the years to the seven-year-old wizard who spent hours in his bedroom dismembering Horklumps and I envy him the journeys to come: from darkest jungle to brightest desert, from mountain peak to marshy bog, that grubby Horklump-encrusted boy would track, as he grew up, the beasts described in the following pages. I have visited lairs, burrows, and nests across five continents, observed the curious habits of magical beasts in a hundred countries, witnessed their powers, gained their trust and, on occasion, beaten them off with my travelling kettle.

The first edition of *Fantastic Beasts* was commissioned back in 1918 by Mr. Augustus Worme of Obscurus Books, who was kind enough to ask me whether I would consider writing an authoritative compendium of magical creatures for his publishing house. I was then but a lowly Ministry of Magic employee and leapt at the chance both to augment my pitiful salary of two Sickles a week and to spend my holidays travelling the globe in search of new magical species. The rest is publishing history: *Fantastic Beasts* is now in its fifty-second edition.

This introduction is intended to answer a few of the most frequently asked questions that have been arriving in my weekly postbag ever since this book was first published in 1927. The first of these is that most fundamental question of all – what is a "beast"?

big hairy thing with too many legs

WHAT IS A BEAST?

The definition of a "beast" has caused controversy for centuries. Though this might surprise some first-time students of Magizoology, the problem might come into clearer focus if we take a moment to consider three types of magical creature.

Werewolves spend most of their time as humans (whether wizard or Muggle). Once a month, however, they transform into savage, four-legged beasts of murderous intent and no human conscience.

The centaurs' habits are not humanlike; they live in the wild, refuse clothing, prefer to live apart from wizards and Muggles alike, and yet have intelligence equal to theirs.

Trolls bear a humanoid appearance, walk upright, may be taught a few simple words, and yet are less intelligent than the dullest unicorn, and possess no magical powers in their own right except for their prodigious and unnatural strength.

We now ask ourselves: which of these creatures is a "being" – that is to say, a creature worthy of legal rights and a voice in the governance of the magical world – and which is a "beast"?

Early attempts at deciding which magical creatures should be designated "beasts" were extremely crude.

Burdock Muldoon, Chief of the Wizards' Council[1] in the fourteenth century, decreed that any member of the magical community that walked on two legs would henceforth be granted the status of "being," all others to remain "beasts." In a

---

1 The Wizards' Council preceded the Ministry of Magic.

spirit of friendship he summoned all "beings" to meet with the wizards at a summit to discuss new magical laws and found to his intense dismay that he had miscalculated. The meeting hall was crammed with goblins who had brought with them as many two-legged creatures as they could find. As Bathilda Bagshot tells us in *A History of Magic*:

> **Little could be heard over the squawking of the Diricawls, the moaning of the Augureys, and the relentless, piercing song of the Fwoopers. As wizards and witches attempted to consult the papers before them, sundry pixies and fairies whirled around their heads, giggling and jabbering. A dozen or so trolls began to smash apart the chamber with their clubs, while hags glided about the place in search of children to eat. The Council Chief stood up to open the meeting, slipped on a pile of Porlock dung and ran cursing from the hall.**

As we see, the mere possession of two legs was no guarantee that a magical creature could or would take an interest in the affairs of wizard government. Embittered, Burdock Muldoon forswore any further attempts to integrate non-wizard members of the magical community into the Wizards' Council.

Muldoon's successor, Madame Elfrida Clagg, attempted to redefine "beings" in the hope of creating closer ties with other magical creatures. "Beings," she declared, were those who could speak the human tongue. All those who could make themselves understood to Council members were therefore invited to join the next meeting. Once again, however, there were problems. Trolls who had been taught a few simple sentences by the goblins proceeded to destroy the hall as before. Jarveys raced around the Council's chair legs, tearing at as many ankles as they could reach. Meanwhile a large delegation of ghosts (who had been barred under Muldoon's leadership on the grounds that they did not walk on two legs, but glided) attended but left in disgust at what they later termed "the Council's unashamed emphasis on the needs of the living as opposed to the wishes of the dead." The centaurs, who under Muldoon had been classified as "beasts" and were now under Madame Clagg defined as "beings," refused to attend the Council in protest at the exclusion of the merpeople, who were unable to converse in anything except Mermish while above water.

Not until 1811 were definitions found that most of the magical community found acceptable. Grogan Stump, the newly appointed Minister for Magic, decreed that a "being" was "any creature that has sufficient intelligence to understand the laws of the magical community and to bear part of the responsibility in shaping those laws."[2] Troll representatives were questioned in the absence of goblins and judged not to understand anything that was being said to them; they were therefore classified as "beasts" despite their two-legged gait; merpeople were invited through translators to become "beings" for the first time; fairies, pixies, and gnomes, despite their humanoid appearance, were placed firmly in the "beast" category.

---

2 An exception was made for the ghosts, who asserted that it was insensitive to class them as "beings" when they were so clearly "has-beens." Stump therefore created the three divisions of the Department for the Regulation and Control of Magical Creatures that exist today: the Beast Division, the Being Division, and the Spirit Division.

Naturally, the matter has not rested there. We are all familiar with the extremists who campaign for the classification of Muggles as "beasts"; we are all aware that the centaurs have refused "being" status and requested to remain "beasts";[3] werewolves, meanwhile, have been shunted between the Beast and Being divisions for many years; at the time of writing there is an office for Werewolf Support Services at the Being Division whereas the Werewolf Registry and Werewolf Capture Unit fall under the Beast Division. Several highly intelligent creatures are classified as "beasts" because they are incapable of overcoming their own brutal natures. Acromantulas and Manticores are capable of intelligent speech but will attempt to devour any human that goes near them. The sphinx talks only in puzzles and riddles, and is violent when given the wrong answer.

Wherever there is continued uncertainty about the classification of a beast in the following pages, I have noted it in the entry for that creature.

Let us now turn to the one question that witches and wizards ask more than any other when the conversation turns to Magizoology: Why don't Muggles notice these creatures?

---

3 The centaurs objected to some of the creatures with whom they were asked to share "being" status, such as hags and vampires, and declared that they would manage their own affairs separately from wizards. A year later the merpeople made the same request. The Ministry of Magic accepted their demands reluctantly. Although a Centaur Liaison Office exists in the Beast Division of the Department for the Regulation and Control of Magical Creatures, no centaur has ever used it. Indeed, "being sent to the Centaur Office" has become an in-joke at the Department and means that the person in question is shortly to be fired.

you liar

A BRIEF HISTORY OF MUGGLE AWARENESS OF FANTASTIC BEASTS

Astonishing though it may seem to many wizards, Muggles have not always been ignorant of the magical and monstrous creatures that we have worked so long and hard to hide. A glance through Muggle art and literature of the Middle Ages reveals that many of the creatures they now believe to be imaginary were then known to be real. The dragon, the griffin, the unicorn, the phoenix, the centaur – these and more are represented in Muggle works of that period, though usually with almost comical inexactitude.

However, a closer examination of Muggle bestiaries of that period demonstrates that most magical beasts either escaped Muggle notice completely or were mistaken for something else. Examine this surviving fragment of manuscript, written by one Brother Benedict, a Franciscan monk from Worcestershire:

> Todaye while travailing in the Herbe Garden, I did push aside the basil to discover a Ferret of monstrous size. It did not run nor hide as Ferrets are wont to do, but leapt upon me, throwing me backwards upon the grounde and crying with most unnatural fury, "Get out of it, baldy!" It did then bite my nose so viciously that I did bleed for several Hours. The Friar was unwilling to believe that I had met a talking Ferret and did ask me whether I had been supping of Brother Boniface's Turnip Wine. As my nose was still swollen and bloody I was excused Vespers.

Evidently our Muggle friend had unearthed not a ferret, as he supposed, but a Jarvey, most likely in pursuit of its favourite prey, gnomes.

Imperfect understanding is often more dangerous than ignorance, and the Muggles' fear of magic was undoubtedly increased by their dread of what might be lurking in their herb gardens. Muggle persecution of wizards at this time was reaching a pitch hitherto unknown and sightings of such beasts as dragons and Hippogriffs were contributing to Muggle hysteria.

It is not the aim of this work to discuss the dark days that preceded the wizards' retreat into hiding.[4] All that concerns us here is the fate of those fabulous beasts that, like ourselves, would have to be concealed if Muggles were ever to be convinced there was no such thing as magic.

The International Confederation of Wizards argued the matter out at their famous summit meeting of 1692. No fewer than seven weeks of sometimes acrimonious discussion between wizards of all nationalities were devoted to the troublesome question of magical creatures. How many species would we be able to conceal from Muggle notice and which should they be? Where and how should we hide them? The debate raged on, some creatures oblivious to the fact that their destiny was being decided, others contributing to the debate.[5]

At last agreement was reached.[6] Twenty-seven species, ranging in size from dragons to Bundimuns, were to be hidden from Muggles so as to create the illusion that they had never existed

---

4 Anyone interested in a full account of this particularly bloody period of wizarding history should consult *A History of Magic* by Bathilda Bagshot (Little Red Books, 1947).
5 Delegations of centaurs, merpeople, and goblins were persuaded to attend the summit.
6 Except by the goblins.

outside the imagination. This number was increased over the following century, as wizards became more confident in their methods of concealment. In 1750, Clause 73 was inserted in the International Code of Wizarding Secrecy, to which wizard ministries worldwide conform today:

> Each wizarding governing body will be responsible for the concealment, care, and control of all magical beasts, beings, and spirits dwelling within its territory's borders. Should any such creature cause harm to, or draw the notice of, the Muggle community, that nation's wizarding governing body will be subject to discipline by the International Confederation of Wizards.

MAGICAL BEASTS IN HIDING

It would be idle to deny that there have been occasional breaches of Clause 73 since it was first put in place. Older British readers will remember the Ilfracombe Incident of 1932, when a rogue Welsh Green dragon swooped down upon a crowded beach full of sunbathing Muggles. Fatalities were mercifully prevented by the brave actions of a holidaying wizarding family (subsequently awarded Orders of Merlin, First Class), when they immediately performed the largest batch of Memory Charms this century on the inhabitants of Ilfracombe, thus narrowly averting catastrophe.[7]

---

7 In his 1972 book *Muggles Who Notice*, Blenheim Stalk asserts that some residents of Ilfracombe escaped the Mass Memory Charm. "To this day, a Muggle bearing the nickname 'Dodgy Dirk' holds forth in bars along the south coast on the subject of a 'dirty great flying lizard' that punctured his lilo."

The International Confederation of Wizards has had to fine certain nations repeatedly for contravening Clause 73. Tibet and Scotland are two of the most persistent offenders. Muggle sightings of the yeti have been so numerous that the International Confederation of Wizards felt it necessary to station an International Task Force in the mountains on a permanent basis. Meanwhile the world's largest kelpie continues to evade capture in Loch Ness and appears to have developed a positive thirst for publicity.

These unfortunate mishaps notwithstanding, we wizards may congratulate ourselves on a job well done. There can be no doubt that the overwhelming majority of present-day Muggles refuse to believe in the magical beasts their ancestors so feared. Even those Muggles who do notice Porlock droppings or Streeler trails – it would be foolish to suppose that all traces of these creatures can be hidden – appear satisfied with the flimsiest non-magical explanation.[8] If any Muggle is unwise enough to confide in another that he has spotted a Hippogriff winging its way north, he is generally believed to be drunk or a "loony." Unfair though this may seem on the Muggle in question, it is nevertheless preferable to being burnt at the stake or drowned in the village duckpond.

So how does the wizarding community hide fantastic beasts?

Luckily, some species do not require much wizarding assistance in avoiding the notice of Muggles. Creatures such as the Tebo, the Demiguise, and the Bowtruckle have their own highly effective

---

8 For a fascinating examination of this fortunate tendency of Muggles, the reader might like to consult *The Philosophy of the Mundane: Why the Muggles Prefer Not to Know*, Professor Mordicus Egg (Dust & Mildewe, 1963).

means of camouflage and no intervention by the Ministry of Magic has ever been necessary on their behalf. Then there are those beasts that, due to cleverness or innate shyness, avoid contact with Muggles at all costs – for instance, the unicorn, the Mooncalf, and the centaur. Other magical creatures inhabit places inaccessible to Muggles – one thinks of the Acromantula, deep in the uncharted jungle of Borneo, and the phoenix, nesting high on mountain peaks unreachable without the use of magic. Finally, and most commonly, we have beasts that are too small, too speedy, or too adept at passing for mundane animals to attract a Muggle's attention – Chizpurfles, Billywigs, and Crups fall into this category.

Nevertheless there are still plenty of beasts that, whether willfully or inadvertently, remain conspicuous even to the Muggle eye, and it is these that create a significant amount of work for the Department for the Regulation and Control of Magical Creatures. This department, the second largest at the Ministry of Magic,[9] deals with the varying needs of the many species under its care in a variety of different ways.

Safe Habitats

Perhaps the most important step in the concealment of magical creatures is the creation of safe habitats. Muggle-Repelling Charms prevent trespassers into the forests where centaurs and unicorns live, and on the lakes and rivers set aside for the use of

---

9 The largest department at the Ministry of Magic is the Department of Magical Law Enforcement, to which the remaining six departments are all, in some respect, answerable – with the possible exception of the Department of Mysteries.

merpeople. In extreme cases, such as that of the Quintaped, whole areas have been made unplottable.[10]

Some of these safe areas must be kept under constant wizarding supervision; for example, dragon reservations. While unicorns and merpeople are only too happy to stay within the territories designated for their use, dragons will seek any opportunity to set forth in search of prey beyond the reservation borders. In some cases Muggle-Repelling Charms will not work, as the beast's own powers will cancel them. Cases in point are the kelpie, whose sole aim in life is to attract humans towards it, and the Pogrebin, which seeks out humans for itself.

Controls on Selling and Breeding

The possibility of a Muggle being alarmed by any of the larger or more dangerous magical beasts has been greatly reduced by the severe penalties now attached to their breeding and the sale of their young and eggs. The Department for the Regulation and Control of Magical Creatures keeps a strict watch on the trade in fantastic beasts. The 1965 Ban on Experimental Breeding has made the creation of new species illegal. *but no one's told Hagrid*

Disillusionment Charms

The wizard on the street also plays a part in the concealment of magical beasts. Those who own a Hippogriff, for example, are bound by law to enchant the beast with a Disillusionment Charm to distort the vision of any Muggle who may see it. Disillusionment Charms should be performed daily, as their effects are apt to wear off.

---

10 When an area of land is made unplottable, it is impossible to chart on maps.

Memory Charms

When the worst happens and a Muggle sees what he or she is not supposed to see, the Memory Charm is perhaps the most useful repair tool. The Memory Charm may be performed by the owner of the beast in question, but in severe cases of Muggle notice, a team of trained Obliviators may be sent in by the Ministry of Magic.

The Office of Misinformation

The Office of Misinformation will become involved in only the very worst magical-Muggle collisions. Some magical catastrophes or accidents are simply too glaringly obvious to be explained away by Muggles without the help of an outside authority. The Office of Misinformation will in such a case liaise directly with the Muggle prime minister to seek a plausible non-magical explanation for the event. The unstinting efforts of this office in persuading Muggles that all photographic evidence of the Loch Ness kelpie is fake have gone some way to salvaging a situation that at one time looked exceedingly dangerous.

WHY MAGIZOOLOGY MATTERS

The measures described above merely hint at the full scope and extent of the work done by the Department for the Regulation and Control of Magical Creatures. It remains only to answer that question to which we all, in our hearts, know the answer: Why do we continue, as a community and as individuals, to attempt to protect and conceal magical beasts, even those that are savage and untameable? The answer is, of course: to ensure that future generations of witches and wizards enjoy their strange beauty and powers as we have been privileged to do.

I offer this work as a mere introduction to the wealth of fantastic beasts that inhabit our world. Seventy-five species are described in the following pages, but I do not doubt that some time this year yet another will be discovered, necessitating a fifty-third revised edition of *Fantastic Beasts and Where to Find Them*. In the meantime I will merely add that it affords me great pleasure to think that generations of young witches and wizards have grown to a fuller knowledge and understanding of the fantastic beasts I love through the pages of this book.

MINISTRY OF MAGIC
CLASSIFICATIONS

The Department for the Regulation and Control of Magical Creatures gives classifications to all known beasts, beings, and spirits. These offer an at-a-glance guide to the perceived dangerousness of a creature. The five categories are as follows:

Ministry of Magic (M.O.M.) Classification

XXXXX	Known wizard killer / *or anything Hagrid likes* impossible to train or domesticate
XXXX	Dangerous / requires specialist knowledge / skilled wizard may handle
XXX	Competent wizard should cope
XX	Harmless / may be domesticated
X	Boring

In some cases I have felt an explanation for the classification of a particular beast is necessary and have added footnotes accordingly.

An A–Z of Fantastic Beasts

ACROMANTULA

M.O.M. Classification: XXXXX ✗✗✗✗✗✗✗✗

The Acromantula is a monstrous eight-eyed spider capable of human speech. It originated in Borneo, where it inhabits dense jungle. Its distinctive features include the thick black hair that covers its body; its legspan, which may reach up to fifteen feet; its pincers, which produce a distinctive clicking sound when the Acromantula is excited or angry; and a poisonous secretion. The Acromantula is carnivorous and prefers large prey. It spins dome-shaped webs upon the ground. The female is bigger than the male and may lay up to one hundred eggs at a time. Soft and white, these are as large as beach balls. The young hatch in six to eight weeks. Acromantula eggs are defined as Class A Non-Tradeable Goods by the Department for the Regulation and Control of Magical Creatures, meaning that severe penalties are attached to their importation or sale.

This beast is believed to be wizard-bred, possibly intended to guard wizard dwellings or treasure, as is often the case with magically created monsters.[1] Despite its near-human intelligence,

---

[1] Beasts capable of human speech are rarely self-taught; an exception is the Jarvey. The Ban on Experimental Breeding did not come into effect until this century, long after the first recorded sighting of an Acromantula in 1794.

the Acromantula is untrainable and highly dangerous to wizard and Muggle alike.

Rumours that a colony of Acromantula has been established in Scotland are ~~unconfirmed~~.

confirmed by Harry Potter and Ron Weasley

ASHWINDER

M.O.M. Classification: XXX

The Ashwinder is created when a magical fire[2] is allowed to burn unchecked for too long. A thin, pale-grey serpent with glowing red eyes, it will rise from the embers of an unsupervised fire and slither away into the shadows of the dwelling in which it finds itself, leaving an ashy trail behind it.

The Ashwinder lives for only an hour and during that time seeks a dark and secluded spot in which to lay its eggs, after which it will collapse into dust. Ashwinder eggs are brilliant red and give off intense heat. They will ignite the dwelling within minutes if not found and frozen with a suitable charm. Any wizard realising that one or more Ashwinders are loose in the house must trace them immediately and locate the nest of eggs. Once frozen, these eggs are of great value for use in Love Potions and may be eaten whole as a cure for ague.

Ashwinders are found worldwide.

AUGUREY (also known as Irish Phoenix)

M.O.M. Classification: XX

The Augurey is a native of Britain and Ireland, though sometimes found elsewhere in northern Europe. A thin and mournful-looking bird, somewhat like a small and underfed vulture in

---

2 Any fire to which a magical substance such as Floo powder has been added.

appearance, the Augurey is greenish black. It is intensely shy, nests in bramble and thorn, eats large insects and fairies, flies only in heavy rain, and otherwise remains hidden in its tear-shaped nest.

The Augurey has a distinctive low and throbbing cry, which was once believed to foretell death. Wizards avoided Augurey nests for fear of hearing that heart-rending sound, and more than one wizard is believed to have suffered a heart attack on passing a thicket and hearing an unseen Augurey wail.[3] Patient research eventually revealed, however, that the Augurey merely sings at the approach of rain.[4] The Augurey has since enjoyed a vogue as a home weather forecaster, though many find its almost continual moaning during the winter months difficult to bear. Augurey feathers are useless as quills because they repel ink.

BASILISK (also known as the King of Serpents)

M.O.M. Classification: XXXXX

The first recorded Basilisk was bred by Herpo the Foul, a Greek Dark wizard and Parselmouth, who discovered after much experimentation that a chicken egg hatched beneath a toad would produce a gigantic serpent possessed of extraordinarily dangerous powers.

The Basilisk is a brilliant green serpent that may reach up to fifty feet in length. The male has a scarlet plume upon its head. It has exceptionally venomous fangs but its most dangerous means

---

3 Uric the Oddball is known to have slept in a room containing no fewer than fifty pet Augureys. During one particularly wet winter, Uric became convinced by the moaning of his Augureys that he had died and was now a ghost. His subsequent attempts to walk through the walls of his house resulted in what his biographer Radolphus Pittiman describes as a "concussion of ten days' duration."

4 See *Why I Didn't Die When the Augurey Cried* by Gulliver Pokeby, 1824 (Little Red Books).

of attack is the gaze of its large yellow eyes. Anyone looking directly into these will suffer instant death.

If the food source is sufficient (the Basilisk will eat all mammals and birds and most reptiles), the serpent may attain a very great age. Herpo the Foul's Basilisk is believed to have lived for close on nine hundred years.

The creation of Basilisks has been illegal since medieval times, although the practice is easily concealed by simply removing the chicken egg from beneath the toad when the Department for the Regulation and Control of Magical Creatures comes to call. However, since Basilisks are uncontrollable except by Parselmouths, they are as dangerous to most Dark wizards as to anybody else, and there have been no recorded sightings of Basilisks in Britain for at least four hundred years. *that's what you think*

BILLYWIG

M.O.M. Classification: XXX

The Billywig is an insect native to Australia. It is around half an inch long and a vivid sapphire blue, although its speed is such that it is rarely noticed by Muggles and often not by wizards until they have been stung. The Billywig's wings are attached to the top of its head and are rotated very fast so that it spins as it flies. At the bottom of the body is a long thin sting. Those who have been stung by a Billywig suffer giddiness followed by levitation. Generations of young Australian witches and wizards have attempted to catch Billywigs and provoke them into stinging in order to enjoy these side effects, though too many stings may

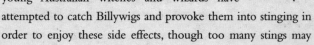

cause the victim to hover uncontrollably for days on end, and where there is a severe allergic reaction, permanent floating may ensue. Dried Billywig stings are used in several potions and are believed to be a component in the popular sweet Fizzing Whizbees.

BOWTRUCKLE

M.O.M. Classification: XX last time I eat them then

The Bowtruckle is a tree-guardian creature found mainly in the west of England, southern Germany, and certain Scandinavian forests. It is immensely difficult to spot, being small (maximum eight inches in height) and apparently made of bark and twigs with two small brown eyes.

The Bowtruckle, which eats insects, is a peaceable and intensely shy creature but if the tree in which it lives is threatened, it has been known to leap down upon the woodcutter or tree-surgeon attempting to harm its home and gouge at their eyes with its long, sharp fingers. An offering of woodlice will placate the Bowtruckle long enough to let a witch or wizard remove wand-wood from its tree.

BUNDIMUN

M.O.M. Classification: XXX

Bundimuns are found worldwide. Skilled at creeping under floorboards and behind skirting boards, they infest houses. The presence of a Bundimun is usually announced by a foul stench of decay. The Bundimun oozes a secretion which rots away the very foundations of the dwelling in which it is found.

The Bundimun at rest resembles a patch of greenish fungus with eyes, though when alarmed it will scuttle away on its numerous spindly legs. It feeds on dirt. Scouring charms will rid a house of an infestation of Bundimuns, though if they have been allowed to grow too large, the Department for the Regulation and Control of Magical Creatures (Pest Sub-Division) should be contacted before the house collapses. Diluted Bundimun secretion is used in certain magical cleaning fluids.

CENTAUR

M.O.M. Classification: XXXX[5]

The centaur has a human head, torso, and arms joined to a horse's body which may be any of several colours. Being intelligent and capable of speech, it should not strictly speaking be termed a beast, but by its own request it has been classified as such by the Ministry of Magic (see the Introduction to this book).

The centaur is forest-dwelling. Centaurs are believed to have originated in Greece, though there are now centaur communities in many parts of Europe. Wizarding authorities in each of the countries where centaurs are found have allocated areas where the centaurs will not be troubled by Muggles; however, centaurs stand in little need of wizard protection, having their own means of hiding from humans.

The ways of the centaur are shrouded in mystery. They are generally speaking as mistrustful of wizards as they are of Muggles and indeed seem to make little differentiation between us. They live in herds ranging in size from ten to fifty members. They are reputed to be well-versed in magical healing, divination, archery, and astronomy.

---

5 The centaur is given an XXXX classification not because it is unduly aggressive, but because it should be treated with great respect. The same applies to merpeople and unicorns.

CHIMAERA

M.O.M. Classification: XXXXX

The Chimaera is a rare Greek monster with a lion's head, a goat's body, and a dragon's tail. Vicious and bloodthirsty, the Chimaera is extremely dangerous. There is only one known instance of the successful slaying of a Chimaera and the unlucky wizard concerned fell to his death from his winged horse (see page 42) shortly afterwards, exhausted by his efforts. Chimaera eggs are classified as Class A Non-Tradeable Goods.

so Hagrid'll be getting some any time now

CHIZPURFLE

M.O.M. Classification: XX

Chizpurfles are small parasites up to a twentieth of an inch high, crablike in appearance, with large fangs. They are attracted by magic and may infest the fur and feathers of such creatures as Crups and Augureys. They will also enter wizard dwellings and attack magical objects such as wands, gradually gnawing their way through to the magical core, or else settle in dirty cauldrons, where they will gorge upon any lingering drops of potion.[6] Though Chizpurfles are easy enough to destroy with any of a number of patented potions on the market, severe infestations may require a visit from the Pest Sub-Division of the Department for the Regulation and Control of Magical Creatures, as Chizpurfles swollen with magical substances will prove very hard to fight.

---

6 In the absence of magic, Chizpurfles have been known to attack electrical objects from within (for a fuller understanding of what electricity is, see *Home Life and Social Habits of British Muggles,* Wilhelm Wigworthy, Little Red Books, 1987). Chizpurfle infestations explain the puzzling failure of many relatively new Muggle electrical artifacts.

CLABBERT

M.O.M. Classification: XX

The Clabbert is a tree-dwelling creature, in appearance something like a cross between a monkey and a frog. It originated in the southern states of America, though it has since been exported worldwide. The smooth and hairless skin is a mottled green, the hands and feet are webbed, and the arms and legs are long and supple, enabling the Clabbert to swing between branches with the agility of an orangutan. The head has short horns, and the wide mouth, which appears to be grinning, is full of razor-sharp teeth. The Clabbert feeds mostly on small lizards and birds.

The Clabbert's most distinctive feature is the large pustule in the middle of its forehead, which turns scarlet and flashes when it senses danger. American wizards once kept Clabberts in their gardens to give early warning of approaching Muggles, but the International Confederation of Wizards has introduced fines which have largely ended this practice. The sight of a tree at night full of glowing Clabbert pustules, while decorative, attracted too many Muggles wishing to ask why their neighbours still had their Christmas lights up in June.

CRUP

M.O.M. Classification: XXX

The Crup originated in the southeast of England. It closely resembles a Jack Russell terrier, except for the forked tail. The Crup is almost certainly a wizard-created dog, as it is intensely loyal to wizards and ferocious towards Muggles. It is a great scavenger, eating anything from gnomes to old tyres. Crup licences may be obtained from the Department for the Regulation and Control of Magical Creatures on completion of a simple test to prove that the applicant wizard is capable of controlling the Crup in Muggle-inhabited areas. Crup owners are legally obliged to remove the Crup's tail with a painless Severing Charm while the Crup is six to eight weeks old, lest Muggles notice it.

DEMIGUISE

M.O.M. Classification: XXXX

The Demiguise is found in the Far East, though only with great difficulty, for this beast is able to make itself invisible when threatened, and can be seen only by wizards skilled in its capture.

The Demiguise is a peaceful herbivorous beast, something like a graceful ape in appearance, with large, black, doleful eyes more often than not hidden by its hair. The whole body is covered with long, fine, silky, silvery hair. Demiguise pelts are highly valued as the hair may be spun into Invisibility Cloaks.

DIRICAWL

M.O.M. Classification: XX

The Diricawl originated in Mauritius. A plump-bodied, fluffy-feathered, flightless bird, the Diricawl is remarkable for its method of escaping danger. It can vanish in a puff of feathers and reappear elsewhere (the phoenix shares this ability; see page 32).

Interestingly, Muggles were once fully aware of the existence of the Diricawl, though they knew it by the name of "dodo." Unaware that the Diricawl could vanish at will, Muggles believe they have hunted the species to extinction. As this seems to have raised Muggle awareness of the dangers of slaying their fellow creatures indiscriminately, the International Confederation of Wizards has never deemed it appropriate that the Muggles should be made aware of the continued existence of the Diricawl.

DOXY

(sometimes known as Biting Fairy)

M.O.M. Classification: XXX

The Doxy is often mistaken for a fairy (see page 16) though it is a quite separate species. Like the fairy, it has a minute human form, though in the Doxy's case this is covered in thick black hair and has an extra pair of arms and legs. The Doxy's wings are thick, curved, and shiny, much like a beetle's. Doxies are found throughout northern Europe and America, preferring cold climates. They lay up to five hundred eggs at a time and bury them. The eggs hatch in two to three weeks.

Doxies have double rows of sharp, venomous teeth. An antidote should be taken if bitten.

DRAGON

M.O.M. Classification: XXXXX

Probably the most famous of all magical beasts, dragons are among the most difficult to hide. The female is generally larger and more aggressive than the male, though neither should be approached by any but highly skilled and trained wizards. Dragon hide, blood, heart, liver, and horn all have highly magical properties, but dragon eggs are defined as Class A Non-Tradeable Goods.

There are ten breeds of dragon, though these have been known to interbreed on occasion, producing rare hybrids. Pure-bred dragons are as follows:

ANTIPODEAN OPALEYE

The Opaleye is a native of New Zealand, though it has been known to migrate to Australia when territory becomes scarce in its native land. Unusually for a dragon, it dwells in valleys rather than mountains. It is of medium size (between two and three tonnes). Perhaps the most beautiful type of dragon, it has iridescent, pearly scales and glittering, multi-coloured, pupil-less eyes, hence its name. This dragon produces a very vivid scarlet flame, though by dragon standards it is not particularly aggressive and will rarely kill unless hungry. Its favourite food is sheep, though it has been known to attack larger prey. A spate of kangaroo killings in the late 1970s were attributed to a male Opaleye ousted from his homeland by a dominant female. Opaleye eggs are pale grey and may be mistaken for fossils by unwary Muggles.

CHINESE FIREBALL
(sometimes known as Liondragon)

The only Oriental dragon has a particularly striking appearance. Scarlet and smooth-scaled, it has a fringe of golden spikes around its snub-snouted face and extremely protuberant eyes. The Fireball gained its name for the mushroom-shaped flame that bursts from its nostrils when it is angered. It weighs between two and four tonnes, the female being larger than the male. Eggs are a vivid crimson speckled with gold, and the shells are much prized for use in Chinese wizardry. The Fireball is aggressive but more tolerant of its own species than most dragons, sometimes consenting to share its territory with up to two others. The Fireball will feast on most mammals, though it prefers pigs and humans.

COMMON WELSH GREEN

The Welsh Green blends well with the lush grass of its homeland, though it nests in the higher mountains, where a reservation has been established for its preservation. The Ilfracombe Incident notwithstanding (see Introduction), this breed is among the least troublesome of the dragons, preferring, like the Opaleye, to prey on sheep and actively avoiding humans unless provoked. The Welsh Green has an easily recognisable and surprisingly melodious roar. Fire is issued in thin jets. The Welsh Green's eggs are an earthy brown, flecked with green.

HEBRIDEAN BLACK

Britain's other native dragon is more aggressive than its Welsh counterpart. It requires a territory of as much as a hundred square miles per dragon. Up to thirty feet in length, the Hebridean Black is rough-scaled, with brilliant purple eyes and a line of shallow but razor-sharp ridges along its back. Its tail is tipped by an arrow-shaped spike and it has batlike wings. The Hebridean Black feeds mostly on deer, though it has been known to carry off large dogs and even cattle. The wizard clan MacFusty, who have dwelled in the Hebrides for centuries, have traditionally taken responsibility for the management of their native dragons.

HUNGARIAN HORNTAIL

Supposedly the most dangerous of all dragon breeds, the

12 *you're not kidding*

Hungarian Horntail has black scales and is lizardlike in appearance. It has yellow eyes, bronze horns, and similarly coloured spikes that protrude from its long tail. The Horntail has one of the longest fire-breathing ranges (up to fifty feet). Its eggs are cement-coloured and particularly hard-shelled; the young club their way out using their tails, whose spikes are well developed at birth. The Hungarian Horntail feeds on goats, sheep and, whenever possible, humans.

NORWEGIAN RIDGEBACK ~~Baby Norbert~~

The Norwegian Ridgeback resembles the Horntail in most respects, though instead of tail spikes it sports particularly prominent jet-black ridges along its back. Exceptionally aggressive to its own kind, the Ridgeback is nowadays one of the rarer dragon breeds. It has been known to attack most kinds of large land mammal and, unusually for a dragon, the Ridgeback will also feed on water-dwelling creatures. An unsubstantiated report alleges that a Ridgeback carried off a whale calf off the coast of Norway in 1802. Ridgeback eggs are black and the young develop fire-breathing abilities earlier than other breeds (at between one and three months).

PERUVIAN VIPERTOOTH

This is the smallest of all known dragons, and the swiftest in flight. A mere fifteen feet or so in length, the Peruvian Vipertooth is smooth-scaled and copper-coloured with black ridge markings. The horns are short and the fangs are particularly venomous. The Vipertooth will feed readily on goats and cows, but has such a liking for humans that the International Confederation of Wizards was forced to send in exterminators in the late nineteenth century to reduce Vipertooth numbers, which had been increasing with alarming rapidity.

ROMANIAN LONGHORN

The Longhorn has dark-green scales and long, glittering golden horns with which it gores its prey before roasting it. When powdered, these horns are highly valued as potion ingredients. The native territory of the Longhorn has now become the world's most important dragon reservation, where wizards of all nationalities study a variety of dragons at close range. The Longhorn has been the subject of an intensive breeding programme because its numbers have fallen so low in recent years, largely because of the trade in its horns, which are now defined as a Class B Tradeable Material.

SWEDISH SHORT-SNOUT

The Swedish Short-Snout is an attractive silvery-blue dragon whose skin is sought after for the manufacture of protective gloves and shields. The flame that issues from its nostrils is a brilliant blue and can reduce timber and bone to ash in a matter of seconds. The Short-Snout has fewer human killings to its name than most dragons, though as it prefers to live in wild and uninhabited mountainous areas, this is not much to its credit.

UKRAINIAN IRONBELLY

The largest breed of dragon, the Ironbelly, has been known to achieve a weight of six tonnes. Rotund and slower in flight than the Vipertooth or the Longhorn, the Ironbelly is nevertheless extremely dangerous, capable of crushing dwellings on which it lands. The scales are metallic grey, the eyes deep red, and the talons particularly long and vicious. Ironbellies have been subject to constant observation by the Ukrainian wizarding authorities ever since an Ironbelly carried off a (mercifully empty) sailing boat from the Black Sea in 1799.

DUGBOG

M.O.M. Classification: XXX

The Dugbog is a marsh-dwelling creature found in Europe and North and South America. It resembles a piece of dead wood while stationary, though closer examination will reveal finned paws and very sharp teeth. It glides and slithers through marshland, feeding mainly on small mammals, and will do severe injury to the ankles of human walkers. The Dugbog's favourite food, however, is Mandrake. Mandrake-growers have been known to seize the leaves of one of their prize plants only to find a bloody mangled mess below owing to the attentions of a Dugbog.

ERKLING

M.O.M. Classification: XXXX

The Erkling is an elfish creature which originated in the Black Forest in Germany. It is larger than a gnome (three feet high on average), with a pointed face and a high-pitched cackle that is particularly entrancing to children, whom it will attempt to lure away from their guardians and eat. Strict controls by the German Ministry of Magic, however, have reduced Erkling killings dramatically over the last few centuries and the last known Erkling attack, upon the six-year-old wizard Bruno Schmidt, resulted in the death of the Erkling when Master Schmidt hit it very hard over the head with his father's collapsible cauldron.

ERUMPENT

M.O.M. Classification: XXXX

The Erumpent is a large grey African beast of great power. Weighing up to a tonne, the Erumpent may be mistaken for a rhinoceros at a distance. It has a thick hide that repels most charms and curses, a large, sharp horn upon its nose and a long, rope-like tail. Erumpents give birth to only one calf at a time.

The Erumpent will not attack unless sorely provoked, but should it charge, the results are usually catastrophic. The Erumpent's horn can pierce everything from skin to metal, and contains a deadly fluid which will cause whatever is injected with it to explode.

Erumpent numbers are not great, as males frequently explode each other during the mating season. They are treated with great caution by African wizards. Erumpent horns, tails, and the Exploding Fluid are all used in potions, though classified as Class B Tradeable Materials (Dangerous and Subject to Strict Control).

FAIRY

M.O.M. Classification: XX

The fairy is a small and decorative beast of little intelligence.[7] Often used or conjured by wizards for decoration, the fairy generally inhabits woodlands or glades. Ranging in height from one to five inches, the fairy has a minute humanoid body, head,

---

7 Muggles have a great weakness for fairies, which feature in a variety of tales written for their children. These "fairy tales" involve winged beings with distinct personalities and the ability to converse as humans (though often in a nauseatingly sentimental fashion). Fairies, as envisaged by the Muggle, inhabit tiny dwellings fashioned out of flower petals, hollowed-out toadstools, and similar. They are often depicted as carrying wands. Of all magical beasts the fairy might be said to have received the best Muggle press.

and limbs but sports large insectlike wings, which may be transparent or multi-coloured, according to type.

The fairy possesses a weak brand of magic that it may use to deter predators, such as the Augurey. It has a quarrelsome nature but, being excessively vain, it will become docile on any occasion when it is called to act as an ornament. Despite its humanlike appearance, the fairy cannot speak. It makes a high-pitched buzzing noise to communicate with its fellows.

The fairy lays up to fifty eggs at a time on the underside of leaves. The eggs hatch into brightly coloured larvae. At the age of six to ten days these spin themselves a cocoon, from which they emerge one month later as fully formed winged adults.

FIRE CRAB

M.O.M. Classification: XXX

Despite its name, the fire crab greatly resembles a large tortoise with a heavily jewelled shell. In its native Fiji, a stretch of coast has been turned into a reservation for its protection, not only against Muggles, who might be tempted by its valuable shell, but also against unscrupulous wizards, who use the shells as highly prized cauldrons. The fire crab does, however, have its own defence mechanism: It shoots flames from its rear end when attacked. Fire crabs are exported as pets but a special licence is necessary.

FLOBBERWORM

M.O.M. Classification: X

The Flobberworm lives in damp ditches. A thick brown worm reaching up to ten inches in length, the Flobberworm moves very little. One end is indistinguishable from the other, both producing the mucus from which its name is derived and which is sometimes used to thicken potions. The Flobberworm's preferred food is lettuce, though it will eat almost any vegetation.

FWOOPER

M.O.M. Classification: XXX

The Fwooper is an African bird with extremely vivid plumage; Fwoopers may be orange, pink, lime green, or yellow. The Fwooper has long been a provider of fancy quills and also lays brilliantly patterned eggs. Though at first enjoyable, Fwooper song will eventually drive the listener to insanity[8] and the Fwooper is consequently sold with a Silencing Charm upon it, which will need monthly reinforcement. Fwooper owners require licences, as the creatures must be handled responsibly.

GHOUL

M.O.M. Classification: XX

The ghoul, though ugly, is not a particularly dangerous creature. It resembles a somewhat slimy, buck-toothed ogre, and generally resides in attics or barns belonging to wizards, where it eats spiders and moths. It moans and occasionally throws objects around, but is essentially simple-minded and will, at worst, growl alarmingly at anyone who stumbles across it. A Ghoul Task Force exists at the Department for the Regulation and Control of

---

8 Uric the Oddball attempted at one time to prove that Fwooper song was actually beneficial to the health and listened to it for three months on end without a break. Unfortunately the Wizards' Council to which he reported his findings were unconvinced, as he had arrived at the meeting wearing nothing but a toupee that on closer inspection proved to be a dead badger.

Magical Creatures to remove ghouls from dwellings that have passed into Muggle hands, but in wizarding families the ghoul often becomes a talking point or even a family pet.

GLUMBUMBLE

M.O.M. Classification: XXX

The Glumbumble (northern Europe) is a grey, furry-bodied flying insect that produces melancholy-inducing treacle, which is used as an antidote to the hysteria produced by eating Alihotsy leaves. It has been known to infest beehives, with disastrous effects on the honey. Glumbumbles nest in dark and secluded places such as hollow trees and caves. They feed on nettles.

GNOME

M.O.M. Classification: XX

The gnome is a common garden pest found throughout northern Europe and North America. It may reach a foot in height, with a disproportionately large head and hard, bony feet. The gnome can be expelled from the garden by swinging it in circles until dizzy and then dropping it over the garden wall. Alternatively a Jarvey may be used, though many wizards nowadays find this method of gnome-control too brutal.

GRAPHORN

M.O.M. Classification: XXXX

The Graphorn is found in mountainous European regions. Large and greyish purple with a humped back, the Graphorn has two very long, sharp horns, walks on large, four-thumbed feet, and has an extremely aggressive nature. Mountain trolls can occasionally be seen mounted on Graphorns, though the latter do not seem to take kindly to attempts to tame them and it is more common to see a troll covered in Graphorn scars. Powdered Graphorn horn is used in many potions, though it is immensely expensive owing to the difficulty in collecting it. Graphorn hide is even tougher than a dragon's and repels most spells.

GRIFFIN

M.O.M. Classification: XXXX

The griffin originated in Greece and has the front legs and head of a giant eagle, but the body and hind legs of a lion. Like sphinxes (see page 39), griffins are often employed by wizards to guard treasure. Though griffins are fierce, a handful of skilled wizards have been known to befriend one. Griffins feed on raw meat.

GRINDYLOW

M.O.M. Classification: XX

A horned, pale-green water demon, the Grindylow is found in lakes throughout Britain and Ireland. It feeds on small fish and is aggressive towards wizards and Muggles alike, though merpeople have been known to domesticate it. The Grindylow has very long fingers, which, though they exert a powerful grip, are easy to break.

HIPPOCAMPUS

M.O.M. Classification: XXX

Originating in Greece, the hippocampus has the head and

forequarters of a horse, and the tail and hindquarters of a giant fish. Though the species is usually to be found in the Mediterranean, a superb blue roan specimen was caught by merpeople off the shores of Scotland in 1949 and subsequently domesticated by them. The hippocampus lays large, semi-transparent eggs through which the Tadfoal may be seen.

HIPPOGRIFF

M.O.M. Classification: XXX

The Hippogriff is native to Europe, though now found worldwide. It has the head of a giant eagle and the body of a horse. It can be tamed, though this should be attempted only by experts. Eye contact should be maintained when approaching a Hippogriff. Bowing shows good intentions. If the Hippogriff returns the greeting, it is safe to draw closer.

The Hippogriff burrows for insects but will also eat birds and small mammals. Breeding Hippogriffs build nests upon the ground into which they will lay a single large and fragile egg, which hatches within twenty-four hours. The fledgling Hippogriff should be ready to fly within a week, though it will be a matter of months before it is able to accompany its parent on longer journeys.

HORKLUMP

M.O.M. Classification: X

The Horklump comes from Scandinavia but is now widespread throughout northern Europe. It resembles a fleshy, pinkish mushroom covered in sparse, wiry black bristles. A prodigious breeder, the Horklump will cover an average garden in a matter of

has Hagrid read this book?

days. It spreads sinewy tentacles rather than roots into the ground to search for its preferred food of earthworms. The Horklump is a favourite delicacy of gnomes but otherwise has no discernible use.

IMP

M.O.M. Classification: XX

The imp is found only in Britain and Ireland. It is sometimes confused with the pixie. They are of similar height (between six and eight inches), though the imp cannot fly as the pixie can, nor is it as vividly coloured (the imp is usually dark brown to black). It does, however, have a similar slapstick sense of humour. Its preferred terrain is damp and marshy, and it is often found near river banks, where it will amuse itself by pushing and tripping the unwary. Imps eat small insects and have breeding habits much like the fairies, though imps do not spin cocoons; the young are hatched fully formed at around one inch in length.

JARVEY

M.O.M. Classification: XXX

The Jarvey is found in Britain, Ireland, and North America. It resembles an overgrown ferret in most respects, except for the fact that it can talk. True conversation, however, is beyond the wit of the Jarvey, which tends to confine itself to short (and often rude) phrases in an almost constant stream. Jarveys live mostly below ground, where they pursue gnomes, though they will also eat moles, rats, and voles.

JOBBERKNOLL

M.O.M. Classification: XX

The Jobberknoll (northern Europe and America) is a tiny blue, speckled bird which eats small insects. It makes no sound until the moment of its death, at which point it lets out a long scream made up of every sound it has ever heard, regurgitated backwards. Jobberknoll feathers are used in Truth Serums and Memory Potions.

KAPPA

M.O.M. Classification: XXXX Snape hasn't read this either

The Kappa is a Japanese water demon that inhabits shallow ponds and rivers. Often said to look like a monkey with fish scales instead of fur, it has a hollow in the top of its head in which it carries water.

The Kappa feeds on human blood but may be persuaded not to harm a person if it is thrown a cucumber with that person's name carved into it. In confrontation, a wizard should trick the Kappa into bowing – if it does so, the water in the hollow of its head will run out, depriving it of all its strength.

KELPIE

M.O.M. Classification: XXXX
This British and Irish water demon can take various shapes, though it most often appears as a horse with

bulrushes for a mane. Having lured the unwary onto its back, it will dive straight to the bottom of its river or lake and devour the rider, letting the entrails float to the surface. The correct means to overcome a kelpie is to get a bridle over its head with a Placement Charm, which renders it docile and unthreatening.

The world's largest kelpie is found in Loch Ness, Scotland. Its favourite form is that of a sea serpent (see page 38). International Confederation of Wizard observers realised that they were not dealing with a true serpent when they saw it turn into an otter on the approach of a team of Muggle investigators and then transform back into a serpent when the coast was clear.

KNARL

M.O.M. Classification: XXX

The Knarl (northern Europe and America) is usually mistaken for a hedgehog by Muggles. The two species are indeed indistinguishable except for one important behavioural difference: If food is left out in the garden for a hedgehog, it will accept and enjoy the gift; if food is offered to a Knarl, on the other hand, it will assume that the householder is attempting to lure it into a trap and will savage that householder's garden plants or garden ornaments. Many a Muggle child has been accused of vandalism when an offended Knarl was the real culprit.

KNEAZLE

M.O.M. Classification: XXX

The Kneazle was originally bred in Britain, though it is now exported worldwide. A small catlike creature with flecked, speckled, or spotted fur, outsize ears, and a tail like a lion's, the Kneazle is intelligent, independent, and occasionally aggressive, though if it takes a liking to a witch or wizard, it makes an excellent pet. The Kneazle has an uncanny ability to detect unsavoury or suspicious characters and can be relied upon to guide its owner safely home if they are lost. Kneazles have up to eight kittens in a litter and can interbreed with cats. Licences are required for ownership as (like Crups and Fwoopers) Kneazles are sufficiently unusual in appearance to attract Muggle interest.

LEPRECHAUN (sometimes known as Clauricorn)

M.O.M. Classification: XXX

More intelligent than the fairy and less malicious than the imp, the pixie, or the Doxy, the leprechaun is nevertheless mischievous. Found only in Ireland, it achieves a height of up to six inches and is green in colour. It has been known to create crude clothing from leaves. Alone of the "little people," leprechauns can speak, though they have never requested reclassification as "beings." The leprechaun bears live young and lives mostly in forest and woodland areas, though it enjoys attracting Muggle attention and as a consequence features almost as heavily as the fairy in Muggle literature for children. Leprechauns produce a realistic goldlike substance that vanishes after a few hours, to their great amusement. Leprechauns eat leaves and, despite their reputation as pranksters, are not known ever to have done lasting damage to a human. *but not mine. R.W.*

LETHIFOLD (also known as Living Shroud)

M.O.M. Classification: XXXXX

The Lethifold is a mercifully rare creature found solely in tropical climates. It resembles a black cloak perhaps half an inch thick (thicker if it has recently killed and digested a victim), which glides along the ground at night. The earliest account we have of a Lethifold was written by the wizard Flavius Belby, who was fortunate enough to survive a Lethifold attack in 1782 while holidaying in Papua New Guinea.

Near one o'clock in the morning, as I began at last to feel drowsy, I heard a soft rustling close by. Believing it to be nothing more than the leaves of the tree outside, I turned over in bed, with my back to the window, and caught sight of what appeared to be a shapeless black shadow sliding underneath my bedroom door. I lay motionless, trying sleepily to divine what was causing such a shadow in a room lit only by moonlight. Undoubtedly my stillness led the Lethifold to believe that its potential victim was sleeping.

To my horror, the shadow began to creep up the bed, and I felt its slight weight upon me. It resembled nothing so much as a rippling black cape, the edges fluttering slightly as it slithered up the bed towards me. Paralysed with fear, I felt its clammy touch upon my chin before I sat bolt upright.

The thing attempted to smother me, sliding inexorably up my face, over my mouth and nostrils, but still I struggled, feeling it wrapping its coldness about me all the while. Unable to cry for assistance, I groped for my wand. Now dizzy as the thing sealed itself about my face, incapable of drawing breath, I concentrated with all my might upon the Stupefying Charm and then – as that failed to subdue the creature, though blasting a hole in my bedroom door – upon the Impediment Hex, which likewise availed me naught. Still struggling madly, I rolled sideways and fell heavily to the floor, now entirely wrapped in the Lethifold.

I knew that I was about to lose consciousness completely as I suffocated. Desperately, I mustered up my last reserve of energy. Pointing my wand away from

> myself into the deadly folds of the creature, summoning the memory of the day I had been voted President of the local Gobstones Club, I performed the Patronus Charm.
>
> Almost at once I felt fresh air upon my face. I looked up to see that deathly shadow being thrown into the air upon the horns of my Patronus. It flew across the room and slithered swiftly out of sight.

As Belby so dramatically reveals, the Patronus is the only spell known to repel the Lethifold. Since it generally attacks the sleeping, though, its victims rarely have a chance to use any magic against it. Once its prey has been successfully suffocated, the Lethifold digests its food there and then in their bed. It then exits the house slightly thicker and fatter than before, leaving no trace of itself or its victim behind.[9]

LOBALUG

M.O.M. Classification: XXX

The Lobalug is found at the bottom of the North Sea. It is a simple creature, ten inches long, comprising a rubbery spout and a venom sac. When threatened, the Lobalug contracts its venom sac, blasting the attacker with poison. Merpeople use the Lobalug as a weapon and wizards have been known to extract its poison for use in potions, though this practice is strictly controlled.

---

9 The number of Lethifold victims is almost impossible to calculate since it leaves no clues to its presence behind it. Easier to calculate is the number of wizards who have, for their own unscrupulous purposes, pretended to have been killed by Lethifolds. The most recent instance of such duplicity occurred in 1973 when the wizard Janus Thickey vanished, leaving only a hastily written note on the bedside table reading "oh no a Lethifold's got me I'm suffocating." Convinced by the spotless and empty bed that such a creature had indeed killed Janus, his wife and children entered a period of strict mourning, which was rudely interrupted when Janus was discovered living five miles away with the landlady of the Green Dragon.

MACKLED MALACLAW

M.O.M. Classification: XXX

The Malaclaw is a land-dwelling creature found mostly on rocky coastlines around Europe. Despite its passing resemblance to the lobster, it should on no account be eaten, as its flesh is unfit for human consumption and will result in a high fever and an unsightly greenish rash.

The Malaclaw can reach a length of twelve inches and is light grey with deep-green spots. It eats small crustaceans and will attempt to tackle larger prey. The Malaclaw's bite has the unusual side effect of making the victim highly unlucky for a period of up to a week after the injury. If you are bitten by a Malaclaw, all bets, wagers, and speculative ventures should be cancelled, as they are sure to go against the victim.

MANTICORE

M.O.M. Classification: XXXXX

The manticore is a highly dangerous Greek beast with the head of a man, the body of a lion, and the tail of a scorpion. As dangerous as the Chimaera, and as rare, the manticore is reputed to croon softly as it devours its prey. Manticore skin repels almost all known charms and the sting causes instant death.

MERPEOPLE (also known as Sirens, Selkies, Merrows)

M.O.M. Classification: XXXX[10]

Merpeople exist throughout the world, though they vary in appearance almost as much as humans. Their habits and customs remain as mysterious as those of the centaur, though those wizards who have mastered the language of Mermish speak of

---

10 See classification footnote for centaur.

highly organised communities varying in size according to habitat, and some have elaborately constructed dwellings. Like the centaurs, the merpeople have declined "being" status in favour of a "beast" classification (see Introduction).

The oldest recorded merpeople were known as sirens (Greece) and it is in warmer waters that we find the beautiful mermaids so frequently depicted in Muggle literature and painting. The selkies of Scotland and the Merrows of Ireland are less beautiful ugly, but they share that love of music which is common to all merpeople.

MOKE

M.O.M. Classification: XXX

The Moke is a silver-green lizard reaching up to ten inches in length and is found throughout Britain and Ireland. It has the ability to shrink at will and has consequently never been noticed by Muggles.

Moke skin is highly prized among wizards for use as moneybags and purses, as the scaly material will contract at the approach of a stranger, just as its owner did; Moke-skin moneybags are therefore very difficult for thieves to locate.

MOONCALF

M.O.M. Classification: XX

The Mooncalf is an intensely shy creature that emerges from its burrow only at the full moon. Its body is smooth and pale grey, it has bulging round eyes on top of its head, and four spindly legs with enormous flat feet. Mooncalves perform complicated dances on their hind legs in isolated areas in the moonlight. These are believed to be a prelude to mating (and often leave intricate geometric patterns behind in wheat fields, to the great puzzlement of Muggles).

Watching Mooncalves dance by moonlight is a fascinating experience and often profitable, for if their silvery dung is collected before the sun rises and spread upon magical herb and flower beds, the plants will grow very fast and become extremely strong. Mooncalves are found worldwide.

MURTLAP

M.O.M. Classification: XXX

The Murtlap is a ratlike creature found in coastal areas of Britain. It has a growth upon its back resembling a sea anemone. When pickled and eaten, these Murtlap growths promote resistance to curses and jinxes, though an overdose may cause unsightly purple ear hair. Murtlaps eat crustaceans and the feet of anyone foolish enough to step on them.

NIFFLER

M.O.M. Classification: XXX

The Niffler is a British beast. Fluffy, black, and long-snouted, this burrowing creature has a predilection for anything glittery. Nifflers are often kept by goblins to burrow deep into the earth for treasure. Though the Niffler is gentle and even affectionate, it can be destructive to belongings and should never be kept in a house. Nifflers live in lairs up to twenty feet below the surface and produce six to eight young in a litter.

NOGTAIL

M.O.M. Classification: XXX

Nogtails are demons found in rural areas right across Europe,

Russia, and America. They resemble stunted piglets with long legs, thick, stubby tails, and narrow black eyes. The Nogtail will creep into a sty and suckle an ordinary sow alongside her own young. The longer the Nogtail is left undetected and the bigger it grows, the longer the blight on the farm into which it has entered.

The Nogtail is exceptionally fast and difficult to catch, though if chased beyond the boundaries of a farm by a pure white dog, it will never return. The Department for the Regulation and Control of Magical Creatures (Pest Sub-Division) keeps a dozen albino bloodhounds for this purpose.

NUNDU

M.O.M. Classification: XXXXX

This East African beast is arguably the most dangerous in the world. A gigantic leopard that moves silently despite its size and whose breath causes disease virulent enough to eliminate entire villages, it has never yet been subdued by fewer than a hundred skilled wizards working together.

OCCAMY

M.O.M. Classification: XXXX

The Occamy is found in the Far East and India. A plumed, two-legged winged creature with a serpentine body, the Occamy may reach a length of fifteen feet. It feeds mainly on rats and birds, though has been known to carry off monkeys. The Occamy is aggressive to all who approach it, particularly in defence of its eggs, whose shells are made of the purest, softest silver.

PHOENIX

M.O.M. Classification: XXXX[11]

The phoenix is a magnificent, swan-sized, scarlet bird with a long golden tail, beak, and talons. It nests on mountain peaks and is found in Egypt, India, and China. The phoenix lives to an immense age as it can regenerate, bursting into flames when its body begins to fail and rising again from the ashes as a chick. The phoenix is a gentle creature that has never been known to kill and eats only herbs. Like the Diricawl (see page 9), it can disappear and reappear at will. Phoenix song is magical; it is reputed to increase the courage of the pure of heart and to strike fear into the hearts of the impure. Phoenix tears have powerful healing properties.

PIXIE

M.O.M. Classification: ~~XXX~~ **but XXXXXXX if you're Lockhart**

The pixie is mostly found in Cornwall, England. Electric blue in colour, up to eight inches in height and very mischievous, the pixie delights in tricks and practical jokes of all descriptions. Although wingless, it can fly and has been known to seize unwary humans by the ears and deposit them at the tops of tall trees and buildings. Pixies produce a high-pitched jabbering intelligible only to other pixies. They bear live young.

PLIMPY

M.O.M. Classification: XXX

The Plimpy is a spherical, mottled fish distinguished by its two

---

11 The phoenix gains a XXXX rating not because it is aggressive, but because very few wizards have ever succeeded in domesticating it.

long legs ending in webbed feet.
It inhabits deep lakes where it
will prowl the bottom in search
of food, preferring water snails.
The Plimpy is not particularly
dangerous, though it will nibble

the feet and clothing of swimmers. It is considered a pest by
merpeople, who deal with it by tying its rubbery legs in a knot;
the Plimpy then drifts away, unable to steer, and cannot return
until it has untied itself, which may take hours.

POGREBIN

M.O.M. Classification: XXX

The Pogrebin is a Russian demon, barely a foot tall, with a hairy
body but a smooth, oversized grey head. When crouching, the
Pogrebin resembles a shiny, round rock. Pogrebins are attracted to
humans and enjoy tailing them, staying in their shadow and
crouching quickly should the shadow's owner turn around. If a
Pogrebin is allowed to tail a human for many hours, a sense of
great futility will overcome its prey, who will eventually fall into
a state of lethargy and despair. When the victim stops walking and
sinks to their knees to weep at the pointlessness of it all, the
Pogrebin will leap upon them and attempt to devour them.
However, it is easy to repulse the Pogrebin with simple hexes or
Stupefying Charms. Kicking has also been found effective.

PORLOCK

M.O.M. Classification: XX

The Porlock is a horse-guardian found in Dorset, England, and in Southern Ireland. Covered in shaggy fur, it has a large quantity of rough hair on its head and an exceptionally large nose. It walks on two cloven feet. The arms are small and end in four stubby fingers. Fully grown Porlocks are around two feet high and feed on grass.

The Porlock is shy and lives to guard horses. It may be found curled in the straw of stables or else sheltering in the midst of the herd it protects. Porlocks mistrust humans and always hide at their approach.

PUFFSKEIN

> *I had one of them once*
> *what happened to it?*
> *Fred used it for Bludger practice*

M.O.M. Classification: XX

The Puffskein is found worldwide. Spherical in shape and covered in soft, custard-coloured fur, it is a docile creature that has no objection to being cuddled or thrown about. Easy to care for, it emits a low humming noise when contented. From time to time a very long, thin, pink tongue will emerge from the depths of the Puffskein and snake through the house searching for food. The Puffskein is a scavenger that will eat anything from leftovers to spiders, but it has a particular preference for sticking its tongue up the nose of sleeping wizards and eating their bogies. This tendency has made the Puffskein much beloved by wizarding children for many generations and it remains a highly popular wizarding pet.

QUINTAPED

(also known as Hairy MacBoon)

M.O.M. Classification: XXXXX

The Quintaped is a highly dangerous carnivorous beast with a particular taste for humans. Its low-slung body is covered with thick reddish-brown hair, as are its five legs, each of which ends in a clubfoot. The Quintaped is found only upon the Isle of Drear off the northernmost tip of Scotland. Drear has been made unplottable for this reason.

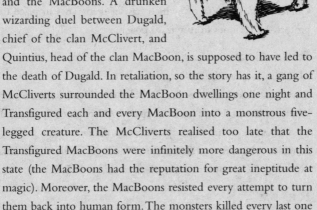

Legend has it that the Isle of Drear was once populated by two wizarding families, the McCliverts and the MacBoons. A drunken wizarding duel between Dugald, chief of the clan McClivert, and Quintius, head of the clan MacBoon, is supposed to have led to the death of Dugald. In retaliation, so the story has it, a gang of McCliverts surrounded the MacBoon dwellings one night and Transfigured each and every MacBoon into a monstrous five-legged creature. The McCliverts realised too late that the Transfigured MacBoons were infinitely more dangerous in this state (the MacBoons had the reputation for great ineptitude at magic). Moreover, the MacBoons resisted every attempt to turn them back into human form. The monsters killed every last one of the McCliverts until no human remained on the island. It was only then that the MacBoon monsters realised that in the absence of anyone to wield a wand, they would be forced to remain as they were forevermore.

Whether this tale is true or not will never be known. Certainly there are no surviving McCliverts or MacBoons to tell us what happened to their ancestors. The Quintapeds cannot talk and have strenuously resisted every attempt by the Department for the Regulation and Control of Magical Creatures to capture a

35

specimen and try to untransfigure it, so we must assume that if they are indeed, as their nickname suggests, Hairy MacBoons, they are quite happy to live out their days as beasts.

RAMORA

M.O.M. Classification: XX

The Ramora is a silver fish found in the Indian Ocean. Powerfully magical, it can anchor ships and is a guardian of seafarers. The Ramora is highly valued by the International Confederation of Wizards, which has set many laws in place to protect the Ramora from wizard poachers.

RED CAP

M.O.M. Classification: XXX

These dwarflike creatures live in holes on old battlegrounds or wherever human blood has been spilled. Although easily repelled by charms and hexes, they are very dangerous to solitary Muggles, whom they will attempt to bludgeon to death on dark nights. Red Caps are most prevalent in northern Europe.

RE'EM

M.O.M. Classification: XXXX

Extremely rare giant oxen with golden hides, the Re'em are found both in the wilds of North America and the Far East. Re'em blood gives the drinker immense strength, though the difficulty in procuring it means that supplies are negligible and rarely for sale on the open market.

RUNESPOOR

M.O.M. Classification: XXXX

The Runespoor originated in the small African country of

Burkina Faso. A three-headed serpent, the Runespoor commonly reaches a length of six or seven feet. Livid orange with black stripes, the Runespoor is only too easy to spot, so the Ministry of Magic in Burkina Faso has designated certain forests unplottable for the Runespoor's sole use.

The Runespoor, though not in itself a particularly vicious beast, was once a favourite pet of Dark wizards, no doubt because of its striking and intimidating appearance. It is to the writings of Parselmouths who have kept and conversed with  these serpents that we owe our understanding of their curious habits. It transpires from their records that each of the Runespoor's heads serves a different purpose. The left head (as seen by the wizard facing the Runespoor) is the planner. It decides where the Runespoor is to go and what it is to do next. The middle head is the dreamer (Runespoors may remain stationary for days at a time, lost in glorious visions and imaginings). The right head is the critic and will evaluate the efforts of the left and middle heads with a continual irritable hissing. The right head's fangs are extremely venomous. The Runespoor rarely reaches a great age, as the heads tend to attack each other. It is common to see a Runespoor with the right head missing, the other two heads having banded together to bite it off.

The Runespoor produces eggs through its mouths, the only known magical beast to do so. These eggs are of immense value in the production of potions to stimulate mental agility. A black market in Runespoor eggs and in the serpents themselves has flourished for several centuries.

SALAMANDER

M.O.M. Classification: XXX

The salamander is a small fire-dwelling lizard that feeds on flame. Brilliant white, it appears blue or scarlet depending upon the heat of the fire in which it makes its appearance.

Salamanders can survive up to six hours outside a fire if regularly fed pepper. They will live only as long as the fire from which they sprang burns. Salamander blood has powerful curative and restorative properties.

SEA SERPENT

M.O.M. Classification: XXX

Sea serpents are found in the Atlantic, Pacific, and Mediterranean seas. Though alarming in appearance, sea serpents are not known ever to have killed any human, despite hysterical Muggle accounts of their ferocious behaviour. Reaching lengths of up to a hundred feet, the sea serpent has a horselike head and a long snakelike body that rises in humps out of the sea.

SHRAKE

M.O.M. Classification: XXX

A fish covered entirely in spines and found in the Atlantic Ocean. The first shoal of Shrake is believed to have been created as a revenge against Muggle fisherfolk who had insulted a team of sailing wizards in the early 1800s. From that day on, any Muggles fishing in that particular patch of sea have found their nets come

up ripped and empty owing to the Shrakes swimming deep
below.

SNIDGET

M.O.M. Classification: XXXX[12]

The Golden Snidget is an extremely rare, protected species of
bird. Completely round, with a very long, thin beak and
glistening, jewel-like red eyes, the Golden Snidget is an extremely
fast flier that can change direction with uncanny speed and skill,
owing to the rotational joints of its wings.

The Golden Snidget's feathers and eyes are so highly prized
that it was at one time in danger of being hunted to extinction
by wizards. The danger was recognised in time and the species
protected, the most notable factor being the substitution of the
Golden Snitch for the Snidget in the game of Quidditch.[13]
Snidget sanctuaries exist worldwide.

SPHINX

M.O.M. Classification: XXXX

The Egyptian sphinx has a human head on a lion's body. For over
a thousand years it has been used by witches and wizards to guard
valuables and secret hideaways. Highly intelligent, the sphinx
delights in puzzles and riddles. It is usually dangerous only when
what it is guarding is threatened.

---

12 The Golden Snidget gains a XXXX rating not because it is dangerous but because
severe penalties are attached to its capture or injury.

13 Anyone interested in the role played by the Golden Snidget in the development of
the game of Quidditch is advised to consult *Quidditch Through the Ages* by Kennilworthy
Whisp (Whizz Hard Books, 1952).

STREELER

M.O.M. Classification: XXX

The Streeler is a giant snail that changes colour on an hourly basis and deposits behind it a trail so venomous that it shrivels and burns all vegetation over which it passes. The Streeler is native to several African countries, though it has been successfully raised by wizards in Europe, Asia, and the Americas. It is kept as a pet by those who enjoy its kaleidoscopic colour changes, and its venom is one of the few substances known to kill Horklumps.

TEBO

M.O.M. Classification: XXXX

The Tebo is an ash-coloured warthog found in Congo and Zaire. It has the power of invisibility, making it difficult to evade or catch, and is very dangerous. Tebo hide is highly prized by wizards for protective shields and clothing.

TROLL

M.O.M. Classification: XXXX

The troll is a fearsome creature up to twelve feet tall and weighing over a tonne. Notable for its equally prodigious strength and stupidity, the troll is often violent and unpredictable. Trolls originated in Scandinavia but these days they may be found in Britain, Ireland, and other areas of northern Europe.

Trolls generally converse in grunts that appear to constitute a crude language, though some have been known to understand and even to speak a few simple human words. The more intelligent of the species have been trained as guardians.

There are three types of troll: mountain, forest, and river. The mountain troll is the largest and most vicious. It is bald, with a pale-grey skin. The forest troll has a pale-green skin and some specimens have hair, which is green or brown, thin, and straggly. The river troll has short horns and may be hairy. It has a purplish skin, and is often found lurking beneath bridges. Trolls eat raw flesh and are not fussy in their prey, which ranges from wild animals to humans.

UNICORN

M.O.M. Classification: XXXX[14]

The unicorn is a beautiful beast found throughout the forests of northern Europe. It is a pure white, horned horse when fully grown, though the foals are initially golden, and turn silver before achieving maturity. The unicorn's horn, blood, and hair all have highly magical properties.[15] It generally avoids human contact, is more likely to allow a witch to approach it than a wizard, and is so fleet of foot that it is very difficult to capture.

WEREWOLF S *aren't all bad*

M.O.M. Classification: XXXXX[16]

The werewolf is found worldwide, though it is believed to have originated in northern Europe. Humans turn into werewolves only when bitten. There is no known cure, though recent developments in potion-making have to a great extent alleviated

---

14 See footnote on centaur classification.

15 The unicorn, like the fairy, has received an excellent Muggle press – in this case justified.

16 This classification refers, of course, to the werewolf in its transformed state. When there is no full moon, the werewolf is as harmless as any other human. For a heartrending account of one wizard's battle with lycanthropy, see the classic *Hairy Snout, Human Heart* by an anonymous author (Whizz Hard Books, 1975).

the worst symptoms. Once a month, at the full moon, the otherwise sane and normal wizard or Muggle afflicted transforms into a murderous beast. Almost uniquely among fantastic creatures, the werewolf actively seeks humans in preference to any other kind of prey.

WINGED HORSE

M.O.M. Classification: XX–XXXX

Winged horses exist worldwide. There are many different breeds, including the Abraxan (immensely powerful giant palominos), the Aethonan (chestnut, popular in Britain and Ireland), the Granian (grey and particularly fast) and the rare Thestral (black, possessed of the power of invisibility, and considered unlucky by many wizards). As with the Hippogriff, the owner of a winged horse is required to perform a Disillusionment Charm upon it at regular intervals (see Introduction).

YETI (also known as Bigfoot, the Abominable Snowman)

M.O.M. Classification: XXXX

A native of Tibet, the yeti is believed to be related to the troll, though no one has yet got close enough to conduct the necessary tests. Up to fifteen feet in height, it is covered head to foot in purest white hair. The yeti devours anything that strays into its path, though it fears fire, and may be repulsed by skilled wizards.

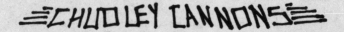